Love Finds You
in
Charm
OHIO

Love Finds You
in
Charm
OHIO

BY ANNALISA DAUGHETY

summerside
PRESS

Dedication

· · · · · · · · · · · · · · · · ·

To my mother, Vicky Daughety, who stood behind me every
step of the way and always encouraged me to follow my dreams.
You've always been my hero. I love you, Mom!

To my grandparents, H.B. & Ermyl Pearle. Your house has
always been one of my favorite places, full of love and laughter.
I love you both!

Special Thanks

· · · · · · · · · · · · · · · · · ·

Special thanks to: Connie Troyer, Susan Downs, Rachel Meisel, Sandy Gaskin, Christine Lynxwiler, Jan Reynolds, Megan Reynolds, Lynda Sampson, and all of my co-workers at NFT—especially Emily Joyner and Mandy Scherer.

"I can do all things through Christ who strengthens me."
PHILIPPIANS 4:13 NKJV

The cozy village of Charm, Ohio, is nestled among the rolling hills of Holmes County, home to the largest Amish settlement in the world. Originally called Stevenson, the town acquired its own post office in 1885 and officially changed its name. Many tourists come to Charm each year to take in the beautiful scenery, visit an Amish farm, eat homemade food, stay in quaint B and Bs, and enjoy the *clip-clop* of passing buggies. Charm's local businesses cater to visitors and offer a variety of handmade Amish goods including quilts, artwork, and furniture. One of the most popular is family-owned Keim Lumber, which has been in business for nearly a century. This 120,000-square-foot hardware and lumberyard store employs many Amish and Mennonite craftsmen. Visitors also enjoy home cooking at Grandma's Homestead Restaurant, gifts and souvenirs from Charm General Store, quilting supplies at Miller's Dry Goods, and beautiful Amish craftsmanship at Ole Mill Furniture. Over the second weekend in October, at the height of Ohio's beautiful autumn season, the town hosts its annual Charm Days, a festival with a heart. Proceeds from Charm Days fund an organization whose mission is to assist local families in need. For these reasons and more, many folks find that the small country village of Charm truly lives up to its name.

Chapter One

....

Emma

The bright red convertible zoomed down the highway, and Emma relished the way the warm, salty breeze felt against her skin. A glimmer of the Pacific Ocean caught her eye as she rounded a sharp curve. With the next gust of air, her white kapp *blew from its place atop her head, and her wavy auburn hair was set free in the wind. The sensation startled her, and she laughed as she reached for the radio. The loud sound of rock music surrounded her, and she could feel the beat pulsing through the leather seat. As the sparkling ocean came into her view, she noticed a familiar figure standing on the roadside, waving her over to the side of the road where he stood. He lowered his designer sunglasses and gave her a slow, lazy grin.*

Johnny Depp.

"Going my way?" Emma asked in what she hoped was a sultry voice.

Johnny gave her another smile and jumped in the passenger seat without even opening the door. "Be my date to the Oscars?" he asked as she put the car into gear.

"I'd love to!" she exclaimed and pointed the convertible toward the Hollywood sign.

"Emma. Emma? EMMA!"

Emma Miller slammed the *People* magazine closed and tossed

it onto the desk as if it were the hot potato and she didn't want to be put out of the game. One glance into the narrowed eyes of her sister, Abby, told her she was in trouble. Again. The only bright point in the familiar scenario was the satisfaction that the frequent frowns Abby bestowed upon her sister would certainly cause her to be old and wrinkly first. And as the older one, Emma took great delight in the thought.

"One of the students brought this to school today, and I confiscated it," Emma explained. "I was just looking through it to make sure there wasn't anything so bad in it that I might need to talk to his parents about." *And to see what the movie stars had worn on the last red carpet.* "I guess he picked it up from a tourist or something."

"Really? So that's why you didn't come home? I was getting worried when you didn't meet me for our chores." Abby sounded as miffed as she looked. As the always-punctual sister, she seemed to see Emma's tardiness as a personal insult.

"Sorry." Emma didn't sound sorry, even to her own ears. But for once, Abby let it slide. Emma decided to try making nice. "Did you have a good day at work?"

Abby worked in a quilt shop in town. "*Jah.* It was a good day." She narrowed her eyes at Emma. "Until you forgot to come home."

They stepped out into the early May sunshine. Their family buggy waited outside of Pleasant Creek School, where Emma taught. "I'll drive." Emma started toward the buggy.

"No way. I don't have a death wish." Abby rushed past her, hopped in, and grabbed the reins. "You never pay attention to where you're going."

One little buggy accident and she wants to banish me to a lifetime in the passenger seat. "Fine. But I'm just as capable as you." Emma climbed in beside her sister. "And you know it was the horse's fault."

Abby let out a tiny snort. "Of course it was." Her mouth turned upward in a smile as she turned her blue-eyed gaze to the road ahead.

Emma sank back against the hard black seat and listened to the familiar *clip-clop* of the horse's hooves against the pavement. Lately, it seemed that each day was a repeat of the previous one. She glanced over at Abby. A tendril of her pale blonde hair escaped from her kapp, its corkscrew curl bouncing with each step the horses took. How did she manage to stay so content?

A cyclist caught her attention as he pedaled toward the horse and buggy. The man on the bike was clad in a bright turquoise jersey and black cycling shorts, the late afternoon sunlight glinting off his shiny black helmet.

Emma waved and turned around backward in her seat, watching him speed away.

"Emma. Turn around right now. You're acting like a silly girl. What would people think if they saw you behaving that way?"

Emma faced the front and furrowed her brow. "I was just watching him. It isn't a crime." She knew she should be ashamed of herself for purposely upsetting her sister. But sometimes Abby's perfection drove her crazy.

"You should only have eyes for one man and you know it. Jacob is wonderful. You should be the happiest girl in town."

If you only knew.

Emma knew she shouldn't question things. She should strive to join the church, marry a nice Amish man, and raise a passel of well-behaved Amish children. It all sounded so good. And to someone like Abby, it really was a dream lifestyle. But for Emma…well, for Emma it wasn't quite that simple.

Day in and day out, she saw the same old pasture fences surrounding neighboring farms. Boring. Emma wanted to experience a life outside of her small community. She wanted to drive a sporty car and wear designer jeans. Sometimes she wondered what it would be like to have short, highlighted hair like she'd seen in the magazines at the checkout lines whenever she got the chance to go to town. But Emma knew as well as anyone that those feelings were way out of place in Shipshewana, Indiana. Even though she tried, she couldn't help but wonder what else the world might have to offer.

She took another glance at the fence near her home. *If the fence protects me, as I've always been taught, why do I feel more like it's keeping me in?*

Abby pulled the buggy around to the barn.

"Thomas!" Abby called. "Can you put the horse and buggy away?"

At twelve, their brother was already making plans for what he would do when he had his own buggy. But for now, he was content to take care of theirs.

"Sure." Thomas dropped the shovel he'd been holding and bounded over. Caring for the horses was his favorite chore.

Chores were a way of life for Emma, just as they were for all her Amish neighbors. But she knew she'd never be as accomplished at keeping house as Abby. When they were younger, she'd speculated that their parents must've picked her up on the side of the road as a baby. There was no way she and Abby belonged in the same family.

Abby emerged from the house with an overflowing laundry basket. With her creamy skin and rosy cheeks, she reminded Emma of a porcelain doll. "We'd better get busy if we want to get finished before dark." She grabbed a white cotton shirt from the basket. "If you'd paid attention to the time, we'd already be halfway through by now."

Emma fought the urge to roll her eyes. At least they had hanging out clothes down to an art. Ever since they were tall enough to reach the line, Abby had held the clothes up and Emma had clipped them in place.

"Just think. Someday soon, you'll be doing laundry for your own family," Abby bubbled. "I just know that you and Jacob will get married, and before you know it, you'll have a home to care for." She pulled an apron from the basket and shook it out. "Isn't that exciting?"

Emma held the clothespin ready but didn't speak. She'd been toying with the idea of telling Abby the truth. Maybe it was time to come clean. And maybe, if her feelings were finally out in the open, she'd be able to shake the anxiety that had been building inside her lately. She clipped the apron into place and took a deep breath. Now was as good a time as any. "I don't know if I would want to marry Jacob, even if he asked." Emma slid down to the ground beside the basket of clothespins and shut her eyes, waiting for the response she knew was coming.

"What? Have you lost your mind?" Abby dropped the sheet she was holding and stared down at her sister, a look of horror on her face. "What's the matter with you?"

Well, for starters, I've been unhappy for a while. And no one seems to notice or care. Why hadn't she tried to sugarcoat her announcement? She'd known Abby wouldn't take it well. "No, I haven't lost my mind. I'm having second thoughts, though. About everything." Emma played with the tie on her kapp, wondering how much she should share. "Jacob is a great guy. Believe me, I know that. We've grown up together." She shrugged. "He'll make a wonderful husband." A sigh came from her mouth of its own volition. "For someone."

Abby opened her mouth to speak, but Emma cut her off. "That's not all." She chewed on her lip for a second, willing herself to just get it out. "I love my family. I love the people in this town, who've known me since I was a baby. But the truth is—I'm not sure it's what I want for my life."

Emma threw herself back on the ground and stared up at the sky. If only the lush green grass could swallow her up. Or even better, turn her into someone more like Abby.

Chapter Two

. . . .

Abby

Abby Miller never got angry. Irritated, yes, but never angry. And for her entire life, it had almost always been Emma who'd caused the irritation. But listening to Emma go on and on about leaving her life behind made Abby seethe.

"Emma, Jacob is the perfect man. You have a wonderful life here. Would you seriously think about giving it all up?" Abby tried to keep her voice steady. She didn't want Emma to know just how upset she was.

Emma let out a huge sigh. "Sometimes, yes. I think a lot about giving it up." Her brown eyes filled with tears, and Abby immediately regretted her anger. Her sister was hurting. How had she missed the signs? Even though they didn't always understand each other, they'd always shared everything.

Abby watched Emma as she lay in the grass, looking up at the blue sky. She remembered when they were kids and they would spread a quilt in the backyard then stretch out and look up at the sky, finding shapes in the puffy white clouds. Things sure were simpler then.

"See that?" Emma pointed out a white line, high in the sky. Abby could barely make out the airplane in front of it. "The other day in class, Ike Bellar raised his hand and asked me how a plane stays up in the air and if it feels like you're going really fast when you're in one."

Abby gave her sister a tiny smile. Ike was one of Emma's favorite students, and she often entertained the family with stories of his schoolhouse antics.

"I couldn't answer him. Because I don't know how it feels. I've never been in an airplane, and I never will." Emma propped herself up on her elbow. "Neither will anyone else in our family. And sometimes I get very frustrated about those things." Sadness washed over her face like rain. "And sometimes I want to book the first flight out of here."

Abby felt as if she'd been stung. "You shouldn't think about things like that." She reached for a clothespin and began snapping it. "You were born here." *Clip, clip.* "You belong here." *Clip, clip.* "You have a wonderful life, and if you'll act right, it will be an even better life when you become Jacob's wife." The clothespin flew from her hand.

"I know you think the world of Jacob. I do, too. But I can't change how I feel."

Abby felt so weak, she wanted to lie down in the cool grass and forget the words her sister had said. Instead, she snatched another apron from the basket. "It's more than just Jacob. You're talking about leaving your family behind." She looked down at the sister who exasperated her so much, and a lump rose in her throat. "Leaving me behind. And for what?" She shook her head. "Adventure?"

Emma slowly rose to her feet. "I'm sorry, Ab. I'm not sure what to say." She fastened the apron onto the line, but Abby could tell her mind was a million miles away. "It's just a feeling inside me. Like there's a storm brewing inside my stomach and brain."

Abby could relate to that. Her own stomach felt like a whirlwind was spinning through it. She automatically reached back into the clothes basket.

Emma touched her arm. "Please don't mention it to *Mamm* or *Dat*. They have their own worries. I'll deal with things on my own. It's my life and I'm a grown woman who is capable of making her own decisions."

Even though her sister had always been a little rebellious, Abby had never doubted that she'd make the right choice in the end. But after hearing her today, and seeing the torn expression on her face, she wasn't so sure. She intended to do whatever she could to make sure Emma didn't make a decision that they'd both end up regretting. "Okay, if that's what you think is best." She forced a lighthearted tone past the lump in her throat. "But remember, you have a family who loves you. We don't want you to 'jump the fence.'" She grabbed the last piece of laundry from the basket and held it to the line for Emma to clip.

"Abby! Emma!" Mamm called from the house. "It's time to get supper on the table."

As they started toward the house, Emma stopped and turned toward her sister. "Promise me that you won't say anything to them."

"I'm not happy about it, but I won't tell." Abby held the door open and watched her sister walk down the hallway. Their dat had always said his girls were exact opposites. From the way they looked, to the way they acted, it had been that way since they were babies. Even so, Emma was her best friend. And the thought of her going away and not returning made Abby feel like she'd been kicked in the stomach. She'd seen it happen to other families. The hole left by a family member who chose to go into the world never really filled, no matter how much time passed.

She was determined to find a way to prevent Emma from making what would be the biggest mistake of her life. Maybe all her sister needed was a little change of pace. A plan already forming in her head, Abby hurried to the kitchen.

Chapter Three

Kelly

Kelly Bennett put one last pair of shoes into her new Louis Vuitton suitcase. Did her dad really think that expensive new luggage would make up for missing her college graduation? Regardless of the reason behind the gift, she had to admit it was nice luggage. Certainly better than the tattered L.L. Bean backpack she'd been using. Was it really only one summer ago when she'd been backpacking across Europe without a care in the world? Things had sure changed since then.

She glanced around the empty dorm room. It was just a shell of the colorful, vibrant room it had been for the past four years. Once all the posters and photos were off the walls and the matching bedspreads were packed away, it was really a sad-looking place.

"You ready?" Her roommate Michelle rushed in, her cheeks flushed from the heat. It had taken them many loads to get all their things downstairs. Moving was always exhausting, especially without a lot of help. Thankfully, Michelle's parents had stayed after graduation and offered the use of their SUV.

"This is the last of it." Kelly zipped the suitcase. "I can't believe this day is finally here." She lifted the suitcase off of the twin mattress and placed it on the floor.

"I know what you mean. But at least we still have grad school standing between us and the *real* world, right?"

Kelly laughed. "Yes. We can still be irresponsible students for a couple more years. Thank goodness for that. And thanks for letting me store the rest of my stuff at the apartment for the summer."

Michelle smiled and twisted her long dark hair into a bun. "Not a problem. And for the millionth time, are you *sure* you don't want to live with me this summer?" The two of them would share an off-campus apartment in the fall while they were in graduate school. But Michelle had been nice enough to let Kelly store her things at the apartment for the summer, even though she wouldn't actually be paying rent. It had been a relief to find out their friend Maria was planning on taking classes over the summer. Maria had needed a place to stay and had offered to sublet the room from Kelly. That was one less worry, at least.

Kelly nodded. "I'll be fine. It will do me good to get away. Besides, I'll be able to save a lot of money, and now that I'll be paying my own tuition, I'll need it."

Michelle sighed. "I'm sorry life has been so hard for you lately. But I'm still not convinced you need to do something drastic. I'm afraid you're in for a miserable summer."

When Kelly had told Michelle her plan to go live in Amish Country for the summer, her friend had displayed a rather strong reaction. "Why would you do something like that to yourself? I don't care if you have had a tough year. You're going to go crazy out in the middle of nowhere," Michelle had said, her gorgeous face twisted in horror.

The past year had been one for the record books. Her senior year of college was supposed to have been perfect. But as soon as she'd stepped off of the plane from Europe, things had begun falling apart. First, her parents divorced. Then, she'd had a near-fatal car accident. The toll of those two things combined had contributed to her losing the scholarship to graduate school that had been all but in the bag. The final straw was when her boyfriend of three years, Nick, had dumped her for his ex. Yes, she was certain that if the *Guinness Book of World Records* had a Worst Year Ever category, she'd win hands down.

So maybe living among the Amish would be good for her. At least for a few months. Plus, her grandmother's sister could use the help. Aunt Irene ran a bed-and-breakfast, but maintaining the place was starting to be too much for the elderly woman to handle alone. So, when she'd offered for Kelly to come and stay, rent free, in exchange for a few household chores, Kelly had jumped at the chance.

"Don't worry about me. I'll be fine. It will be a growing experience." She tried to sound sure, but the words sounded hollow even to her own ears.

Michelle clearly wasn't convinced. "Whatever. But the offer stands. Once you get sick of a simple lifestyle, you can crash on the couch for the rest of the summer." She brightened. "And then, next fall, we're going to have the best time ever. Our own place. Hot guys with real jobs. It's going to be a blast. We'll make up for your stinky senior year."

Kelly managed a grin and followed Michelle down the hallway without even a second glance at the room she'd called home for the past year. She was ready to start a new chapter.

Chapter Four

Emma

"Miss Emma, are you sad about somethin'?" Nine-year-old Ike trotted over to Emma's desk, a thoughtful expression on his freckled face.

"I'm not sad, Ike, but there are a lot of things on my mind." She straightened the papers in front of her, glad the school day was over.

"What kinds of things?" Ever the questioner, Ike was rarely satisfied with the answers his teacher gave him.

"Well, there are a few things troubling me right now. Grown-up stuff." Emma had always hated that kind of response when she was young and was ashamed to be using it now, especially on such a sharp kid. She stood up and guided him toward the door, hoping to avoid further questioning.

"Trouble?" Ike waited as she closed the door. "My mamm always says 'don't trouble trouble till trouble troubles you.'" His mouth turned upward and his gap-toothed smile made her feel better.

"Your mamm is a wise woman." Emma watched as Ike ran to catch up with his brothers. She started the short walk home, lost in thought. Had she been troubling trouble? Maybe. But not on purpose.

If only Emma could be as lighthearted as a nine-year-old again. And her worries were even worse now that she'd told Abby what was weighing on her mind. In the two weeks since she'd confessed her doubts to Abby, she'd had to put up with non-stop questioning about her decision.

Abby had been quick to let her know that she hadn't once doubted their life. She trusted their parents, trusted God, and had never felt the least bit tempted to see what else was out there. This knowledge only made Emma feel worse. What was wrong with her?

She and Abby had always been different, even as children. When Emma was ten and Abby a year younger, they'd entered a baking contest. Abby's cake had been made from scratch, just as the rules stated. It was a beautiful cake, even their mamm had said so, and she was known for her baked goods. Emma's was a disaster from the beginning. In desperation, she'd finally gone over to her grandparents' house, snuck into the kitchen, and snatched one of the lemon meringue pies her *mammi* had baked. She'd tried to pass it off as her own, but one look and no one believed she'd baked it. Abby's cake won. And Emma was in heaps of trouble when their mamm found out what she'd done. Dat, on the other hand, had chuckled when he thought no one was looking. Emma had seen his broad shoulders shaking, though, and it had taken some of the sting out of her punishment to know that he at least found her antics laugh worthy.

As she got closer to home, she passed a vivid display of spring flowers blooming. There may not be any place more beautiful than Shipshewana in the spring. *Not that I have anywhere to compare it to.* Emma tried to push the negative thought away as she reached the house.

"Good afternoon, Emma." Mamm was bustling about the kitchen, cleaning the spots that only she could see. "You got some mail today." She motioned toward the counter.

Emma spotted the envelope. She'd know that loopy script anywhere. "It's from Lydia Ann." She eagerly ripped it open.

Mamm looked up with curiosity. "I hope she's doing well." She grabbed a broom and began to sweep the kitchen floor. She hovered near the counter, though, and Emma knew she was waiting to hear the contents of the letter. Lydia Ann didn't write often, so there must be news.

Lydia Ann was four years older than Emma, and even though they didn't see each other often anymore, Emma had fond memories of her from childhood. Lydia Ann, Emma, and Abby used to spend a couple of weeks each summer with their grandparents and always had such fun. When Emma returned home, it felt like she'd been on a real adventure.

> Dear Emma,
>
> Greetings from Charm, Ohio! We're already starting to be bombarded by tourists, and I'm trying to get the quilt shop ready for the rush. I hope you're doing well. I'll bet you're glad school is about to be out for the summer. By the time you receive this letter, you should have only a few days left.
>
> The girls and I are still coping with Levi's death, but we're finally starting to adjust. Having two small children and a store to run is tough, but it keeps me too busy to dwell on how much I miss him.
>
> Do you know of anyone who might be interested in coming to Charm for the summer? I could really use the help, both with the girls and the store. I can't pay too much,

but I can provide free room and board. Ask Abby and your mamm if they know of anyone. Tell everyone I said "hello" and that I miss them. You are always in my prayers.

Love,

Lydia Ann

"It sounds like Lydia Ann is having a tough time." Emma laid the letter down. "It must be hard to lose a husband at such a young age." Levi had died last year after losing a battle with cancer. Now Lydia Ann was raising their four-year-old twin girls alone. Emma's own problems seemed small in comparison.

Mamm leaned the broom against the wall and sat down. "She's known a lot of sadness in her young life." The little lines around her blue eyes were more prominent than normal as she squinted to read Lydia Ann's print.

"Do you know of anyone who could go help her out?" Emma asked once Mamm was through reading.

Her mother looked thoughtful. "I'm not sure. Abby already has a job. And Sarah isn't old enough to be of much help."

That was true. At only eight years old, Emma's youngest sibling would likely be more of a hindrance than a help.

"But you…" Mamm trailed off and looked at Emma expectantly.

"Me?" Emma's voice squeaked. "You think I should go?"

"Go where?" Abby entered the kitchen and grabbed an apple from the bowl. She eyed her older sister curiously.

"Lydia Ann needs some help in Charm. The summer will be busy and she's got those two little ones." Mamm stood and handed the letter to Abby. "I think Emma should go help her out. It's only for a few weeks." She resumed her sweeping as if it were a done deal.

"Jah, I think that's a wonderful idea." Abby glanced at Emma, her blue eyes wide. "You'd have a great time with Lydia Ann, and I'm sure Jacob would understand. Especially since you'd be coming back to him soon." She smiled sweetly.

Something in Abby's voice made Emma peer at her sister a little closer. She seemed very satisfied with herself.

The two of them locked eyes and Abby looked away first. *She's guilty of something.* Emma was sure of it. What had her sister done?

Abby backed out of the room and sped down the hall toward her room.

Emma watched her sister's departing figure. She noticed Mamm watching their interaction with interest. "I'd promised I'd help out in the quilt store here this summer. I'd better make sure Abby really doesn't mind if I'm away for a while." She hurried toward Abby's room.

"Abby," she hissed, "did you somehow set this up?"

Little Miss Innocent perched on her bed and crossed her legs. "If I did, it was only for your own good." She pushed away a blonde tendril that had escaped from her kapp. "Besides, Lydia Ann does need the help, and you need to come to terms with things. Staying in Charm for the summer and sorting everything out is much better than running away from your family and the man who loves you." Her round eyes narrowed. "—And who you love."

Maybe she underestimated Abby. All these years, Emma had been pegged as the rebel, but apparently, Abby could cook up schemes of her own. "Did you tell mamm about my doubts?" Emma crossed her arms and tried to read Abby's face.

"Of course not. No need to worry her. I used the quilt shop phone to call Lydia Ann and fill her in, though. We both thought Mamm would immediately think of you as the best candidate to go help out."

Emma sputtered, trying to form words. Sometimes her little sister was just too much.

"You've only got cold feet. Nothing a little time away won't cure." Abby smoothed the pink Dahlia quilt on her bed. "I guarantee, by the end of the summer, you'll be missing your life here so bad, you'll never give leaving another thought."

Emma sank down into the rocking chair beside the bed. Unless she was prepared to leave town under the cover of night and run away, it looked like a trip to Charm was in her future. And as much as she'd been weighing her options lately, she wasn't ready to run away just yet. She studied her hands in her lap as if they contained the answer to life's problems.

"It's more than just cold feet. Sometimes I feel trapped here, and I'm dying to see more of what else is out there." She looked at Abby intently. "Charm for the summer does give me a temporary way out, though." Temporary being the key. Maybe it would buy her some time to figure things out. And she might meet some interesting people. "*If* I decide to go, I'm only going because Lydia Ann can truly use the help. I'll still feel the same way about things when I get back."

Abby reached over and patted her on the arm. A very patronizing little pat. "That's fine. If you still feel the same way when you get back, maybe then you should rethink some things." She stood. "Come on. There are more chores to do before supper." She turned to walk off.

Emma stuck her tongue out at Abby's retreating figure. Maybe not the most mature thing she'd ever done, but Abby sure had a way of getting underneath her skin.

Chapter Five

·······················

Emma

Ever since she was a small girl, there had always been one place she could go to think. And after the surprising invitation from Lydia Ann, she needed to get away from the prying eyes of her sister and the constant chatter of Sarah and Thomas. So after the supper dishes were cleaned, Emma darted out of the house and into the barn.

Once inside, the sharp scent of hay filled her nose. She quietly closed the door behind her, trying not to disturb the animals that were in for the night. She went into an empty stall and sat down on a hay bale. Her trusty flashlight was hidden in a nook along the wall. Over the years, she'd spent countless years hiding out in the barn, praying, reading, or just thinking.

Tonight, she needed to make a decision about Charm. Even though Abby was behind the scheme, there was no doubt that Lydia Ann could use the help. Plus, Emma had to admit that a change of scenery might do her some good.

The barn door creaked as it swung open. Emma froze. Just a few minutes alone were all she wanted. Was that too much to ask for?

"Emma?" Dat's deep voice broke the silence in the barn, and the horses stirred. "Are you in here?" His lantern cast weird shadows on the wall.

She poked her head around the stall. "Here I am."

He stepped in front of where she sat and smiled down at her. Mose Miller was tall and broad shouldered. His sharp, angled face probably looked severe to some, but his brown eyes were kind. Emma had her father's eyes, the color of chocolate and shaped like almonds. Each of her siblings had her mother's blue eyes, and she'd always been secretly happy to be the lone brown-eyed one in the bunch.

"I figured you'd be here. Doin' some thinkin'?"

She gave a tiny smile and nodded. "Wonderin' if I should spend the summer in Charm, that's all." At least thinking about summer plans allowed her to stop fretting over what to do about Jacob.

"Mind if I give you some advice?"

As far as Emma could remember, her father had never offered up any advice to her. Sure, he made rules for the family. But he'd never really shared his opinion with her before. Not even when she'd decided between teaching and working in a store.

She nodded. "I'd love to hear what you think."

Mose hung the lantern on the wall and sat down on a hay bale opposite her. He let out a deep sigh and pulled his hat off of his head. "Emma, you've always been a little different than your siblings." His smile reached his eyes. "And different's not always a bad thing. It's just different. I know that you probably question a lot of things here." He turned his hat around and around in his big hands. "I've watched you grow from a funny little girl into a thoughtful young woman. I remember all those nights when you'd sneak out here to read your library books by flashlight. I knew then that we were in for some trouble."

She smiled sheepishly. "You knew what I was doing?"

He chuckled. "Let's just say that I always have a pretty good idea what you're up to." His eyes clouded over. "You remind me so much of Clara." He stopped twirling the hat and shook his head.

Clara was her father's younger sister. Lydia Ann's mother. She'd been killed a few years ago in a fire, and Emma had watched her father's private grief. He'd never told her that she reminded him of Aunt Clara, though. "I do? I don't think we look that much alike."

"It's not your looks that remind me of her, although you did get your coloring from my side of the family. It's your spark. You have a zest for life that Clara always had. She used to test our parents something fierce." He rubbed his beard. "I always promised myself that if I ever had a child like her, I'd try to be more understanding." He raised a thick eyebrow. "Would you say I've succeeded?"

Emma smiled. "I know I've been a bit of a rebel at times. I guess I'll never be as perfect as Abby." Her smile was gone. She'd always been afraid she was a disappointment compared to her sister. Was that what her dat was trying to say?

The big man shook his head. "You can't compare your children. You'll see that someday. Each child is their own person. Life would sure be boring if we were all exactly the same, wouldn't it?"

She nodded. "I guess. I just seem to struggle a little more than some."

"That's what I wanted to talk to you about. I know that you've been spending some time with Jacob Yoder." He looked intently at her and she felt the heat in her face. "Your mamm and his mamm have been wanting to see the two of you make a match practically since you were born."

She was surprised at his knowledge. It went to show that even though someone may be quiet, he could still be keenly observant.

"I know that Jacob is getting ready to join the church. Which tells me that he's probably getting near to being ready to ask someone to be his wife." He peered at her. "And you haven't joined the church yet, although I hope that is the decision you will make. But I also know that just like Clara, you're going to have to make those decisions on your own." He sighed and plopped his hat back on his head. "So my advice to you is that I think you should go to Charm. Spend some time with Lydia Ann. Make some new friends." He stood up. "Emma, I have faith in you. I believe you'll come to the right conclusions." He put a hand on her shoulder. "But I also know that you have to figure it all out for yourself."

He lifted up the lantern and turned to go.

"Dat?"

He paused. "Yes, Emma?"

"I'm glad you gave me your advice. I've decided to go to Charm. But I sure will miss you."

He smiled. "It won't be the same around here without you. And you'll be so busy in Charm with Lydia Ann and the twins, you'll barely have time to blink before the summer will be over. So make the most of it."

* * *

"You're kidding, right?" Jacob's green eyes bored into Emma's. "Three months is a mighty long time. I don't think I've ever gone that long without seeing you."

True. Because I rarely get to go anywhere.

"Lydia Ann needs help with things, school is nearly out, and Abby will be busy working at the quilt store here." The quicker she could get the words out, the quicker the conversation could be over. "And..." She grabbed his hand and took a deep breath. "I have a confession to make." There was no turning back now. "I've been having some doubts about things. I think it will be good for me to go to Charm. Maybe I can figure a few things out."

Jacob's jaw tensed. She could see that he wasn't happy. At all. When Emma had rehearsed the little speech in her head, she'd imagined him being fine and even sharing her feelings. It was amazing how everything could work out perfectly in her imagination but then turn into a disaster when she actually lived it. She'd always had a special knack for disaster, though.

"What do you mean 'doubts'?" he asked quietly. "I'm trying to understand what you're saying here, but I am having a difficult time of it." He dropped her hand and rubbed his forehead as if he'd just developed a huge headache. Named Emma. "Do you mean you're having doubts about me?"

"Really about everything. Abby says I'm crazy." Maybe that would make him feel better. She looked at him. Nope. In fact, now he looked like he felt worse, so she plunged ahead. "I think I'm just..." she trailed off, unsure of exactly what to say. "I guess I feel a little lost. Sometimes I don't know if I want to live in Shipshewana forever." This revelation appeared to be a shocker to Jacob. But at least she was telling him now. Abby had tried to make her promise not to tell him about her unhappiness. But Emma thought it was better to be honest now rather than to spring it on him in August when she returned. At least this way he had some warning.

"Emmy." Jacob said the nickname with such tenderness she was tempted to beg him to forget what she'd just said. But she knew the turmoil inside her was there for a reason, so she kept quiet. "Why haven't you mentioned this to me before?" He furrowed his brow, puzzled.

"I'm not sure." She twisted the hem of her apron and bit her lip. The fact that he hadn't had any idea of her feelings only fueled her desire to get away. If Jacob truly knew her, he should've picked up on her feelings a long time ago. But he hadn't. "I guess I kept thinking these thoughts would go away." She glanced over at him. "But they keep popping up." Like weeds in a flower garden.

"I think you can have a wonderful life here in Shipshewana." Jacob was so sincere, so kind. Emma hated knowing she was the cause of his hurt.

"I'm just confused right now. But I don't want to be unfair to you. I feel like you need to know what's going on in my head." She waited on his response.

He sighed deeply and studied her face. "I believe in you. And I think that you'll make the right decisions about your life." A tear rolled down Emma's cheek and Jacob wiped it away. "I don't doubt for a second that you'll choose your life here over whatever else may be tempting you. That's what I'll be praying for."

Chapter Six

Abby

"Are you nuts?" Abby screeched at her sister. Her insane sister. "I can't believe you told Jacob what was going on." She shook her head. "What if he gets tired of waiting on you?"

"The thought has crossed my mind, but I guess that's a risk I have to take." Emma pulled a black suitcase out of the closet and threw it on her bed. "I'm not going to be dishonest with him. I'm tired of keeping secrets. He deserves to know how I feel before I leave."

For the past hour, Abby had grilled Emma on each word and every look that she and Jacob had exchanged when they said their good-byes. Sometimes Emma acted so outlandish. There was no reason to worry Jacob. "If you would just stop and think about everything, you'd see how foolish you're behaving." Abby perched beside the suitcase and watched her sister pace the floor.

"Maybe you should find a man of your own so you'll worry less about me," Emma shot off.

Abby flinched. How easy that sounded coming from Emma, who had known since she was a child that Jacob was the one for her. She swallowed hard. "I just feel sick to my stomach at the thought of you messing up such a good thing." She folded a light blue dress Emma had thrown on the bed and placed it in the suitcase. "But it worries me even more that you might decide to leave our community.

Promise me you'll think seriously about this. If you decide to leave, our lives will never be the same."

Emma stopped what she was doing, and her expression softened. "Please don't worry about me. Worrying never solved anything." She smiled. "Listen to me. I usually leave sounding like mamm to you, but now I can't help myself."

Abby's own lips turned upward, but it was half-hearted. Why wouldn't Emma take this seriously? "I'll try not to worry. But I just want to make sure you know what you're doing."

Emma sighed and sat down on the other side of the suitcase. She ran her hand over the neat stacks of clothes nestled inside the suitcase. "Look at my things. Light blue, black, gray." She met Abby's eyes. "I know it's wrong. But sometimes I want to wear brighter colors. Emerald green, hot pink, or maybe even red."

Abby played with the edge of the quilt, willing herself to keep cool. Did Emma have to test everything? "Emma, really. Why would you even say such a thing?"

Emma's eyes blazed. "I saw a pair of pink high-heeled sandals in that magazine a couple weeks ago that had little diamonds on top. I could paint my toenails pink to match. I'll bet I could add an extra hem to my dress and no one would ever know." She turned her gaze back to the contents of her suitcase. She knew she was being unreasonable. There was no way she would ever try and wear high heels underneath her dress. She was only trying to get underneath her sister's skin.

The horrified expression on Abby's face told her she'd been a success. "Oh, Emma. I just don't understand you. Why can't you just be normal?"

"I didn't say I wanted to rob a bank. Just that sometimes I wish there were more colors in my life." She shrugged. "Besides, who's to say what's normal?"

Abby closed her eyes. Patience. She needed patience. Once Emma was away, her life would be peaceful. Just as she liked it. She opened one eye and looked at her sister. Emma was staring into the suitcase as if the answers to all of life's questions were inside.

Abby stood up. "You amaze me. I don't know anyone else who gets so caught up in their own thoughts that they totally forget the world around them."

Emma let out a sheepish smile. "I was just making sure I had everything I needed."

"Jah, sure you were. What's really on your mind?"

"I was wondering if I'll ever be happy. Really happy. You know?"

Abby's irritation fled. She put her hand on her sister's shoulder. "I'll pray for you. I know I give you a hard time. But I really do want you to feel good about things."

Emma's smile came quickly. "Thanks, sister. I could use your prayers." She stood and grabbed a smaller black bag out of the closet. "Oh! I have an idea."

"That always means trouble," Abby murmured, but as it always did when it came to Emma's ideas, her curiosity got the best of her. "Tell me anyway."

"You have to come visit Lydia Ann and me this summer."

"Visit?" Abby shook her head. "You know I hate riding the bus, and that's a long way to get someone to drive me." And to be honest, she wasn't much of a traveler anyway. Even as children, Emma had always been thrilled at the prospect of going somewhere new, while Abby preferred staying at home.

"I'll take that as a no then…but I will at least expect a weekly letter from you." She eyed her sister. "Or maybe even a phone call. Surely this will be the summer that Timothy Mast will finally start courting you, and I want to be kept informed."

"I wouldn't get my hopes up if I were you." Abby felt a blush rise to her cheeks. "We're friends. That's all." Timothy had been sweet on Abby for years but was very shy. Abby didn't know how she felt about him, anyway.

Emma's look said she didn't buy that they were just "friends," but Abby chose to ignore the doubt. Based on the limited conversations she'd had with Timothy, she was certain they weren't right for one another. But it was kind of fun to let Emma think she might have a prospect of her own.

"Of course I'll write you. I expect you to do the same. You and Lydia Ann are going to have plenty of fun together." Abby couldn't keep the wistful tone out of her voice. She was looking forward to the peace and quiet. But she felt sad nevertheless. After all, Emma had been around her entire life. It would be an adjustment not to talk to her on a daily basis.

"I'll miss you. And I'll fill you in on every little detail. Although I imagine it will just be a summer filled with selling quilts to tourists and running after the twins." Emma placed the suitcase and bag beside the bedroom door.

"And making important decisions," Abby added, raising her eyebrows for emphasis. Emma's entire life was at stake. Abby just hoped her sister would carefully consider things and not jump headfirst, as she was prone to do.

Chapter Seven

Kelly

The regret had begun to wash over Kelly before she was an hour down the road. Was Michelle right? She could turn her X-Terra around right now and stay in Columbus. What if she were making a huge mistake? She barely knew her aunt. She wouldn't know anyone else in Charm. The thought of being an outsider in what was likely to be a closely knit community was freaking her out a little.

But on the other hand, it would be a nice change. It might be cool to be unknown. The new girl in town. And maybe she could figure out a way to turn her life around.

So, she'd have to put on her best Pollyanna attitude and embrace her decision. She'd spent years second-guessing herself, and where had it gotten her? Changing majors a million times and still not being sure the one she chose was for her. Dating a long string of guys who were totally wrong for her, only to end up with her heart smashed to smithereens. In fact, her knack for bad decisions was part of the reason why she'd decided on graduate school rather than entering the workforce. She'd probably make terrible decisions about a job, too.

The best part about spending the summer in Charm was that it would give her a temporary buffer from the rest of the world. And come August, she'd be back in Columbus at her cool new apartment. She and Michelle had had tons of fun over the last week, getting things settled into the new apartment and figuring out the décor.

Plus, Charm was only a couple of hours from the apartment in Columbus. So if she started to feel too isolated, she could always drive in for a visit. Although, looking at the changing landscape outside her window, she almost felt as if she were entering a different country. After she'd gotten off of I-70, the hustle and bustle of the city had begun to disappear. Now that she was nearing Charm, there were rolling hills and farms. She'd already seen a few buggies.

Kelly had never even ridden a horse, much less been in a buggy. She had gone on a horse-drawn carriage ride one time, though, when she was a little kid. It had been a family vacation to New York. She'd been about seven at the time, and it had been her favorite trip until last summer's European adventure. Although, she supposed the trip had been less of a family vacation and more of her dad having had a business trip that he'd allowed her and her mom to tag along on. Even sixteen years ago, they'd already been dysfunctional. It really was a wonder her parents had waited so long to officially go their separate ways.

Pushing those thoughts from her mind, she hit the button on her steering wheel to change the radio station. A slow country ballad blared from the speaker, and she fumbled to turn off the radio completely. She didn't have any more room in her life for heartbreak, even if it were just in the form of a country song.

The silence was quickly broken by a familiar tune coming from her purse. She recognized Michelle's ringtone. With one hand on the wheel, she blindly felt around inside her purse until she grasped the phone.

"Hello."

"Hey. Just thought I'd see how you were making it."

"You afraid I'm having second thoughts already?"

Michelle laughed. "Okay. You caught me. Are you?"

Kelly decided against confessing her doubts to Michelle. Her friend didn't need any more ammo to try and get her to return to Columbus. "Nope. I'm fine. Looking forward to the peace and quiet." At least that part was true.

"Well, I also have news." Michelle paused. "Nick showed up at the apartment. He thought you might still be there. He seems pretty determined to talk to you."

"I'll bet he does. You didn't tell him where I was going, did you?" Kelly held her breath, hoping against hope that Michelle had kept her destination a secret.

"Yeah...the thing about that. Um." Michelle sighed loudly. "It seems that he e-mailed your mom and asked her for your mailing address for the summer. Told her he'd misplaced it and wanted to surprise you or some such thing."

"And she responded? From her divorce recovery trip through Italy?" Kelly's mom and one of her friends had decided to spend the summer "celebrating freedom," which translated into shopping, eating, and flirting with Italian men. She'd hopped on a plane almost as soon as the diploma was in Kelly's hand. But at least she'd attended the graduation ceremony.

"I guess so. Because he knew. He thought it was pretty funny that you're spending the summer among the Amish."

"He's such a jerk."

"Yes. A jerk that you've been on again/off again with for how many years now?"

Her words were harsh but true. "I don't want to talk about it."

"Well, at least promise me you won't take him back again."

Kelly groaned.

"And what's the deal with your mom telling him where you are, anyway? She knows you broke up, right?"

"She knows. That didn't stop her from trying to invite him to go with us to lunch the day before graduation, though. You know how she loves him." Her mother's affection most likely stemmed from his family being affluent. Because it certainly wasn't because of the way he treated her only daughter.

"Ugh. Sorry. Well, I'll let you get back to the drive. Please keep in touch this summer. You will have cell service, won't you?"

"As far as I know, I will. It isn't a third-world country. And you should totally come to Charm for a visit." Aunt Irene had warned her that cell service could be spotty. But there was no need to tell Michelle. She could always drive until she found a signal.

"Maybe."

They said their good-byes, and Kelly turned her full attention back to the road ahead. Her Garmin estimated it to be another half hour to her destination. That wasn't too far, but the growling in her stomach urged her to speed. The lunch she'd shared with Michelle felt like an eternity ago, and the first thing she was looking forward to upon arrival in Charm was a good meal. Aunt Irene had promised to have supper on the table at seven sharp.

Kelly's grandmother was the kind of cook that made eating at a restaurant seem like slumming. And according to Gram, her sister Irene was even better at it and had even taught her a thing or two. Since Kelly had lost fifteen pounds over the past few months, a summer of home-cooked meals was just what she needed. She had a tall, naturally slender frame, and with the missing fifteen pounds, she had a gaunt look about her that she hated. Slender was fine. Waifish wasn't her best look, though.

Last night on the phone, Aunt Irene had also mentioned a surprise. Kelly couldn't imagine what that might be.

But as long as it was a pleasant surprise, she'd be happy. She'd had enough *un*pleasant surprises to last a lifetime.

Chapter Eight

Emma

Maybe Emma would never be satisfied. All this time she'd wanted to get out of Shipshewana, and now that she was on a bus heading out of town, all she could think about was the stench coming from the seat in front of her. She must have a special talent for being seated on public transportation beside people who have strange smells wafting from them. Old men with gas, mothers holding babies with poopy diapers, people with smelly feet who take off their shoes mid-trip. That was usually the crowd she ended up sitting with during the few trips she'd gone on to visit Lydia Ann or her grandparents. And today was no exception.

She stood halfway up and peered over the seat in front of her. Sardines. *Who brings a can of sardines on a bus? For that matter, who eats sardines straight out of the can?* She covered her nose with one hand and tried to think nice, sweet-smelling thoughts.

The passenger in front of her finally put the sardines away, and the air surrounding Emma cleared. Finally. Emma leaned her head back against the seat and closed her eyes.

A poke to her head jolted her upright. She smoothed her kapp and leaned back again. She must've been bumped accidentally by someone behind her. As soon as she was settled against the seat, it happened again, this time accompanied by a giggle.

Emma turned in her seat. A tiny redheaded boy stood in the seat, his stubby fingers outstretched. The guilty party was not a day over three years old. A woman Emma assumed to be his mother, based on her matching red hair, simply shrugged. Prodding strangers on a bus must not be discipline worthy in their family.

Maybe if the white kapp weren't visible to the child, it wouldn't tempt him. Emma turned back around and sank down in the seat. She closed her eyes again and leaned against the window. Sleep would be welcome.

Just as she began to drift off, a sharp kick caught her in the back. She turned around again to look at the little boy.

"Sorry." His mother smiled. "Long trip and he had some chocolate earlier." Her Southern drawl was out of place in Indiana. Emma wondered what brought her and her little boy to a bus bound for Ohio, but she hated to pry.

"That's okay." Emma smiled at the pair and faced the front once again. But not before she heard the woman whisper, "That lady is a nun in training, so you need to be nice to her or she'll tell God on you."

Emma stifled a laugh. One of the things she loved most about traveling was the chance to be around different types of people. She loved to hear their accents and see their unique styles. She leaned against the window and watched the landscape until the sun went down and there was only darkness outside.

Finally, after several hours in the cramped seat, Emma arrived at her destination. Relief washed over her like a spring rain. She couldn't wait to breathe in the fresh air. It seemed like a lifetime had passed since the van had picked her up from home and taken her to catch the bus.

Emma grabbed her bag and headed toward the door, careful to avoid the kicks the little red-haired boy was aiming at her ankles. She was thankful when his mother finally lifted him from the ground and carried him down the aisle.

She made her way down the bus steps. It would've been nice if there had been a familiar face waiting for her. But Lydia Ann had arranged for a van to pick her up from the station in Dover. Her arrival time was way too late for her to come out with the twins.

Emma collected her luggage and looked around, relieved to see an Englisher holding up a "Miller" sign. She signaled to him and he hurried in her direction.

"Hi, Miss Miller, I'm Derek and I'll be driving you to Charm." He took her suitcase and motioned for her to follow. "How was the bus ride?"

"Smelly, but fine." She grinned and switched her small bag to the other shoulder.

Derek laughed as he hoisted her suitcase into the blue van. "You're my only passenger tonight. Hopefully, it won't be too 'smelly' in here. Climb in."

She didn't know if she'd ever been so happy to be in a clean environment. She sank into the seat and buckled her seat belt. Riding in a vehicle didn't bother her, but it always made Abby a nervous wreck.

"Is the temperature okay?" Derek asked.

Emma adjusted the vent to blow right on her. "Fine, thanks."

He turned the van onto the highway. "Would you like to drive through and get something to eat? Charm is half an hour from here, and it's already well past suppertime."

"Jah, if it's not too much trouble." She tried to keep the excitement out of her voice, but she had a feeling Derek wasn't fooled. She rarely got the chance to eat fast food. Before long, she was happily munching on a cheeseburger and fries, topped off by a chocolate shake.

"Do you mind if I turn on the radio?" Derek glanced over at her.

She shrugged. "That would be okay with me." Emma didn't want to feel pressured to make conversation with a strange man for half an hour, and right now, the only sound in the van was her chewing. Music would be welcome over that. Plus, like the cheeseburger and shake, it wasn't often that she actually got to listen to the radio.

A rap song blasted from the speakers and Derek fumbled to change the station. But not before Emma heard what Mamm would've called "choice words." He finally settled on an upbeat country song. She leaned back against the seat and listened.

The year she was fifteen, Emma's parents had allowed her to keep some of the money she'd made selling vegetables at a roadside stand. She'd used it to buy a secondhand Walkman. She'd kept it hidden underneath her bed, and when everyone else was asleep or out in the barn, she would listen to it at night while she read. To this day, music always made her think of that summer, when she felt like the biggest rebel in town because of her secret radio. One day while they were sweeping and mopping the house, Abby had found it and threatened to tell Mamm and Dat if Emma didn't immediately get rid of it. Emma had been furious and called Abby a spoilsport the rest of the summer.

Emma wondered what Abby was doing. According to the van's clock, it was bedtime at home. So she was probably reading the Bible, as had always been their nightly ritual.

Even though Emma didn't always see eye-to-eye with her sister, she couldn't help but admire her. Abby may have some faults, but at least she knew who she was. She never faltered in her devotion to God and to her family. Sometimes it felt to Emma that Abby should've been the older sister, because she would've been better at being an example.

"Here we are." Derek pulled into a driveway and jarred her back to reality.

She hopped out and collected her things. "Thanks for a pleasant drive." Lydia Ann had pre paid him, so Emma waved good-bye and headed to the porch.

She raised her hand to knock, but before she made contact with the wooden door, it opened.

"Emma!" Lydia Ann looked tired, but good. She enveloped Emma in a tight hug. "I'm so glad to see you."

Stepping back, she grabbed the suitcase. "Here, let me help you with your things."

Emma followed her into the house.

Lydia Ann took the suitcase into a spare bedroom. Returning, she motioned for Emma to follow her back to the living room. "The twins are finally asleep," she said in a low voice. "Are you hungry? Thirsty?" She directed Emma to the kitchen table.

"I'm not the least bit hungry." Emma slid into a chair and explained about supper from the drive-thru window.

Lydia Ann laughed. "Don't make a habit of it. Those cheeseburgers and chocolate shakes can be addictive."

"Is that experience speaking?" It was so nice to see her again.

She grinned. "Let's just say that we all need a treat every now and then. How about some water?"

Emma nodded.

"Well?" Lydia Ann eyed her expectantly once they each had a glass of water. "Abby filled me in on your problem."

"Yes, I'm sure she did." Emma took a long drink, more so she wouldn't have to say anything than from thirst.

Lydia Ann took the hint quite nicely, and Emma remembered how much she'd always loved her cousin. "I'll tell you what. You're probably exhausted, and I know I am. How about we postpone this conversation until we both feel better?"

Emma nodded. "Thanks. I do want to talk to you about it. Hopefully you'll understand better than Abby does. And I'd love to hear your thoughts." Emma drained her glass. "And I want to hear all about what's been going on with you. I can't wait to see Mary and Katie tomorrow."

Lydia Ann took their glasses to the sink. "They've grown by leaps and bounds since you saw them last." She gazed out the dark window over the sink as if she were a million miles away. Emma froze at the look of intense sadness on her face. Then, she remembered. The last time she'd seen the twins was at Levi's funeral.

"Um, Lydia Ann, I'm so sorry. About Levi." Emma never knew what to say to someone who was grieving. Abby was so much better at it. She always knew just what to do.

Lydia Ann jerked her gaze back to Emma. "It's been tough on all of us. Let's talk more after we've rested."

"That sounds good."

* * *

The next morning, the sound of loud voices outside of Emma's room pulled her from a deep sleep. She burrowed deeper into the soft pillow, hoping it was a dream. But a second later, the bedroom door burst open, and Mary and Katie came bounding inside.

The little girls were identical except for a dimple in Katie's cheek. Emma sat up and rubbed her eyes. They were adorable. She couldn't remember ever seeing children who were such a perfect mixture of both parents.

Mary and Katie climbed up on the bed, laughing and giggling.

"My mamm said we could come wake you up." Mary bounced up and down with excitement.

"You're a sleepyhead." This announcement came from Katie, who flashed her dimple and then proceeded to grab Emma's nose. "I've got your nose!" She victoriously holds up Emma's "nose" between her fingers. Mary fell over into gales of giggles.

"I said you could wake Cousin Emma up quietly like little mice." Lydia Ann leaned against the doorframe and shook her head at her girls. She was already neatly dressed for the day. "I tried to let you sleep in a little since you had such a long trip yesterday."

"Thanks." Emma smiled at the girls as they leapt from the bed and ran out of the room, each making a kissing noise at their mother as they passed her by. "Do they do everything at top speed?" She rose and started making the bed.

"Honestly? Yes. They hit the ground running every morning and don't stop. I'm just thankful for their afternoon nap." She helped Emma spread the quilt on the bed. "Except that by that time, I feel like I need a nap, too."

"Well then, I guess it's good that I'm here." Once the bed was finished, Emma dug through her suitcase. "Even if Abby had an ulterior motive for getting me to come on this trip, I'll do all I can to pitch in."

Lydia Ann nodded. "Hopefully we can be of help to each other. Now go get cleaned up and dressed. There's a pot of coffee on, and I'm making pancakes."

"Yum. You don't have to tell me twice." Emma headed into the bathroom to get ready for her first full day in Charm. For the first time in months, that old feeling of restlessness was gone. An adventure was coming her way. And she was ready.

Chapter Nine

....

Abby

Three days. It had only been three days since Emma left town. And already Abby secretly wished she'd gone with her. Of course, she'd never admit it to anyone. Forget about her dislike of travel. It was as quiet as a tomb around the house without Emma there. Even Thomas and Sarah seemed to be quieter than normal.

On Thursday afternoon, Abby sat on a stool in the quilt shop where she worked. It had been a slow day, plenty of time to think and wonder. Mostly about what Emma was up to.

The bell above the door made a jingling sound as someone entered. Abby jumped up to greet the customer, knocking a stack of quilt squares onto the floor.

Jacob Yoder strode toward her, his straw hat firmly on top of his head. His blond hair curled slightly underneath the hat. His square jaw kept his blond locks from making him look childish, but Abby remembered when he'd been a towheaded little boy. She and Emma had known him their entire lives. He and his family were their closest neighbors, and he and Emma were exactly the same age. Now that he was grown, Jacob worked with his father on their family farm.

Abby felt her cheeks flush as if she'd been standing in front of the stove for too long. The worst part about having such pale skin was blushing easily. "Hi, Jacob."

He reached the counter and grinned. "Good afternoon." He nodded toward the brightly colored squares scattered around her. "Do you need some help?"

"No, I can get them. I'm just clumsy today." She managed a weak smile.

"I insist." He walked around the counter to where she stood.

They scooped the squares up from the floor and, after a minute, had restored order to the stack.

"Glad I could be of help." He stepped to the other side of the counter. "I was on my way home and thought I'd stop in to see how you are and if you've heard anything from Emma."

She sighed. "Jah. She made it to Charm with no problem." She leaned her arms on the counter and met his green eyes. "I spoke to her on the phone yesterday."

"I'm glad to hear she made it safely. I was praying for her to have safe travels."

"No need to worry anymore. She's settling in at Lydia Ann's house now and will start her new job in a few days." She began folding a stack of quilt squares.

"Actually, I wonder if that, in and of itself, is reason to worry." Jacob paused for a second. "I'm concerned about her. What do you think is the real reason she's in Charm for the next few months?" His green eyes bored into her, and she broke away from his gaze.

Abby took a deep breath. "Oh. You know Emma. She's always been a little dramatic." She managed a weak grin. "I'd say she probably just wants a little excitement before she settles down. That's all."

He nodded. "So, you really think she'll come back? Do you think she'll ever be happy here?"

She hated to tell him how worried she was. There was no need
to add to his worries. Her sister should be ashamed. "Jah. There's no
doubt in my mind that she'll be back at the end of the summer, as
planned." She reached out and patted his arm. "Don't think another
thing about it. The months will fly by. I'm sure of it." The doubt in
her voice couldn't be masked, but at least Jacob didn't mention it.
"Besides. What's not to love here?"

"Thanks. And let me know if you hear from her, okay?"

"Of course I will." She smiled. "You do the same."

He nodded. "I'll check back with you in a couple of days." With
that, he tipped his hat to her and turned to go.

Abby watched Jacob climb into his buggy. Her sister was playing
with fire. Jacob was an honest, God-fearing man who deserved a
woman who knew what she wanted. Abby was determined to make
Emma see what she was risking.

She picked up the phone from the counter and dialed Lydia
Ann's shop. She disliked using the phone but felt justified because it
was the quickest way she could check up on her sister. Once the last
number was dialed, the phone just rang and rang. No answer. She
sighed and hung up.

The front door burst open and two women entered. Abby
pasted on a smile and went to greet them. Worrying would have
to wait.

* * *

Later that evening, Abby sat at the kitchen table, reading her Bible.
She'd been so caught up lately in what was going on with her sister,

she'd barely given any thought to anything else. How could she best lead Emma back into the fold? She closed her eyes and said a silent prayer. Only God could show her how to help Emma.

"Abby?" Dat's deep voice made her jump.

"Jah. It's me. I know I should be in bed."

He sat down across from her. "You've been sad since Emma left." It was a statement not a question.

Tears sprang into her eyes. "Oh, Dat. I was the one who encouraged her to go, but now…" she trailed off.

"You can't take full responsibility for that. I also encouraged her to go." He looked thoughtful. "And I'd say she wanted to go anyway."

Abby gave him a tiny smile. "I guess she probably did."

"And how about you? Didn't you give any thought to a summer in Charm? I imagine Lydia Ann could use all the help she can get." His brown eyes twinkled at her over the lantern light.

"Oh. You know I'm not much of a traveler. And I'm needed here. Mamm needs me to take up the slack while Emma is away."

"We will always need you here. But I hate to see you poutin' around all summer." He rose from the table. "If you wanted to go, I believe we could arrange for you to stay at Lydia Ann's for at least a few weeks."

He gave her a wink and headed to bed, leaving Abby with only her thoughts.

Chapter Ten

Emma

"I'm sorry you haven't seen much of the town yet." Lydia Ann bustled about, getting the quilt store ready to open.

Emma looked up from the floor where she was helping Katie and Mary get situated with coloring books. "Don't be sorry. I'll learn my way around in no time." She smiled. "Besides, we've had our hands full." She motioned at the girls, who were babbling and coloring. "I don't know how you do it all, Lydia Ann."

Lydia Ann shook her head. "I have a lot of help. When Levi got sick, it seemed like everyone in town pitched in to help us out. And then..." she trailed off and took a breath. "After the funeral, even more people came around." She smiled wanly. "I've been amazed at the outpouring of love. The Lord has truly blessed me and my girls, even through our tragedy."

Emma was flooded with guilt. Mamm and Abby were always asking her to go with them when they took food to a grieving church member. And she always refused. But listening to Lydia Ann talk about how much the outpouring of support meant to her, Emma knew that she would have to change her ways. Maybe sometimes, even if you didn't feel like you were good at handling the grief of others, just showing up was important.

Emma stood up and walked around the little shop. The brightly colored quilts reminded her of the ones in the store where Abby worked. She pushed away the pang of homesickness that hit with that thought. In addition to quilts, there were bolts of fabric, pattern books, homemade dolls, and a few woodcarvings. "You have a lot of neat stuff for sale," she said, crossing to the wall opposite the cash register.

A series of paintings caught her eye.

The first two colorful paintings were of quilts. Emma had never seen anything like them before. The intricate lines and details of the quilts were perfectly captured in the paintings. The third painting was a landscape. She recognized the location immediately as Charm. "These paintings are beautiful."

Lydia Ann glanced up from where she was cutting fabric. "Aren't they, though? They are big sellers as well. Tourists especially love the quilt paintings. The artist is local, so the landscape paintings are popular, too, because of their authenticity. In fact, I think they are often displayed at stores and galleries in Sugarcreek and Berlin and other larger towns nearby."

Emma was impressed. Although she'd never been very artistic, she'd always had an admiration for those who were. She often thought an artist must have such a fun job, being surrounded by all the colors of the rainbow.

"Mamm!" one of the twins called from the back of the store.

"Can you watch things out here for a second?" Lydia Ann asked.

Emma smiled. "Jah. That's what I'm here for." She made her way over to the counter, pausing for a moment to admire another painting.

The bell jingled over the door, and she looked up, anxious to greet her first customer. A tall, handsome man entered the store.

His brown eyes twinkled as he got closer to the counter. The tanned, smooth face told her he wasn't married. "Good mornin'." His smile reached his eyes and was so infectious, Emma smiled back.

"Mornin'. Is there something I can help you find?" She wrinkled her forehead. What would a man like him need from a quilt store? "Fabric? Buttons?" She was at a loss. "Maybe a pattern?"

He chuckled. "I'm not much of a quilter. Although my mamm would probably be delighted if I took her some supplies."

"Noah!" Lydia Ann exclaimed as she hurried to the counter. "I thought I heard a voice out here." She reached the counter and motioned toward Emma. "I guess you've already met my cousin?" she asked.

He shook his head. "We were just getting around to that." He nodded at Emma. "Noah Weaver." The dimple in his cheek was a great contrast to his angular jaw.

She gave him a smile. "Emma Miller. Pleased to meet you."

"Emma lives near Shipshewana but is visiting Charm for the summer," Lydia Ann explained. "She's going to help me here and with the girls."

Noah nodded. "Welcome to our town." He grinned. "Has Lydia Ann shown you around yet?"

Emma shook her head. "I've only been here a few days and we haven't had a chance just yet. We will soon, though."

Noah nodded. "Good."

Lydia Ann cleared her throat. "Actually, Noah, if you have a little time today, maybe you could give her the grand tour."

A tiny gasp escaped from Emma. She cast a sideways glance at Lydia Ann, but her cousin was looking at Noah. "Oh. That's…"

Before she could decline, Noah cut her off. "It would be my pleasure." He turned toward Emma and flashed her another brilliant smile. "How about I come back around noon?"

Lydia Ann jumped in. "That sounds perfect. And I'll bet I know two little girls who would love to spend some time outdoors." She waved her arm around the nearly deserted store. "I'll manage just fine here alone while you're gone."

"That will be fun. Mary and Katie can help me show Emma the town." Noah grinned again at Emma.

Emma was speechless. She couldn't remember the last time she'd been talked around, as if she were invisible. She watched as Lydia Ann walked Noah to the door, speaking in hushed tones. Before he left, he tipped his hat in Emma's direction. "See you in a bit."

The door had barely closed before she began sputtering. "Lydia Ann, you shouldn't have forced that man to give me a tour. I would've been perfectly happy waiting until you had time or I could have even gone exploring on my own."

Lydia Ann regarded her with a twinkle in her eyes. "Noah doesn't mind." She picked up a roll of thread that had fallen to the floor. "Mary and Katie love spending time with him, and they will be thrilled to get to go along. So it isn't like I'm sending you off all alone with a man you just met."

Emma wasn't convinced. "Who is he, anyway?"

"Noah's mamm and Levi's mamm are sisters. Noah was Levi's favorite cousin." She paused. "Noah took Levi's death pretty hard. And he's been of great help this past year, stopping by to see if I need anything done around the house. In fact, that's why he was here. He's going to do some repair work at the house over these next weeks.

He was a great friend to Levi." Her eyes clouded over for a moment. "He's a little older than you, but it wouldn't hurt you to make a friend here." She brightened. "Besides, spending time in the company of a handsome man isn't a bad thing."

Emma felt the hot blush creeping over her face. She had noticed. He was quite handsome in a more rugged way than most of the men she knew from back home.

Lydia Ann giggled. "Well, that settles it. You're going on a tour."

She had wanted to meet new and interesting people. And after all, this was supposed to be an adventure. So, she guessed allowing a stranger to give her a tour of the town wasn't such a wild idea. She wondered for a fleeting second what Abby would say but quickly pushed the thought away.

Chapter Eleven

....

Kelly

The One Charming Inn reminded Kelly of a postcard. *Quaint* was how she'd described it in the text message she'd sent to Michelle once she'd finally arrived. Her first few days had been spent exploring the grounds and visiting with her aunt. The white, two-story house had a huge wraparound porch, which had quickly become her favorite place. And she couldn't remember the last time she'd been so enveloped in silence. Maybe never. There were no honking horns. No alarms. No trains. And even better, she hadn't heard a single angry word since she'd arrived. Just peace and quiet. She'd even begun to find the sound of the horses' hooves on the road soothing.

She poured herself a cup of coffee in the large kitchen. Although she'd never been much of a cook, she could certainly picture herself attempting to try, if only to get to use the double oven. She peeked out the window over the sink and spotted a rabbit hopping across the grass. She quickly walked out to the porch and perched on a wooden rocking chair, happy to watch the rabbit scurry along the yard. For miles around, all she could see were rolling green hillsides, farmlands, and white houses. The inn was about a half-mile east of downtown Charm. And except for the occasional tourist, the only traffic was the horse-and-buggy variety.

There was one tiny problem. It seemed that relaxation was eluding her, even in such a peaceful place. For some reason, she'd had the idea that as soon as she was away from her "regular" life, her troubles would melt away. But they hadn't.

In fact, they'd intensified. Maybe she just wasn't used to being so still. There was literally nothing to do but think. And when she thought, it was about all the things troubling her. Was her mom okay? Could she forgive her dad? Would Nick track her down? And was being a librarian really what she wanted to do with her life?

She leaned her head against the rocker and sighed. While she'd never been one much for dramatics, a little part of her would like to fall down right there on the porch and kick and scream like a toddler. It might not have solve anything, but it sure would feel good.

"Well, someone looks like they're having a heaping serving of bitter with their coffee," Aunt Irene said, stepping out onto the porch. "Are you okay, honey?"

Kelly shrugged. "I'm sure I will be. I'm just trying to sort some things out."

Irene sat down in a rocker and looked at her great-niece. Even though her face was wrinkled, her eyes were still a sparkling blue. Her snow-white hair was swept into a bun. She reminded Kelly of Aunt Bea from *The Andy Griffith Show*. Except maybe a little older. Irene reached over and patted Kelly on the hand. "There, there, my dear. It will all be okay. Believe me, the good Lord never gives you more than you can handle."

Kelly managed a tiny smile. "I guess not." Talking about God made her feel uncomfortable. She hadn't stepped foot into a church since she left for college, and she wasn't quite sure where He fit into her life. "So, is it always so quiet around here?"

Irene nodded. "Most of the time. Every now and then, I'll have guests who have children. That certainly livens things up. But most people who stay here are looking to get away." She glanced over at her great niece. "You know?"

"Yes. I'm just not sure about all the silence." In the dorm, there were always voices, music, TV, and phones ringing non-stop.

Irene chuckled. "It's a funny thing, isn't it? Sometimes you just can't get away from your problems no matter how far you run. I guess the silence can be a little daunting at first." Irene slowly rose from the chair. "But maybe now you can learn to really listen to your heart."

Kelly sighed. Maybe. Either that or the silence would just drive her mad. "I start work at the bookmobile on Monday. Thanks for getting me the job."

Irene nodded. "I figured you'd want to keep as busy as possible. Plus, if I remember correctly from your childhood, you love books." She smiled. "And it will be a good way for you to get out and meet some people from the community. Now, I'd better go finish my grocery list."

The job at the bookmobile had been the surprise her aunt had in store for her, and it had been a nice one. Sure, she'd have plenty of things to do around the inn to keep her busy. But working at the bookmobile a couple of days a week would be a nice change of pace. And she did love books. In fact, she had a stack of "to be read" books sitting on the little nightstand beside her bed. These past few months there hadn't been much time for pleasure reading.

But maybe that was all about to change. Kelly stood and followed Aunt Irene back into the house.

Chapter Twelve

Emma

The fluttering in her stomach began just before noon. What was she doing, going off with a man she didn't know? Even if he was a close friend of Lydia Ann's, he was still a complete stranger as far as she was concerned. For all her outlandish talk, Emma had always been shy around people she didn't know very well. It took her some time to warm up to new people. She took a deep breath.

"Are you okay?" Lydia Ann asked.

"What? Oh. Yes. I'm fine."

"Do you think you can stop tapping your foot then?" Lydia Ann motioned to the floor.

Emma smiled. She'd not even noticed her tapping. "Sorry." She stopped the tapping.

"Nervous tic?" Lydia Ann chuckled. "You'll be fine. He's quite a nice fellow. And he's a talker, so I suspect you'll not have to say much."

Emma grinned. "Well, maybe I am a little nervous." She shrugged. "I haven't really spent that much time alone with a man."

Lydia Ann looked surprised. "What? I thought you had a steady beau back home." She eyed Emma suspiciously. "At least, that's what Abby said."

Of course Abby had told Lydia Ann that. "Jacob." She sighed. "We've never really talked about our feelings. It seems like we're always just thrown together." She played with the hem of her apron. "Abby is much more enthused about the prospect of us getting married than I am."

"So he's…" Lydia Ann trailed off and gave her a puzzled look.

"He's wonderful. Really. If I had to sit here and make a list of the perfect man, it would be like I described him to a tee."

"But maybe he's not perfect for you?" Lydia Ann asked.

Emma bit her lip and nodded. "Exactly. Besides that, I think I frustrate him." She smiled. "And I always have, ever since we were little kids. He tells me I'm too complicated."

"So why did you start spending time together in the first place?"

"My matchmaking sister got involved. She arranged for him to drive me home from a singing a few months ago, and ever since then, it was just sort of a pattern we fell into."

"But do you think he feels differently about things than you do?"

Emma made a face. "That's the thing. I'm not a hundred percent certain how he feels. And honestly, when I came here, I sort of hoped I'd learn to feel differently about him. Let's just say it would make my life much easier if I found myself head over heels for him."

Lydia Ann laughed. "The heart wants what it wants, though. You can't make yourself have feelings for someone just because he has the right qualities. There's a little more to it than that."

Emma grinned. "If only it were that easy. Right?"

Lydia Ann nodded. "I suppose that would make things easier. But maybe not as much fun."

The bell above the door rang and Emma looked up from the fabric she was folding. Noah Weaver sauntered in, a broad smile on his face.

"Ladies." He nodded at them. "Emma, are you ready to be a tourist?" He gave her a playful grin. "I may not be much of a tour guide, but I'll give it a shot."

She nodded. "I'm sure you'll be fine."

"Mary, Katie," Lydia Ann called. "Noah is here."

The little girls came running from the back of the store, giggling and chattering. "We're ready," Katie said.

Emma glanced at Lydia Ann. "We won't be gone long."

"Have fun," Lydia Ann called as Noah held the door open.

Emma hesitated for a moment. It wasn't too late to back out. She glanced up at Noah and his brown eyes met hers. What she saw in them reassured her. She'd be safe stepping out of her comfort zone with this man.

* * *

They stepped out on the sidewalk and Emma blinked against the bright sun.

"Come on, girls, let's go," Noah said. He held out his hands and each twin took hold of a hand.

"Will you hold my other hand?" Katie looked up at Emma.

"Of course, sweetie, I'd love to." Emma held out her hand and Katie grabbed it.

As they headed down the sidewalk holding hands, Emma knew that any stranger seeing them would assume they were just a family going for a walk. The thought jolted her, but she reminded herself that this was no different than going for a walk with Jacob. Easier really, considering no one wanted Noah to marry her. Her cheeks flamed at the thought.

Noah looked at her over the twins' heads. "Are you okay? Your face is a little…"

She nodded and felt her face grow hotter. "I'm fine."

The twins chattered to each other, and Emma could feel a slight breeze as they strolled down the sidewalk looking in the shop windows. It soothed her face, and after a few moments, she relaxed a little.

Noah glanced at her. "So, what really brings you to Charm?" They strolled slowly along.

"Oh, you know. Lydia Ann needed some help." She glanced down at the girls. Was it that transparent that she had an ulterior reason for being here?

"You're very kind to come all this way to pitch in."

She smiled. "I hope to be of great help to them. And I thought spending the summer in a new place sounded like it could be fun." That was enough explaining.

"New places always do have a certain pull, don't they?" he asked, almost more to himself than to her. "Okay, before our tour begins, how about I give you a little background?"

"That sounds perfect."

He stopped and pointed toward the road that led to Charm from Millersburg. "In the mid-1800s, this area was a crossroads of sorts. There was an old Indian trail that ran through here, and at some point, someone built a blacksmith shop here. After that initial business was opened, a little town sprang up around it. It was originally known as Stevenson."

He had a good storytelling voice. It was deep and gravelly. Since Emma had always loved history, his tale was right up her alley. In fact, she kept a running list of historical locations she would like to visit someday. Every time she read about a new place that interested her, she added it to her "places Emma wants to visit" list. Even though she didn't know for sure if she'd ever get the chance, she thought it was important to have dreams.

"After a post office was established in the late 1800s, the name was changed to Charm. Has a nice ring to it, wouldn't you say?" He grinned. "These days, there are scores of tourists who come through here, wanting to see Amish country. I suspect you'll see a lot of them this summer." They started walking again.

"This is Charm View School," Noah said.

"We're going to school soon," Mary said. "Aren't we, Katie?"

"Mamm says we will when we get older." Katie nodded confirmation.

Since school was out for the summer, there were no students around. "It reminds me of the school I teach in back home."

"So you're a teacher? Do you enjoy it?"

"Jah. Very much." She glanced down at the little girls. "Children are so funny. They are free with their thoughts and actions in a way I miss being able to be."

He nodded, his green eyes on her face. "I know what you mean. Spending time with these two has taught me a lot." He grinned down at them. "A couple of weeks ago when I stopped by the store, they served me tea from one of their little toy tea sets. I had to drink every last drop."

She laughed. "That must've been a sight to see."

"Will you have a tea party with us?" Katie tugged on her hand. "When we get home?"

"Maybe not today, but I will have a tea party with you." Emma smiled at her.

"So, what's next?" She looked up at Noah.

He chuckled. "Keepin' me on track. I like that." They continued walking and finally came to a stop. "This is Grandma's Homestead Restaurant." The parking lot adjacent to the restaurant was full of cars, trucks, and a few buggies. "It's a favorite with tourists, but the locals eat here sometimes, too. You'll have to try it."

She nodded. "That sounds good."

"And next door to the Homestead is the Charm General Store," he said, pointing to the store. "You can get just about everything there. Groceries, household items…and they have great ice cream." He looked over at her then glanced down at the twins with a twinkle in his eyes.

"Ice cream?" Mary echoed. "We love ice cream!"

Katie nodded in agreement.

"Let's wait a little on that. We've still got a little farther to walk." Noah smiled down at the girls. "We need to cross the street. Everybody hold a hand."

Katie slipped her hand back into Emma's, and Mary did the same with Noah. They waited for a buggy to go by, and then crossed. They stopped at the bottom of a steep hill. "Does everyone feel like climbing?" Noah asked.

"I do," Katie said.

"I do," Mary echoed.

The four of them climbed the hill and walked into a large parking lot. Emma was amazed at the rows of buggies and cars in the lot.

"Charm also has a booming material business. This is Keim Lumber, where I work. We do business all over the United States."

"Wow. That's a big place." Emma could see that the business encompassed several buildings. He nodded. "It seems even larger on the inside. And there's a place inside called Carpenters Café, where you can have lunch or just a root beer float."

Emma smiled. "Why am I getting a feeling ice cream is one of your favorite things?"

He shrugged. "I guess you pick up on the important stuff." He glanced at the twins. "Who wants to go inside and have some ice cream?"

Both girls excitedly agreed, and they headed into the cool building. While the twins were looking through the clear glass at the ice cream flavors, Emma and Noah found a small table where they could see the girls.

"So do you enjoy your work?" Emma asked as Noah pulled her chair out for her.

He grinned at her. "Very much. I was fortunate to work alongside Levi for a while." He shook his head. "It's not the same without him." He sat down across from her.

The sadness in his voice was evident. "I'm sorry." She wondered if Levi had realized when he was alive what an impact he was having on those around him.

She glanced out the huge windows. May was a beautiful time of year. The sky was clear and the sun was out. Emma sighed. On a day such as this, it was easy to forget her troubles. She closed her eyes, picturing miles of blue water.

"Penny for your thoughts?" Noah brought her out of her daydream.

"This is the kind of day that makes me want to see the ocean. To hear the waves crashing all around."

"The ocean? Have you been there?"

She shook her head. "Only in my dreams."

His grin grew wider. "Someday you will."

The last thing she needed was encouragement in her silly ideas. Just ask Abby.

In a few minutes the twins came to the table followed by a young waitress bearing a tray with a scoop of bubblegum ice cream in one dish and a scoop of chocolate in the other. She took their orders for root beer floats and headed off.

"I picked bubblegum," Katie said. "But Mary wanted chocolate."

"But I'm going to eat part of hers and she's going to eat part of mine," Mary explained to them. "That's what we always do."

After they finished their ice cream, the four of them headed back out into the sunlight, contented and full. The twins walked in front chattering to each other.

"Well, is this enough sightseeing for today?" Noah asked as they strolled slowly toward Lydia Ann's store at the other end of town.

"I think so, especially with the extra ice cream treat. This has been nice." Her mouth turned upward in a smile. "Thank you for taking the time to show me around."

"It has been my pleasure. I hope you find what you're looking for in Charm."

She bristled. "I'm not looking for anything here. I'm just helping out a family member who needs me." Her words came out sharper than she intended. Why hadn't she just kept her mouth shut? Abby always chided her for speaking without thinking.

"I don't mean to offend you, but I see the look in your eyes. You're running from something." She opened her mouth to protest, but he cut her off. "I know you don't know me very well. And you may think it inappropriate for a near stranger to speak this way to you. But I've been there." He regarded her with serious green eyes. "If you decide you need someone to talk to about things, I'll be glad to listen."

Emma wrinkled her forehead and shook her head. "I'm fine." She pushed open the door to the quilt shop and ushered the twins inside. "Thanks again for the tour."

He tipped his hat to her. "I suspect I'll see you again soon."

She turned and watched as he walked away. He didn't have the right to question her reasons for being here. Even if he thought he might understand. Lost in thought, she walked toward the counter.

"Whoa. Someone has a color to her cheeks," Lydia Ann said as Emma reached the counter. "Is that just from the sunshine... or something else?" She peered at her cousin.

Emma shook her head. "Oh, it's nothing." Nothing she wanted to talk about anyway. "It was a nice tour. I think Charm is a neat town." She smiled. "Now, what did I miss while I was gone?"

Lydia Ann looked at her for a long moment as if she were still trying to read Emma's expression.

"Really," Emma insisted, "we had a fine time. There's nothing more to say." There was no need to tell Lydia Ann how disconcerting it was that Noah had been able to read her so well. Months had gone by at home with her feeling downright depressed, and no one had noticed. Not Jacob, not Abby. Although, based on the conversation she'd had with Dat before coming to visit Charm, she suspected her father might've picked up that something wasn't right.

Lydia Ann finally looked satisfied. "You didn't miss much. You have a letter from Abby, though."

Emma grinned. "Checking up on me again." She shook her head. "You've got to hand it to her. When my sister sets her mind to something, she usually gets her way."

Lydia Ann laughed. "True. Things have always had a way of working out for Abby."

Emma eagerly tore into the letter, suddenly anxious to hear what was going on back home.

Chapter Thirteen

Abby

Abby watched as Jacob divided the kids up into two teams. He
always tried to make the teams even so neither side would have
an easy victory. That was one of the things that she admired about
him—one more of the many reasons she was so sure he would be
the perfect match for Emma.

She glanced down at the colorful quilt she was relaxing on. It
was right here on this very spot, maybe even on this very quilt, that
she had developed her plan to make sure Emma and Jacob both
realized they belonged together.

She sifted through the reasons again—they both loved children.
Emma was an elementary school teacher, and it was the perfect job
for her. She was full of energy and loved to play games and read
stories to her students. And Jacob was the same way. Watching
him, surrounded by kids of all ages, organizing them into teams,
showed how patient he was with children. She, on the other hand,
preferred selling quilts and souvenirs to the English tourists that
came to town. And Emma and Jacob were both athletic. Given the
choice, both of them would rather be outdoors than inside. Even as
little girls, Abby had always preferred dolls and coloring, but Emma
would play volleyball or kickball with the boys until mamm made
her quit. Abby grinned, thinking about the time Emma had tried

to convince mamm to let her wear pants so she could climb trees better.

"Thomas, go see if David wants to play." Jacob called to her brother. Jacob's hair seemed to be even curlier than normal in the early-summer heat. She imagined Jacob and Emma, standing together. With Jacob's fair hair and skin, and Emma's dark hair and eyes, even their coloring complemented each other. Not like herself. When she and Jacob went places together, people probably assumed they were brother and sister.

Thomas interrupted her thoughts as he came running over.

"David can't play because he let the dog eat half of his mamm's pot roast and now he's in big trouble." Thomas gave her a grin. "Come on, Abby. We just need one more player to make the teams even. Puh-lee-z?" he begged, giving the word three syllables. "Even Sarah is playing."

Abby looked at the crowd of players who stood waiting for her decision. Jacob had divided them up as evenly as he could, given the disparity of ages and sizes of the players. The youngest were nine-year-old Ike Bellar and Abby's sister Sarah, whose ninth birthday was right around the corner. Jacob was the oldest player, followed by Ike's brothers, eighteen-year-old Jonah and fifteen-year-old Josiah.

"I wish Emma were here." Abby rose from the quilt she had placed on the ground in anticipation of watching the volleyball game. "I'm awful at this and every one of you knows it."

Thomas laughed. "Yeah, you are, but Emma isn't here so you have to play."

"Stand right here." Jacob pointed to a spot right beside him. "You remember how to play, right? If the ball comes your way, you

can just tap it in the air and I'll hit it over." He grinned at her."
Or you can pound it over the net yourself."

Abby took her place, trying to ignore the flutters in her
stomach. Anything athletic made her so nervous. She hated
looking foolish in front of others. The first few balls went to
other players and she was grateful. Maybe no one would hit it to
her since they all knew how bad of a player she was. She would
probably miss the ball, even if it were hit right to her. As the game
went on, she relaxed slightly. So far, all she had to do was move
out of the way and let the players on either side of her hit the ball.
Jacob was especially good about stepping in to hit any balls that
came in her direction. She noticed that even Sarah was able to hit
it up high enough for the taller ones to tap over the net. She must
take after Emma.

Abby was in the middle row when one of the Bellar boys from
the other team served the ball. It flew through the air, aiming for
her. It seemed like it was drawn to her like a magnet. Her eyes
widened, but she didn't move. Her legs felt like they were made of
concrete.

"You can do it, Abby," Thomas hollered.

She raised her arms up, preparing to strike. This was it. She
should have known that, eventually, the ball would come her way.
She closed her eyes tightly as the ball came closer. It thwacked
hard against her forehead with a loud smacking sound. Pain seared
through her, and she stumbled backward. Abby hit the ground with
a thud so hard it knocked the breath right out of her.

She heard the gasps from the other players. "Oh, no." Sarah's soft
voice seemed to come from far away. "Should I go get Dat?"

Abby hated to be the center of attention. She tried to sit up so she could stop Sarah from telling their parents, but it was too painful. She dropped back down and closed her eyes tightly, willing the pain to subside. When she finally opened her eyes, Jacob's bright green eyes stared back. His brows were knitted together as he peered at her. His face was inches from hers. She closed her eyes again quickly.

"Maybe you need to give her that mouth-to-mouth recesssa… recess… recess thing like the paramedics showed us at school," Ike Bellar shouted.

Abby could feel the blood rushing to her face. She jerked her eyes open to meet Jacob's again. Could she be more embarrassed?

Jacob's mouth quirked slightly in a half smile. "No, Ike. I think she's breathing okay." He turned to the group hovering around her. "Maybe everyone needs to back away and give her some air, all right?"

Abby tried to decide the best way to remove herself from this situation without becoming the laughingstock of her family and friends. She knew better than to attempt playing volleyball.

Jacob leaned toward her again, and she could feel his breath on her face. "Just wait a couple of minutes and let me clear everyone out. Then you'll be able to get up in peace." He turned to Thomas and Sarah, who wore matching worried looks on their faces. "She's fine. It just knocked the breath out of her." He glanced at the rest of the group. "Why don't we all take a water break while Abby gets her breath back?"

She watched from her prone position as everyone but Jacob, Sarah, and Thomas went to get some water. Jacob reached for her hands and pulled her up to a sitting position.

"I'm fine," Abby said to her younger siblings. "Really. Jacob's right, it just knocked the breath out of me." She took Jacob's hand, and he helped her to stand. "It's just so embarrassing to be such a klutz."

"You're not a klutz," Jacob reassured her. "You just missed the ball. Next time, keep your hands and arms closer together."

"You've told me that all my life," Abby grumbled. "There won't be a next time. Sports are not my thing. And everyone here knows it."

Jacob grinned at her. "Yeah, I remember when we were kids and you tried to play." He turned to Sarah. "I've been picking her up off the ground since before you were born, Sarah. Every time she played, it ended like this."

"No more volleyball?" Ike asked as the rest of the players bounded over.

"I think I'll just sit and watch if that's okay." Abby settled back down on her quilt to watch the uneven teams finish the game.

"Drink this." Jacob held out a glass of water. "It will make you feel all better. That and the fact that you're officially exempt from playing." He grinned. "Did you take that ball to the head so you'd have an excuse to leave the game?" he teased.

She took a sip of water. "You caught me," she said with a smile. She motioned to her still stinging forehead. "All these years, I haven't really been klutzy, just trying to get out of playing sports."

He laughed. "Yeah, right."

"I'll bet you're wishing Emma was here. She could've helped lead your team to victory." Abby wanted to make sure her sister stayed in the forefront of his mind. In fact, she considered it her own personal duty to make sure he didn't forget about her.

Jacob shrugged. "She is a good player." He knelt down beside her. "Are you sure you're okay?" he asked.

She nodded. "I'll be fine. Go play."

He grinned and jogged off to join the game.

Abby held the cool water glass to her stinging head and watched as Jacob aced a serve. Her sister was a blessed girl.

Chapter Fourteen

Emma

"Did Noah show you any of the bookmobile stops?" Lydia Ann asked as they tidied up from a rush of afternoon tourists.

"No." Emma's sprits rose at the thought of library books. "Please tell me where it will be, though. I've always loved to read."

Lydia Ann laughed. "I believe that's the most excited I've seen you today. One of the stops isn't too far from the shop, at Charm School. You can walk there. I'm not sure which days it will be there, though."

Emma smiled. "Great. I think I'll walk over later this afternoon and see if I can find it. I'd love to have a good book to read." She sighed.

Lydia Ann was silent for a long moment. "Are you sure everything went okay with Noah? You've been awfully quiet since you went sightseeing. Did he say something to upset you?" Her brown eyes were full of concern. "Because that isn't like him."

Emma shrugged. "Not really. He just..." she trailed off. "He wanted to know what I was running from."

Lydia Ann stopped folding a yellow and pink baby quilt and looked at Emma. "Well? I didn't want to be nosy as soon as you stepped foot in town, but I'm sort of wondering that myself."

Emma shook her head. "It isn't exactly like that." She sank onto a stool behind the counter. "I guess I'm having a hard time accepting that this is really my life." She gave a lopsided smile. "That sounds silly, I know. It's just that I've spent my whole life waiting on something to happen to me, you know? And now I find that it's time for me to grow up and join the church and marry some suitable young man." She felt the tears welling up in her eyes. "But I'm not ready. I still feel like I haven't learned who I am yet."

Lydia Ann was quiet for long moment. "Your feelings aren't out of place." She walked around the counter and grasped Emma's hand. "I hope you do figure things out. And you're welcome to stay with me as long as you need while doing so."

Emma was relieved. She'd been afraid Lydia Ann would react like Abby and just try and gloss over everything. If there was one thing she didn't need, it was another person treating her as if she were somehow tarnished because she had questions that needed answering. She knew herself well enough to know that, even if she ignored them, they wouldn't go away. The doubts would linger, and that was a burden she didn't want to spend a lifetime bearing.

"Thanks." She rose from the wooden stool. "Do you mind if I walk down to see if the bookmobile is there? I'll be right back."

"Sure." Lydia Ann smiled. "Here, take my library card and check out a couple of books for the twins." She shuffled through a drawer and came up with a plastic card. "They love to have new books to look through." She gestured around the store. "And now that the rush is over, the rest of the afternoon will probably be slow, so take your time."

Card in hand, Emma walked quickly in the direction Lydia Ann had pointed. She hoped the bookmobile would be there today. She had to laugh at herself over how thrilled she was at the prospect of something new to read.

She'd grown up reading the classics. *Little Women* had transported her into a world where she'd imagined herself as Jo, the fiery oldest sister. *The Secret Garden* had made her long for a garden retreat of her own. *The Diary of Anne Frank* had made her feel as if she could actually see the secret staircase behind which Anne and her family lived. Of course, in recent years, she'd been mesmerized by stories of love—lost and found. *Gone with the Wind* had delighted her until the end. Even now, she liked to pretend that Rhett and Scarlett had remained happy and together. Jane Austen was one of her favorite authors, and Emma never could decide which kind of man she'd rather meet. Right now, it was a toss-up between Mr. Darcy and Mr. Knightley.

As soon as she saw the bookmobile, she developed a spring in her step. It was a treat that it happened to be there today. She stopped in her tracks when she heard the sounds coming from inside the bookmobile. Great sobs, the kind that come when a heart is breaking. For a moment, Emma hesitated. Maybe she should come back later. She nervously looked around. Not a soul in sight. She sighed. The proper thing to do would be to leave. She didn't want to intrude on what was obviously a private moment.

She thought of Lydia Ann, telling her about the community coming together to support her after her husband's death. Maybe the right thing to do was to go inside and see if she could be of help. She squared her shoulders and stepped inside.

An English girl about her age was crumpled in a heap of books, her shoulders shaking. Her long, wavy red hair flowed around her shoulders. She wore denim pants that came right below her knees, a bright green tank top, and flip-flops on her feet. As if sensing that someone had entered, she looked up with red-rimmed eyes.

"S–sorry," she stammered and tugged on a lock of red hair. Before Emma could say a word, the girl hiccupped and grasped a shelf above her. As she pulled herself up, the shelf slid forward and books spilled all around her. The clattering noise they made as they hit the floor seemed to ricochet around the inside of the makeshift library.

When silence settled like a blanket on the room, Emma and the girl stared at each other. A dimple appeared in the girl's cheek for a brief second, but it was enough to set Emma's mouth to twitching. Suddenly they were both laughing uncontrollably.

"I'm sorry," the redhead gasped finally. "You must think I'm crazy."

Emma shook her head as her own chuckles stopped. She'd forgotten how good it felt to just let the laughter come. "Sometimes you just have to laugh."

The girl nodded, tears still wet on her cheeks. "Have you ever felt like your life was falling apart?"

Emma reached down to pick up a book to buy time. She considered offering a platitude about God taking care of everything. Instead, she straightened and met the girl's green-eyed gaze directly. "Unfortunately, yes."

The girl motioned toward the shelf and books on the floor. "And then it seems like everything you touch starts falling apart, too?" She swiped at her cheeks with the back of her hand. "That seems to be my life these days." She rose daintily from the midst of the chaos, careful not to touch anything around her. "I'm Kelly, by the way."

Chapter Fifteen

. . . .

Kelly

How mortifying. Not a single person had stepped foot into the bookmobile all day. And, of course, right when Kelly decided to have a tiny nervous breakdown, someone decided they needed a library book. A cry fest right in the middle of a bookmobile—and on her first day on the job—wasn't exactly what she had planned when she'd gotten out of bed this morning.

It was all supposed to have been so simple. She'd driven to Millersburg that morning, picked up the bookmobile, and gone on the scheduled route. After an hour or two in each place, she was supposed to move on to her next scheduled stop. Easy, breezy.

Except for the barrage of text messages she'd gotten from Nick, proclaiming his undying love and pleading for a second chance. And then, she'd received an e-mail from her mother, who said she'd met her very own Adonis and was being wined and dined all over Italy. The phone call from her dad had been the final straw. She should've known better than to answer it. He'd offered a flimsy excuse for missing her college graduation. He'd been out of town for work. Most dads would find a way to take a few hours off and watch their only daughter graduate. But not him. Clearly, work came first, as it always had.

She glared at her iPhone. It had been the bearer of each of those things. They say don't shoot the messenger, but she was sorely tempted to toss it out of the window on the trip back to Millersburg to pick up her SUV.

She glanced at the Amish girl, who stood watching her, undoubtedly shell-shocked from witnessing such an emotional outburst. Did Amish people have emotional outbursts? Kelly wasn't sure.

The girl wore a long, light blue dress with a matching apron, which nearly reached the floor. Clean, white tennis shoes peeked out from underneath the hem. A white cap covered her head, but Kelly could see the pretty auburn color of her hair. The young woman stepped forward and offered Kelly her hand. "Nice to meet you. I'm Emma Miller," she said with a faint accent. Pennsylvania Dutch, Kelly thought, but again, she wasn't certain. Maybe she should've picked up an *Amish for Dummies* book before she came to town.

Kelly shook Emma's outstretched hand, surprised at the firm grip. She would've expected something softer from this gentle-looking girl.

Emma pointed at the shelf and books on the ground. "And I believe I understand exactly what you mean about everything you touch falling apart." She gave a wry smile. "I have that same problem."

Kelly seriously doubted it. What kind of turmoil could this girl possibly have? "Well, please feel free to look around. I'll just stack these up."

Emma was at her side in a flash. "I'll help. It will go much quicker that way."

"Thanks." Kelly was taken aback. She was used to doing things on her own. Her mind drifted back to the day she'd moved out of the dorm. So many boxes, so few hands to help lift them. She'd been jealous of her classmates, who were surrounded by laughing family members, all pitching in to help their respective graduates move on to the next chapter of their lives. But she'd only had Michelle and Michelle's parents to help.

"I'm glad to finally meet someone from Charm," Kelly said once they had restored order to the pile of books. "I've only been in town for a week, but I haven't really met anyone local yet." With the exception of a few guests at the One Charming Inn, she'd only had Aunt Irene to talk to.

Emma looked sheepish. "Oh, I'm not from Charm. I'm just staying here for the summer." She brightened. "I arrived last week as well."

"Cool." Kelly smiled. "Guess we're both newcomers then." She sighed.

"Um," Emma started, "I don't mean to be rude, but you have black streaks running down your face."

Kelly groaned. "This stupid mascara is supposed to be waterproof." She grabbed her red bag from where it sat on the counter and began digging through it. She finally came up with a compact and looked at herself in the mirror. Not only did she have mascara smeared down her face, but her eyes were also red and puffy. She sank to the floor again. "I have to apologize for the way I look." She began trying to wipe the smears away. "It's been a bad day." She looked up at Emma. "Oh, who am I kidding? It's been a bad year."

Emma flashed a tentative smile. "I heard you crying. Are you okay?"

Kelly took a deep breath. "No, but I will be. Someday. At least that's what they tell me."

"They?" asked Emma.

"You know." Kelly shrugged. "All of those well-meaning people who say that they understand how I feel or who say they've been where I am."

"And, exactly where is that?"

Kelly grimaced. "If I only knew." She glanced up at Emma's serious expression. Great. She'd freaked out the Amish girl. "Don't worry about me, though. Really."

Emma bit her lip. "So, what brought you to Charm?"

Kelly explained about Aunt Irene and the inn. She left out the philandering boyfriend and abandoning parents. No need to delve into those stories.

"It's nice that you're helping your aunt. I'm sure she appreciates it."

"Yeah. It's nice to be able to help her. She doesn't have any kids of her own, so when my gram mentioned it, I jumped at the chance." She pulled at her tank top strap. It wasn't revealing or anything, but next to Emma, she felt very underdressed. "Plus, I'm saving money for graduate school."

"Oh? What are you going to study?"

"Believe it or not, library science." Kelly gestured around the bookmobile. "So this is sort of a practice run, so to speak."

"I see." Emma gave a slow smile. "I think it would be fun to work among books all day." She looked wistful. "And to go to college." The last part was said with such sadness, Kelly felt a tinge of embarrassment. From the little she knew from Aunt Irene, most Amish young people only went to school through the eighth grade. After that, they joined the workforce and were trained for their specific jobs.

"I guess."

The twangy sound of Rascal Flatts made both girls jump. Kelly pulled her cell phone out of her pocket. "Sorry. Text message." She pushed a button to read the message. "*Grrr.*" She rolled her eyes.

Emma looked at her with interest. "Is everything okay?"

"Actually, no." She held up her phone. "He makes me want to scream."

"Must be boyfriend troubles."

"Ex-boyfriend, actually. But trouble with a capital T." Kelly sank down onto a stepstool and put her head in her hands.

"My sister says that emotional outbursts aren't good. But I think when you hold things inside for too long, it could make you feel even worse." Emma plopped down onto the bookmobile floor. "Why don't you tell me your troubles?"

Kelly managed a tiny smile. "You sure you want to hear?" She was surprised by how happy she was to have some company. And there was something about Emma that she immediately liked. It was kind of like freshman year, when she'd met Michelle for the first time. Some people you just instinctively know would be good friends.

Emma nodded. "I'm a great listener."

The door to the bookmobile burst open. A little boy who looked to be about five years old entered with a young Amish woman. Kelly jumped up to greet them.

The woman pointed at the child. "Do you have any books for a new reader?"

"The children's books are in this section," she said, pointing to three shelves filled with brightly colored books.

The child began eagerly pulling books from the shelf and handing them to the woman.

Kelly walked over to where Emma had risen from her spot on the floor. "Maybe things are finally going to get busy around here."

"At least that will keep your mind off of things." Emma smiled.

"Right. At least until the next text message. If I were smart, I'd just turn the thing off." She gave Emma a sheepish grin. "But it's hard to do. Listen, there's only one person staying at the inn right now, so Aunt Irene won't need my help tonight. Any chance you might like to meet me at the Homestead?" The restaurant was one of the few places in town to get a meal. In one of the travel guides she'd found at the inn, Kelly had read good reviews of the food and service.

"I've never been there." Emma paused. "Let me check with my cousin first. I need to make sure she didn't have anything planned."

"Okay. How about this? I'll be in the parking lot of the Homestead around five. If you're able to make it, just meet me there. Otherwise, I can just eat by myself." Kelly really hoped Emma could make it. She'd never been one of those people who was comfortable eating alone.

"That sounds good. And I'm sure Lydia Ann won't mind. I just need to run it by her first." Emma smiled.

"Hope to see you at five then." Kelly watched as Emma stepped out of the bookmobile and set off down the street.

Who would've thought that she'd make friends with an Amish girl? Kelly was thrilled to have potential plans, no matter who they were with. And Emma seemed nice. Different from anyone she'd known before, but that was probably a good thing. After all, hadn't Kelly come to Charm for a change of pace?

Chapter Sixteen

Emma

The surprise was written all over Lydia Ann's face. "An English girl?" she'd asked. "What could you possibly have to talk to her about?"

"Ach, Lydia Ann. You sound like Abby. Kelly is new in town, just like me," Emma had said as they gathered the little girls' toys and prepared things for the trip back to Lydia Ann's house.

"Okay." Lydia Ann had shrugged. "I guess I do have some friends who are Englishers. But they're older."

Emma wasn't sure what that had to do with anything. But she'd finally convinced Lydia Ann that she'd be fine. She wasn't running off to live among the English or anything. Just meeting what seemed to be a sad, lonely girl at a restaurant.

She was happy to walk to the Homestead, since it was a nice evening. The sun was still out, and the warm breeze seemed to carry Emma along. Besides, it wasn't too far from Lydia Ann's shop. Emma planned on asking Kelly to give her a ride home.

She passed the Charm General Store and remembered Noah telling her about their ice cream. She smiled in spite of herself. He'd certainly gotten under her skin.

"Hey!" Kelly was sitting on a wooden bench in front of the restaurant. She rose as Emma walked near. "I'm glad you were able to come. I wish I were one of those people who didn't feel stupid eating out alone, but I've never been able to do that."

Emma laughed. "I don't blame you. Although, every now and then, I think that might be kind of peaceful."

They made their way inside. There were several people seated at tables, likely tourists from the assortment of states represented on the license plates in the parking lot. Even so, the place wasn't too crowded, and Emma spotted a number of empty tables. The young Amish hostess showed them to a table for two near a window and handed them menus.

"Did your afternoon get busier after I left?" Emma inquired after a few minutes of silence as they looked at the menus. She'd already decided on the fried chicken, mashed potatoes, and green beans. Her mouth watered at the thought.

"Not too much. A few more people." Kelly twisted her red hair into a bun and secured it with a ponytail holder she'd had on her wrist. "Maybe people have to get used to the new schedule or something."

"Maybe. And I realized after I left that I didn't even check out a book. Next time the bookmobile is in town I will." Emma grinned.

"I'm so sorry." Kelly groaned. "It's my fault for distracting you with my dramatics."

The waitress came over and took their orders. She left steaming rolls and apple butter on the table. "Yummy." Kelly plucked a roll from the basket and put a heaping serving of apple butter on it. "This may be the best thing I've ever put in my mouth," she said after she took a bite.

Emma grinned. "You should taste my mamm's cooking. I enjoy eating out sometimes, but nothing can compare to her meals."

This was the truth. Emma had tried for years to learn to cook like Mamm. Abby could replicate a few of the dishes, but so far, Emma's didn't quite have the same touch.

"Well, my mother considers boiling water to be cooking." Kelly shook her head. "Let's just say that I hope I didn't get my domestic ability from her." She took another bite of bread. "Although, I'm afraid that I did. I can't even make toast without burning it."

"I'm the same way."

Kelly narrowed her eyes.

"Okay, maybe I can make toast." Emma grinned. "But I'm certainly not the cook my mamm is—or my sister."

"I thought all Amish women were supposed to be fantastic cooks."

Emma laughed. "Yes, it seems that way. Except for maybe me." She shrugged. "My mammi always says it will come to me in time. When Abby and I were small, we'd go stay at her house and she'd try to teach us to make homemade bread."

"Mammi?"

"My mamm's mother." Emma grinned. "Bread and dessert are about the only things I cook well." She grinned. "I just hope by the time I have a family of my own, I'll have finally learned, otherwise my family will have to live off of rolls and cakes."

Kelly's green eyes clouded over. "So are you about to get married or something?"

Emma was taken aback. "No. Not at all." She thought for a moment about Abby's insistence that she and Jacob would be published in the fall. Why couldn't her sister leave well enough alone?

"Oh." Kelly sighed. "Me neither. In fact, I'm light years away."

The waitress appeared at their table with two steaming platters. "Who had the fried chicken?" she asked.

Emma raised a hand. "I did. Danki," she said as the heaping plate was placed in front of her. "Your meat loaf looks delicious," Emma said, eyeing Kelly's plate as the waitress set it down.

Emma bowed her head and said a silent prayer for her food. When she opened her eyes, Kelly was watching her curiously. Emma smiled. "Just thanking God for my meal."

Kelly nodded. "I figured. It's nice that you remember to do that." She looked glum.

"Well, it has become second nature to me, I guess. I talk to God throughout the day." Emma shrugged. "So it seems natural for me to thank Him for the blessing of food before I eat it."

Kelly gave her a tiny smile. "That's cool." She took a bite of meat loaf.

It had been a long time since Emma had met any new people. In fact, she'd been around most everyone in her community her whole life. And most of them had experienced similar upbringings to hers. She wasn't sure what to talk to Kelly about. Maybe Lydia Ann was right. Having only their new-in-town status in common might not get them very far, conversation wise. Emma took a bite of her potatoes. Not as delicious as Mamm's, but very good. "So, where did you grow up?" she finally asked Kelly.

"Cincinnati. But I'd always wanted to attend Ohio State for college, so I live in Columbus now." She paused for a drink of water. "My parents met there. I guess that is one reason why I chose the school. I grew up hearing stories about their college days and it sounded so much fun."

"And was it?"

"Yes. And no." Kelly smiled. "I know how that must sound. The first couple of years were great. I loved finally feeling like I was on my own. And then I started dating Nick. That all went well for a little while."

"Nick is your...?" Emma trailed off.

"Oh. He's my ex." She rolled her eyes. "The one I got the text message from while you were in the bookmobile." She shook her head. "He has been texting me like crazy. Especially once he figured out that I wouldn't actually answer his phone calls. Since then, it's been non-stop texts." She looked quizzically at Emma. "Do you know about texting?"

Emma grinned. "Believe it or not, there are some Amish people who have cell phones. Of course, it is for business purposes, but still. It is becoming more common to see." She pushed her green beans around the plate with her fork. "I don't have one or anything. And I've never sent a text message. But I know the concept."

"Well, sometimes I wish texting had never been invented. I mean, don't get me wrong. Sometimes it's great to be constantly connected." She picked up her phone from where it was lying on the table. "But the downside is I can't ever really get away," she said with disgust.

"I can't imagine. Although I think that would be sort of nice. Like on the days when I'm staying late at school and won't be home—it would be neat to be able to send a message to my mamm to let her know."

"Yeah, it is convenient. But still. People text me all hours of the night. And when I'm not getting a text, my phone is ringing. And don't even get me started on Facebook." She laughed.

"It just sounds like you have a lot of people who want to talk to you. You must have a lot of friends."

"Honestly? I have a large circle of acquaintances. I have a small circle of real friends. You know, the people who really know me." She shrugged. "But I guess everyone is like that."

"What about your family? Are you close to them?" Even though they drove each other crazy sometimes, Emma considered Abby to be her closest friend. And she had a tight bond with Sarah and Thomas, too, which would only strengthen as they grew older.

"I'm an only child, so no brothers or sisters. And my parents were actually both only children, too, so I don't even have cousins. It's just me." She took another bite of meat loaf, chewed, and swallowed. "I wonder sometimes what it would be like to be in a big family, you know? My roommate, Michelle, has that. And whenever I've gone home with her for weekends, it's so loud. There's always something going on, someone telling a story or wanting to go do something." She paused. "I can't imagine having all those people on your side."

Emma had never thought of it like that. She had just the kind of family Kelly was lacking. Siblings, cousins, and lots of extended family. They were always doing things together, even if it was just chores or helping out on someone's farm. And lately all she could think was how it stifled her. But deep down, she knew she'd had more good times than bad. "Don't you enjoy just being on your own? You can do whatever you want. And you must have the undivided attention of your parents. That was probably nice growing up, right?"

Kelly snorted. "I love my parents. Really, I do. But undivided attention meant that I always knew what city they were in and, if

I was lucky, how to reach them in their hotel." She shook her head. "Now that they've split up, I feel like I don't even have a home to go to anymore. That's sort of why I'm here. Gram is in a nursing home, and my great-aunt Irene is really the only other family I have."

Emma sat back, stunned. She'd never known anyone whose parents weren't together. She couldn't imagine what that must be like. Her own parents had differences sometimes, but they were happy, and their love for one another was always apparent. "I'm sorry to hear about your parents."

"Oh, it's okay. Most people I know have gone through it. I sort of thought, since they'd made it nearly twenty-three years, that they'd stick it out. But no. I got back from Europe last summer and Dad had already moved out."

Emma had always wondered about what it was like in Europe. But now was not the time to ask for a travel commentary. "That must have been very difficult for you."

"Luckily, I went straight to school, so I didn't really have to deal with it too much. In fact, it was sort of like it never happened. I was back in the dorm, and not around them, so I didn't have to face the reality."

"So did you ever deal with it?"

"Well, after I'd been back at school for a couple of weeks, Nick and I were fighting." She rolled her eyes. "As usual. But this time, he talked me into riding with him to get something to eat. He was so mad, I should have known better."

"That doesn't sound good," Emma said, her heart pounding at the thought of her new friend in such a situation.

Kelly shook her head. "It was worse than not good. It was awful. He ran a flashing red light and a car broadsided us. On my side."

"Oh no!" Emma gasped.

Kelly's eyes filled with tears. "That was when my life really started to fall apart."

Chapter Seventeen

....

Kelly

Pouring her heart out to a near stranger over a hearty meal wasn't exactly what she'd planned. But once she started, she couldn't seem to stop. "Nick walked away just fine. But I was in bad shape. I had to be airlifted to the hospital, and of course, my parents both got there as soon as they could." That had meant two hours for her mom and two days for her dad. At the time, she'd at least been too sedated to let her dad's lack of urgency hurt her feelings.

The waitress stopped by the table. "Can I get either of you anything else?"

Both girls shook their heads and she walked off.

"Anyway, I wound up having to spend the rest of the semester at home. Thankfully, it was early enough in the semester that I was able to switch into a couple of online classes. And one professor let me take his class as an independent study." She poked the rest of her meatloaf with her fork. "So I didn't fall too far behind and was still able to graduate on time."

"How did it go while you were at home?" Emma's brown eyes were soft with compassion.

"That was when it finally hit me. Dad really didn't live there any longer. And my mom tried to play like it was all okay, but I could tell she was shaken up. There was just an empty feeling to the house that hadn't been there before. And I wound up having to do physical therapy for my right side. It took most of the impact from the other car. Recovering was very painful."

"Do you have a hard time riding in a car now?"

"I did at first. I cringed at every stop sign or red light, scared that it would happen again. But I've finally gotten past it for the most part." Kelly's worst nightmares still included the awful sound of metal on metal, but she didn't want to admit it to Emma.

"What about Nick? I guess he felt pretty bad." Emma propped her elbow up on the table, clearly entranced by the story.

Kelly furrowed her brow. "You'd think so. But he wasn't as guilt-ridden as he probably should've been. I mean, he sent me flowers while I was in the hospital and all, but once I wasn't on campus anymore..." she trailed off, unsure of whether it was okay to tell Emma the whole story. Would it make the Amish girl uncomfortable? She didn't want to be guilty of sharing too much information.

"What happened?" Emma asked. "You can tell me."

"Well, he was back to his old tricks. He always was a real flirt. And I guess without me there, he decided there was no need to stay faithful."

"So he found a new girlfriend?"

"Not exactly. More like he found several new girls to spend time with. And I was at home, in physical therapy and trying to stay on top of classes, none the wiser. Thankfully, Michelle happened to see him out with one of them and she told me about it."

"That must've been awful."

"It was frustrating. I was far away and couldn't do anything. Of course, he said it was all innocent and he was just hanging out as friends." Kelly shook her head. "And then, when I got back to campus this past semester, he was all perfect boyfriend again. Taking me to dinner, bringing me flowers. The whole nine yards." She rolled her eyes. "So of course, I forgave him. But then, right before graduation, he dumped me for one of the girls he'd been spending time with while I was at home. And as much as I hate to admit it, I've been in pieces ever since."

Emma opened her mouth to speak then closed it.

"What? You can say it." Kelly grinned. "Come on. I've just spilled my guts to you. So that gives you license to say what you think."

"Well, it sounds to me like maybe you're better off without him. I've never been in love or anything, but I don't think he treated you very well."

Kelly nodded. "That seems to be the consensus. But walking away from something you've been in for so long is hard. Even if it is toxic to you."

"So that's why you're here?" Emma took a sip of water.

"Yeah. All of it added together. My parents. The wreck. Getting dumped. And then, of course, the big one. Trying to figure out what to do with my life."

"I thought you were going to be a librarian."

"Well, I'm enrolled in the program. But who's to say if that's really what I'm meant to do. I don't know." She slumped in the seat. "It's like I have no direction. I'm drifting. And it isn't a good way to be."

Emma's smile was pensive. "So you're hiding out."

"Exactly. I guess you could say that, for me, being here, surrounded by a simpler way of life, is kind of protective." She sighed. "I don't know. And it probably sounds stupid to you, since you're used to it. I mean, at first, the quiet all around me took some getting used to. But now my mind feels clearer. And I'm not as tense as I was a few weeks ago." She grinned. "It's like the place is called *Charm* for a reason."

* * *

The girls made their way out of the restaurant, Kelly in the lead. She held the door open and let Emma walk through. "So now you know my story. That is what led me here. And, just FYI, you can tell me yours any time. I'm sorry I dominated the conversation." She followed Emma outside. "I guess I needed to get all that off of my chest, and you happened to get caught in the wake."

Emma smiled. "Don't apologize. I enjoyed hearing about your life. I forget sometimes that other people have problems besides just me."

"I'm thinking of making a Wal-Mart run soon. Do you want to go with me to Millersburg one night this week? Then you can feel free to tell me what brought you to Charm." Kelly inhaled the pure, fresh air. This place was amazing. The sun was just beginning to go down and there was the tiniest hint of cool in the air, a welcome respite from the warm day.

"Oh, that would be wonderful. I do need to buy a few things, and Lydia Ann might have a list for me, too."

"Great. Maybe Thursday after work? We can plan on grabbing a bite to eat while we're there."

Emma nodded.

"Emma?" A male voice called out from across the parking lot.

Kelly turned in the direction of the voice. An Amish man was climbing down from a buggy and heading their way. He was tall and muscular, with dark hair and dark eyes. Eyes that seemed to be fixated on Emma. She glanced at her friend and detected a tiny hint of a blush. *Hmm.*

"Noah." Emma's voice came out in a croak. "What are you doing here?"

He sauntered over to where they stood, a grin on his handsome face. Kelly was struck by how white his teeth were against his tanned face. If he weren't wearing traditional Amish clothing and a straw hat, she would've sworn he was a TV star. "I had to drop some things off to Lydia Ann and she told me you were eating here." He nodded his head toward the horse and buggy he'd gotten out of. "I thought I'd see if you wanted a ride home."

"Oh." Emma's brown eyes widened. "That's very nice of you but..." she trailed off and looked at Kelly.

"You know, I actually should be getting back to the inn. I try to clean the kitchen for Aunt Irene after the evening meal." No way was she letting Emma miss out on the chance to spend time with this guy. She didn't know what every Amish girl's dream was, but she at least knew handsome when she saw it. And he was it, in the flesh. She flashed a smile at Noah. "I'm Kelly Bennett. I don't think we've met."

"I'm sorry. I don't know where my manners are." Emma looked sheepish. "Noah, this is Kelly. She is staying with her aunt for the summer at the One Charming Inn. She also works at the bookmobile." She motioned at Noah. "Noah is kin to Lydia Ann's late husband."

"Pleased to meet you." Kelly reached out and shook his hand. "Are you originally from Charm?" she asked.

"Yes, indeed. I was born and raised here."

"I'm glad to finally meet a local. I thought I'd found one in Emma, but found out she's just as new to town as I am."

He grinned. "Well, welcome to town. I'm certain you'll find it a nice place to spend some time. It might be a small place, but there is a lot of heart here." He turned to Emma. "Now, about that ride."

Emma looked frantically at Kelly. "You don't need to go to any trouble."

"It isn't any trouble at all. In fact, I have to drive right past there on my way home." He glanced at Kelly again. "It was nice to meet you." He nodded at Emma. "I'll be waiting in the buggy." He walked off toward the buggy.

Kelly glanced at Emma, who seemed rooted to the pavement. "So why do I get the feeling you aren't going to thank me for pushing for him to give you a ride?"

Emma grimaced. "I barely know him is all."

Kelly was pretty sure that wasn't "all," but she didn't ask for details. This was neither the time nor the place. "Well, I think he's yummy." Her smile faded quickly as her cell phone buzzed. She held it up. "Another text from Nick."

Emma made a face. "Sorry."

"I'm clearly not the person to be giving out advice about choosing men, so maybe you should ride with me instead." She looked at the offending phone. "I ought to get my number changed." She sighed. "Although, knowing Nick, he'd find a way to get it."

"Well, there is no need to worry about me choosing Noah. I'm certain he is only doing a favor for Lydia Ann. He was very close to her husband, so I think he pitches in whenever he can to help her and her kids."

Kelly had seen the way his eyes lit up when they saw Emma, but it really wasn't her place to comment. Some things have to be realized naturally. And her track record did speak for itself. He could be a big jerk for all she knew. "Okay, if you're sure. And if you want to stop by the bookmobile Thursday, we'll make plans to go to Millersburg."

"That sounds good. I'll see you then." Emma walked toward the horse and buggy, where Noah sat waiting.

Kelly's phone buzzed again as she climbed into the SUV. Maybe she was going to have to speak to Nick after all, just to get him to leave her alone. Although, on second thought, he didn't deserve for her to even acknowledge him. Surely he'd get the hint sooner or later. *Here's hoping for sooner.* She pulled out of the parking lot and headed toward the inn.

Chapter Eighteen

Emma

Emma climbed into Noah's waiting buggy. "You really didn't have to do this, you know." She motioned toward Kelly's SUV. "She would've been glad to run me to Lydia Ann's house."

Noah grinned at her. "I know. But I felt like you and I didn't get off to such a great start. I figured I had a little ground to make up."

"I'm just extra-sensitive sometimes."

"Do you have to get right home?" he asked, directing the horse out of the parking lot.

"I don't guess so. I mean, I'm not on a set schedule or anything."

"How about we go out to one of the places I think is the prettiest in the area?"

"Okay. But we don't have much daylight left."

"It won't take long to get there."

They set out, passing Keim Lumber and Charm Engine. Before too long, they stopped near a little pond.

"I like to come fishing here sometimes." Noah grinned. "Do you ever fish?"

"Why, yes, as a matter of fact, I do." She glanced over at him. "Don't tell me you thought I'm one of those girls who is scared of worms." She laughed. "I can even bait my own hook."

He let out a whistle. "Impressive. See, I had you pegged all wrong." He met her eyes. "So, tell me about your life back home. I know you're a teacher. But what else can you tell me about yourself?"

"The usual stuff, I guess. My parents, two sisters, and a brother. I've got some other family nearby, too. I just teach." She shrugged. "That's about it."

"Somehow I doubt that even scratches the surface."

She grinned. "Okay. Well, I like to play sports. I guess I'm too grown up to do much of that anymore. But I used to love volleyball and softball. And I like to fish. And read." She paused. "I'm not a good cook. I don't sew very well. And I can't sing."

He laughed. "Now we're getting somewhere."

"My sister is much better at that kind of stuff than I am." She watched the big orange sun as it slowly began to dip below the tree line. "She tries to be a matchmaker, too."

"Really? So has she tried to matchmake you yet?"

"Oh, yes. She thinks she's already got my future husband all picked out."

"Well, I must say, you don't look too happy about it. Is that what you came to Charm to get away from?"

She met his gaze. "Not exactly." She sighed. "I guess I've just been struggling lately. Trying to figure out where I belong."

Noah nodded. "There's nothing wrong with that. I think we all go through it at one time or another."

She considered the conversation she'd had with Kelly at the Homestead. "Maybe you're right. And you know what's crazy? I thought it had something to do with my being Amish. But my friend from the restaurant has a lot of those same feelings."

"We're all people." He looked at her for a long moment. "So does that mean some of what you struggle with is whether to remain with your family?"

She nodded. "Not that I really want to jump the fence, you know? When most of my friends were going through it, deciding whether they would join the church or go into the world, I didn't give it a second thought. I'd just always felt like I knew what was right for me."

"But now?" he asked.

"I still haven't joined the church back home. I guess I have some questions inside me that needed to be answered first. I want to make sure I make a choice I'm happy with." She furrowed her brow. "So basically I've not made any choice, which in a lot of ways feels even worse. Like a limbo of sorts."

"The best thing you can do is pray about it. Which I'm sure you already know."

Emma smiled. "Prayer has been my only lifeline lately."

"As it often is for many of us. But I understand, probably better than some, where you're coming from."

"You do?" she asked.

"I left Charm for a while a few years ago. I went and lived with a childhood friend who'd left the faith."

She looked at him with wide eyes. "Where did you live?"

"Cleveland. And it wasn't all bad. I traveled some. Tried to fit in." He looked over at her. "But it didn't change who I was. I still knew right from wrong." He shook his head. "It was just stupid. I tried to be someone I'm not. It didn't work out very well."

"But you came back."

He grimaced. "I had to go through some pretty awful stuff before I decided to come back." He met her gaze. "Someday I'll tell you the whole sordid story." He motioned toward the town. "It's getting dark and I should get you home." He grinned. "Besides, if we get to Lydia Ann's soon, we'll be able to see the twins before they go to bed."

"You care a lot about them, don't you?"

He nodded. "I intend to make sure they always know what a great man their dat was. Plus, they're so funny."

For a moment, the only sound was the *clip-clop* of the horse's hooves. Emma looked at Noah's profile. "Thanks for the ride."

He gave her a sideways grin as he prompted the horse to trot. "Tell you what. How about we go fishing soon? Maybe Saturday afternoon? That'll give me the chance to see your hook-baiting skills."

"Sounds like fun." Emma's mouth turned upward in a smile. "As long as you're prepared for the possibility of being out fished."

He laughed. "I can take it."

Emma leaned against the seat and enjoyed the wind against her face. She was already looking forward to Saturday.

Chapter Nineteen

....

Abby

"Excuse me, ma'am." Abby tapped the elegant, blonde Englisher gently on the shoulder. "Is this your child?" She nodded toward the young girl beside her. "She said she is looking for her mother."

"Oh, my goodness." The blonde reached for the child's hand. "Caitlin, I told you to stay right here while I looked at these quilts. Why did you run off?"

The little girl wiped a tear from her cheek. "I was bored, Mommy. You told me to stay here, but there's *nothing* to do." She pulled her hand from her mother's. "And I wanted to do something." Her voice rose to a howl. "I'm tired of being here. I want some ice cream." Then, taking her voice to a new decibel, she yelled, "Ice cream, ice cream, Mommy. You promised."

Abby stifled the urge to cover her ears. It had been this way all day. Irritable children, rude customers. It seemed like some days were just so much worse than others. Must have been a full moon last night. She could barely wait to put the CLOSED sign on the door and head for the peaceful confines of her home. Even doing her chores would be a relief after this day.

The woman looked at Abby apologetically. "Sorry. She's had to spend most of the day in and out of quilt and antique stores."

Caitlin began running up and down the aisle, pulling random objects from the shelf and knocking them to the ground.

"Caitlin Marie Chandler. Stop that right now. Mommy is not going to get you any ice cream."

Abby knew an empty threat when she heard one. The woman's attention was already on a blue and yellow quilt. Caitlin continued her run through the store. Objects fell to the floor with a smack. Abby rounded the corner, thinking she would cut the child off, but the little girl was too fast. She stuck her tongue out at Abby as she rushed past. Abby sighed. She knew when she was beat. The woman finally made her selection and checked out. Abby watched as she grabbed Caitlin's hand and led the grumbling child out the door.

She was relieved when it was time to lock up, even though there was quite a bit of cleaning to do, thanks to the tantrum. She bustled about, cleaning the aisles. Finally. She straightened her light blue dress and tried to tuck a few wayward strands of blonde hair into her kapp. It was no use. This day had left her feeling as if she'd been through a tornado.

Both tourists and locals were strolling down the sidewalk as Abby stepped out into the warm, summer air. She took a deep breath and turned toward home. Now that the days were longer, she had plenty of daylight left to walk the short distance.

"Hey, Abby!"

She recognized the voice and glanced over her shoulder at Jacob, who was walking up behind her. "Hi, Jacob."

"Rough day?" His sympathetic voice soothed her frayed nerves. "You look like you could use a ride home."

"Well…I *was* just thinking about how tired I am. There must have been a full moon or something last night." Abby pushed a curl back under her kapp. "A ride home would be great."

Jacob escorted her to the buggy and gave her a hand up. "If you aren't in a hurry, maybe we can go for a drive." He grinned.

"I'm in no hurry. In fact it'll be nice to relax a bit before I get home." Abby smoothed her apron. "Mamm won't be worried. Sometimes when I walk home I stop at the park and feed the geese."

Jacob smiled. "You won't be any later than usual, then."

"Oh, I don't mind." This was a great opportunity to mention her sister. And to remind Jacob that they were perfect for each other. She cleared her throat. "Have you written Emma yet?"

"Emma?" Jacob glanced at her. "No, why? She hasn't been gone all that long." He looked back at the road. "Besides, she hasn't written me either." He shrugged. "Anyway, she's the one who chose to leave."

Abby searched her mind for the proper response. Surely, Jacob wasn't going to just let Emma go without a word. "Well, yes, but you could at least write her and remind her that you're here."

"Abby, she's known me all my life. She knows I'm here." Jacob sounded exasperated. "Where else would I go?"

"Maybe you should go to Charm and visit her." As soon as the words left Abby's mouth, she was positive that was the perfect answer. "That's it! Why don't you go to Charm?" What better way to convince Emma that they were perfect for each other. Abby could see it all now, Jacob pulling up in front of Lydia Ann's house, sweeping Emma off her feet. How romantic. He would probably ask Emma to marry him right there. Lost in her daydream, she barely heard Jacob's answer.

"Abby, I have a job. Remember? I can't just pack up and leave. Besides, I don't really want to go to Charm." Jacob raised his eyebrows. "So what happened at work today to make you so tired?"

Abby recounted the story of the missing little girl and her temper tantrum. "And you know the worst part?" She didn't wait for his answer. "The mother didn't even realize she was gone." Abby shook her head. "How can you not miss someone you love?"

"Come on, Abby," Jacob chided her. "The child was probably only gone for a few minutes. Besides, it isn't like she left the store or anything." He glanced over at her. "Since it's been such a tough day, how about we grab some ice cream?"

She considered the chores that were waiting on her at home. Grabbing ice cream in the afternoon was more like something Emma would do. But maybe it was time she learned to be more spontaneous. "Yum. That sounds nice. Let's do it."

Jacob turned the buggy toward the local dairy bar.

She tried to relax against the seat and forget about her day. Her mind drifted back to her plan to get Jacob and Emma together. After a moment, she decided to try a new tactic. "Jacob?"

He kept his eyes on the road. "What is it? Did you change your mind about the ice cream?"

"No. Actually…I was just thinking how exciting it would be for Emma if you showed up unexpectedly and surprised her." Abby tried to gauge his reaction. "You could stay with your aunt and uncle who live in Sugarcreek. That wouldn't be a bad drive."

"Ah, I get it. You are missing Emma so much that you want me to take you to visit her." He glanced at her. "Is that it?" He smiled. "Or are you just like that little girl today, so bored here with only me for company that you want to go to Charm yourself?"

"No. Of course not." Abby shook her head. "I'm not bored."

"Good." He pulled the buggy into the parking lot. "Sit tight," he said. "A small vanilla cone?" He grinned.

Every time she came here, she always ordered the same thing. It was thoughtful of him to remember. "Sounds great." She watched as he placed the order at the window. He turned and gave her a wave as he waited. Abby couldn't help but smile. Her tense day was a thing of the past.

Chapter Twenty
. . . .

Kelly

A loud noise filled the room and Kelly sat straight up in bed, her heart pounding. *Get under the bed,* her mind screamed. She flung the bright blue quilt back and jumped out of the bed. As her bare feet hit the cold hardwood floor, reality brought her to her senses. She wasn't in the city, where gunshots in the night might be possible. She was in the small town of Charm, where they were much less likely. The noise that had so rudely awakened her sounded again. This time, it was easily identified as knocks on the door to her room. But *who* would knock on her door at—she plucked her cell phone from the nightstand and peered at it—nine a.m. She wasn't due at the bookmobile today. Surely Aunt Irene hadn't gotten mixed up and thought she was supposed to be on the way to pick it up. Aunt Irene! What if something was wrong with her? Kelly threw a robe over her shorts and T-shirt and dashed to the door, scuffing her feet into a pair of flip-flops.

"Aunt Irene?" she asked, as she flung the door open. Instead of her demure, white-haired aunt, she was face-to-chest with a well-developed set of pecs encased in a Hollister T-shirt. Her eyes traveled upward to the amused light blue eyes of Nick Williams.

"Nick! What are you doing here at the crack of dawn?" She tried to slam the door shut, but he reached out and stopped it

"Hey," he said in the slow, sexy way she'd always found irresistible. Especially when he accompanied it with that half-smile where one corner of his mouth quirked up. "I heard you were out here in Timbuktu, and I came to rescue you."

"What makes you think I want to be rescued?" It would be better if she didn't sound so breathless. She swallowed and tried again. "I'm fine. I came here on purpose. I'm helping my aunt. And how did you find my room anyway?"

He dropped the smile and opted for a serious, steady gaze. Another look once guaranteed to get past her guard. Over the years they'd been dating, she'd seen all of his looks.

"I have a reservation, if you must know. My room is just down the hall. Once I came upstairs, I did a little exploring. Since this was the only closed door, I took a gamble that you were behind it." He winked at her. "Must be fate, don't you think?"

He had made a reservation here? Ugh. And of course, Aunt Irene wouldn't recognize his name and think to warn her. She gave him a steely gaze. He had some nerve.

Nick seemed to sense that he was quickly losing ground. "Listen, can we go somewhere and talk? I mean, seriously? We really need to get the air cleared." His voice was pleading.

"Yeah. The air between us was pretty full of someone named Heather the last time I looked," she answered tartly. "What happened? Did she dump you?"

"Please?" He extended a hand. "Get dressed and come out for

breakfast. I promise, if you hear me out then send me on my way, I'll never bother you again."

"If it's the only way to get rid of you," she answered grudgingly, "I'll go. Now get downstairs and let me get dressed."

A brilliant smile lit his face, but he didn't attempt to touch her. Instead, he turned and strode downstairs.

She slammed the door behind him, seething. Who did he think he was, showing up like this? She took her time getting ready, making sure her makeup was perfect and every hair was in place. She ruffled through the closet, looking for the perfect outfit. After three tries, she finally settled on a pair of khaki shorts and a blue strappy tank top. She slipped on some brown wedge sandals and looked in the mirror one last time. Not bad. She plopped her sunglasses on top of her head and stuffed her cell phone in her tiny purse. Time to go face the jury.

Nick had always been hypercritical about the way she looked. Whenever her appearance didn't meet his standards, he'd let her know. She mentally marshaled her forces. Sending Nick packing should be a pleasure, but she'd tried so many times. He was harder to get rid of than a boomerang. Except when he wanted out. And he certainly was a woman magnet, adding the lure of wealth to the charisma and good looks he possessed. That had always been the problem for Kelly. She knew from the bitter experience of her parents' marriage that one partner being faithful wasn't good enough. No matter how faithful. And she refused to live her parents' life. Nope. The trouble was, Nick had perfected the knack of acting like the sun rose and set with her when it suited his cause. And she would break down and buy into it, only to find out—the hard way—that it was just that. An act. Not today, though. She'd had it. She stepped into the inn's drawing room, and Nick sprang to his feet.

"Country air becomes you, Kel," he said as he opened the door and stood back for her to exit. Instead, she turned to her aunt, who was sipping a cup of coffee and working the puzzle from the paper.

"I'll be back soon, Aunt Irene." She dropped a kiss onto her wrinkled cheek.

"Take your time, sweetie." Her aunt glanced up with a smile before returning to her puzzle. "We'll get to those flowers later this week. Today, you should just enjoy yourself."

Nick held the door of a shiny black Jeep Wrangler and slammed it shut once she'd gotten inside.

"This is new since I saw you last," Kelly observed. Nick usually went for smooth sports cars. This rough and tumble vehicle wasn't his normal style. "Did Heather prefer it to the Corvette?"

Nick slid behind the wheel and adjusted his sunglasses before responding. "You aren't going to cut me any slack, are you?" He shook his head sorrowfully. "If you must know, I smashed the Corvette after I celebrated graduation more than I probably should have."

"You were in another wreck?" She stared searchingly at him. "Were you hurt?"

"This is where—if I were still the self-serving old Nick—I'd lay it on thick and make a play for sympathy." He sent a sardonic smile her way. "But I've changed. And, no, I wasn't hurt badly. I only had a slight concussion. But the car couldn't be salvaged."

"Was—anyone else hurt?" She couldn't help but think of their own accident, which had left her in months of painful therapy. Her right leg still ached on rainy days.

"I was alone. And it was a one-car accident. I wrapped it around a tree."

"Poor tree," she said.

He took one hand from the steering wheel and laid it lightly on hers. "What it did was make me realize I could have gone from this world without you knowing how I feel about you."

Kelly feared he could feel her pulse thudding in her wrist. Surely he wasn't proposing?

"So, I came to make it up with you." He grinned in her direction. "I think we should start seeing each other again."

She hadn't realized she was holding her breath until it came out in a whoosh. Back to square one. They'd been "seeing" each other for years.

He seemed to read her mood. He pulled into an overlook and parked then squeezed her hand before getting out of the Jeep. After opening her door, he led her to a rock and motioned for her to sit. They settled side by side, but she stared into the distance, steeling herself against his magnetism. She so didn't want to go down this path again.

"Kel? Come on." He nudged her shoulder with his. "Look, I know I haven't been fair to you in the past. But I promise that's all changed. I'm a different man. A near-death experience will do that."

"I guess my own near-death experience didn't quite do it for you, huh?"

He winced. "Touché." He lightly grabbed her chin and turned her face toward him. "I'm serious, though. I'm through with all that. My wild oats are sown. I'm ready to settle down."

"So, no more Heathers? Or Jennifers? Or Brandys?" She jerked away from his grip and stubbornly gazed across the valley, her fingers tightly laced together. "And I could go on and on."

"No more. I give you my word. From now on, you're my one and only." He sounded so sincere. And he was saying the very words she longed to hear. And he was so handsome. And funny. *And fickle*, her treacherous heart reminded her. But when he grabbed her hand and tugged her to her feet, she went willingly.

"Brought you something." His whisper tickled her ear. "Close your eyes."

"What?" she asked.

"Hold out your hands and close your eyes and you will get a big surprise," he said in the singsong voice of childhood. And she did.

Nick softly pressed his lips to hers in a feathery kiss before dropping a small package into her outstretched hands.

She opened her eyes slowly. This day had certainly not gone according to plan. She stared at the small blue gift tied with a bright blue bow.

"Go on, open it," Nick urged in a husky voice.

With fingers that trembled slightly, she started to open the box. Leave it to Nick to buy her a gift from Tiffany's to try and woo her back. She stopped. "I don't know about this."

"I do," he said, and it sounded like a promise. Or so she told herself. So she opened the box. And drew in a deep breath as she lifted out a platinum chain with a princess cut diamond pendant hanging from it.

"Is that real?" she asked in a small voice, even though she knew what his answer would be.

"Totally real," he assured her in an amused tone. "I knew it would look perfect on you. Here, let me help you put it on."

She lifted her heavy curtain of red hair and turned around.

The light brush of his hands on her neck and the faint trace of his mint-scented breath were alluring, and she stood with her head bent while he fastened the necklace in place.

Before she could move, he planted a kiss on her neck then turned her into his arms and kissed her lips. When he pulled away, he grinned. "I've missed you."

She let him lead her back to the Jeep and help her inside.

"Now, for that breakfast I promised you," he said after he'd hopped behind the wheel. "Is that Homestead place okay? That was the only eating establishment this one-horse town seemed to have. I dropped Andy off there."

"Andy came with you?" Nick's roommate, Andy, was one of those guys who seemed to have the ability to make everything he touched turn to gold. She'd never been sure how he did it exactly.

"Well, yeah. I needed moral support in case you refused to give it another go." He reached over and took her hand.

"I haven't agreed to anything but breakfast yet," she said sternly.

He waggled his eyebrows at her and headed for town.

Chapter Twenty-one

Emma

Emma was lost in a landscape. She was growing fonder each day of the paintings in Lydia Ann's store. They made her want to pick up a brush and try her hand at painting. Although, based on the drawings she'd done as a child, she knew that wasn't a talent she possessed. But the colors... Oh, the colors! She loved the way they swirled together.

The jingling bell pulled her from her reverie, and she moved forward to greet the customers. Lydia Ann was in the back, settling a dispute between the twins. From what she could gather from their earlier screams, Mary had torn the arm off of Katie's favorite doll. The little girls had seemed content to settle the dispute on their own by arguing, but Lydia Ann had seen fit to step in. Things had gotten much quieter since their mother had intervened.

Kelly stepped inside the shop, followed by two men. Emma's smile froze as she got a good look at the man with Kelly. She was dimly aware there were two men with her, but once her gaze locked on the taller one, all else faded. Even though her perusal of *People* was always short-lived, she recognized that the guy looked enough like Matthew McConaughey to be his twin. Or maybe his younger brother. Emma realized the buzzing in her ears was Kelly's voice. She shook her head slightly and gathered her wits.

"Sorry." She forced her eyes to Kelly's face. "What were you saying?"

"This is Nick," Kelly said, gesturing to the man on her right. "He's my," she paused and looked at Nick, "friend," she said finally. "And this," she said, turning to the Matthew McConaughey look-alike, "is Nick's roommate, Andy."

Emma flashed an uncertain smile at the two Englishers.

"Guys, this is Emma. She's my only friend in Charm."

"Hello." Nick sent a bored nod her way and immediately began looking around the shop. Emma couldn't help but notice his disdain for the merchandise.

Andy held out a hand to shake. "Charmed," he drawled with a smile. "Is every girl in Charm as enchanting as you?"

"Um, no?" Emma smiled uncertainly. "I mean, yes?" After a brief handshake, she pulled her hand from his and cast a desperate glance in Kelly's direction. Her friend was walking around the shop with Nick, and they were speaking in low tones.

"I'm sure they're not or this town would be the tourist capital of the world." His brilliant blue eyes were the color of the ocean. She gulped slightly and sought for a reply. None came, and she just stood, staring back, aware that her face was unbecomingly flushed. If this were one of her daydreams, she would know exactly what to say to have him eating out of her hand.

"Andy, cut it out." Kelly had returned to the scene. "Emma, ignore him. He's originally from Lexington, Kentucky, and he plays up his Southern drawl because it makes the girls swoon. He's always been the biggest flirt on campus. Maybe in the entire USA." She nudged him with her elbow. "I told you not to bother any of the girls around here. They're not used to your high-powered tactics."

That brought Emma to her senses.

"I'm used to such tactics," she asserted. "I mean, we do have men where I come from. And they flirt. I was just—trying to be professional. I am in charge of the shop right now, you know." She attempted to look dignified, knowing a flaming face made that difficult.

"And, just for the record, I wasn't flirting," Andy stated in a serious voice that contained only a hint of the drawl he'd spoken in before. "I was appreciating natural beauty." He took Emma's arm and steered her away from the other two. "Show me around this shop you're in charge of."

Emma had herself under control. What on earth had caused her to act so foolishly over the way some guy looked? She *must* stop looking at movie magazines. Now she'd have to prove she wasn't just a backward girl who wasn't used to flirts.

"Here is our selection of needles." Emma cast her eyes down demurely. "The size you use depends on which project you have in mind. And over here are our patterns. I can show you the local favorites, or—"

"Patterns?" he interrupted. "You're making fun of me, aren't you?" He tilted her chin up to stare deeply into her eyes.

"No. I was just showing you around, like you asked." She chuckled.

"And now you're laughing at me." He pretended to pout.

"Laughing *with* you, perhaps?"

"You really are enchanting." His voice held a note of sincerity it had lacked before.

"Andy," Kelly spoke from behind them, "I'm going to show Nick the rest of town. Are you ready?"

"I think I've already seen the important part." He motioned toward Emma and grinned.

"Emma, can you go with us?" Kelly's voice was filled with resigned amusement. "Andy's so boring when he gets a fixation."

She was a fixation for someone like him? Emma was now completely herself again, free from any form of infatuation. Or so she told herself.

"I need to stay and keep the shop open until Lydia Ann returns."

Lydia Ann entered from the back just as Emma finished speaking.

"Emma, by all means, go with your friends. It's almost lunchtime anyway."

"I can stay if you need me," she replied.

"I'll be fine. Go and enjoy yourself." Lydia Ann smiled impartially at the group and turned to tweak a quilt into place. Left with no dignified recourse, Emma pasted on a smile and left with the others. Andy put a hand to her elbow as if she needed guiding from the shop. She stiffened but resisted the urge to shake it off.

"Don't listen to Kelly," Andy begged in a mock-serious tone. "I don't get fixations. I just know what I like when I see it." He looked pointedly at her. And winked.

"You know, it's hard to know when to take you seriously," she said with disapproval.

"That's what makes me so irresistible." He grinned. "Women like a mystery, you know."

"When I want a mystery, I read a book," she answered tartly.

"Witty as well as beautiful." He nodded in approval. "I like it."

"Hey, you guys coming?" Nick turned to ask.

"We're here," Andy assured him. "Just lead the way and we'll bring up the rear."

They reached the Jeep and Nick opened the passenger door. Emma climbed into the backseat. Kelly began to climb in beside her, but Andy stopped her. "You can have shotgun," he said, grinning as he slid in next to Emma.

Nick started the engine. "So I guess it's the Homestead again?"

"Actually, there's a place called the Carpenters Café inside of Keim Lumber that I hear serves really good sandwiches," Kelly said. "Why don't we grab a bite there?"

At the mention of Keim, Emma's stomach fluttered. Would Noah be working today? What if he saw her with an Englishman? What would he think?

"It doesn't matter to me. Just lead me to food." Nick adjusted his rearview mirror and pulled the Jeep onto the road.

Kelly gave him directions, and they were on their way.

"Do you get to ride in motorized vehicles very often?" Andy spoke directly into her ear, as the wind whipped through the Jeep.

She leaned toward him. "Every now and then. We hire a driver to take us places sometimes. But not on a regular basis."

"Wow. That's cool. You must save a lot on gas."

She shrugged. "I guess."

Nick pulled the Jeep into the parking lot, and they climbed out.

Emma smoothed her dress and tried to tidy her hair. The forceful wind had taken its toll, and she could feel a few loose strands.

As they entered the café, Andy, again, placed his hand at Emma's elbow, in a gesture she still found irritating. She endured it and scooted into the booth, giving him room to sit beside her.

The waitress brought menus over, and Andy leaned toward Emma. "What looks good?" He spoke as if they were on a secret mission together, and Emma instinctively pulled back slightly as she scanned the room. She finally picked up her own menu and stared blindly at it.

As Nick and Kelly ordered, Emma saw him. Noah was sitting alone at a table in the far corner. They locked eyes. He lifted a casual hand in greeting before turning back to his meal.

She waved back, but he was already focused again on the plate in front of him.

Andy nudged her.

"Huh?" She looked around the table and found all eyes on her.

The waitress stood beside the table, her notepad poised, waiting on her order. "Oh. Sorry." She glanced at the menu again. "I'll have the Charmin' Chicken Sandwich, please. And water." The waitress hurried off to the kitchen.

"Emma."

Her head snapped up so fast she felt her jaw crack. Noah was standing beside their table.

"Hello, Noah," she managed. "You remember Kelly."

He nodded. "Nice to see you again."

"And these are her friends, Nick and Andy."

"Welcome to town." He turned to Emma again. "Are we still on for Saturday?"

"Jah. Just come by the store after lunch. I'll be ready."

"Sounds good." He glanced at the newcomers. "I hope you have an enjoyable meal." He tipped his head and left.

"Wow. Next time you think you're hot stuff, Andy, you should think of him and reconsider." Kelly giggled.

Andy groaned. "So you think he's hot stuff, do you?" He smiled. "I'll have you know, *I* can be the strong, silent type."

"You couldn't be silent if your life depended on it." Kelly raised an eyebrow at him. "But you're welcome to try."

"I guess she told you." Nick chuckled.

Emma was thankful for the diversion. She didn't think she could've spoken if her life depended on it. Noah was just a friend. So why did seeing him rattle her so?

The waitress delivered their food, and they settled into a friendly banter. It was obvious the three Englishers were used to hanging out together. She considered the interaction between Kelly and Nick. She could see why her friend had a hard time walking away from him. And Andy was, for lack of a better term, dreamy. But maybe a little too smooth-talking for her.

"There are some really pretty places around here," Kelly said. "It's hard to get used to the sidewalks rolling up before midnight, but the countryside is really worth seeing."

"Emma, give us the down low on the local scenery," Nick said.

"I haven't been here long," she replied, "and I haven't been far out of town. But there's a nice spot a few miles from here with a fishing pond and a nice view of the countryside."

"Perfect," Nick replied. "Let's go have a look." He wiped his mouth, dropped his napkin on the table, and pulled a billfold from his pocket. "I've got this. You guys gather yourselves and let's hit the road."

They slid from the booth, and Andy held out a hand to help Emma up. She stood and smoothed her skirt nervously.

"Um," she began, "actually I probably need to get back to the shop." Even to her own ears, she sounded regretful.

"Come on, Emma." Andy slipped into his Southern drawl again. "We won't be gone much longer." He held the door open for her and they stepped out into the bright sunshine. "Thirty more minutes?" he pleaded.

She felt her resolve melt. "Well, I guess thirty more minutes won't hurt." She smiled. "Let's go."

They climbed into the Jeep and headed toward the pond.

Emma couldn't stifle the guilty thrill that coursed through her as they zoomed along. Had this been a sports car instead of a Jeep, it would have almost fulfilled one of her many daydreams.

"Emma? Is everything all right?" Kelly called from the front seat. "Is he driving too fast for you?" She turned slightly in the seat to look at Emma.

"Everything's fine." Emma forced a smile. She may have been comfortable hanging out with Kelly, but throw in two handsome English guys and a fast vehicle, and she was way out of her element. She glanced down at her simple cotton dress. Would she feel more at ease if she were dressed like them? She must look so out of place.

"Penny for your thoughts," Andy said. He nonchalantly slipped an arm around her shoulder, and she stiffened. Just as casually, he removed his arm but cast her an apologetic look.

"Just enjoying the day is all."

She smiled nervously back at him. However, as the ride continued, she was so caught up in the novelty of speeding down a highway with the wind whipping around her that she forgot her companion in the sheer joy of the freedom. She was struck by a sharp pang of disappointment when they actually came to a stop. The scenery was beautiful, but she would have preferred more of the magical ride.

"We can only stay for thirty minutes," Andy declared as they climbed out of the Jeep. He winked at Emma. "That was the only way we could get our tour guide to come with us."

"I'm hardly a tour guide. In fact, I've only been here one time before."

Kelly raised an eyebrow. "Would that have been with Noah?" She grinned. "I'd let him be my tour guide, that's for sure."

Nick looked at her in disgust. "Come on, you're bruising my ego talking about that guy."

"I dare say it would do your ego some good to be taken down a notch." Kelly paused. "Or maybe two." She looked at him pointedly.

"Now, now." Andy stepped between them. "Let's all play nice or Emma's going to hitch a ride out of here."

"Sorry," Kelly murmured.

"Likewise." Nick held out a hand to Kelly. "How about we call a truce? Tell you what, the rest of the day is your choice."

Kelly's smile was mischievous. "Actually, I have a little job back at the inn you can help me with."

Andy groaned. "Man, what have you gotten us into?"

"An afternoon of weeding. That's what. Hope you brought your work gloves." Kelly laughed.

Emma joined in her laughter. "My mamm always says weeding is good for the soul."

"—Says the girl who's off the hook from an afternoon of manual labor," Andy teased.

"Speaking of which, we should probably get back." Kelly led the way back to the Jeep. "But Emma, if you want to come to the inn tonight for dinner that would be great. I can come pick you up after work if you want." She gestured at the guys. "They're the only two guests at the inn tonight, and I know Aunt Irene won't mind cooking for one more."

"Oh, I don't know," Emma started. She was here to help Lydia Ann, and she'd certainly been doing a lot of running around lately. "I'll need to talk to Lydia Ann first, to make sure she doesn't need me."

Kelly nodded. "Is there a phone at the quilt shop?"

"Jah."

"I'll call you later to find out if you can come."

Emma climbed into the backseat, and Andy hopped in beside her.

"I'd like it if you were at dinner tonight," he said softly, as they began the trip back to town.

Emma gave him a tiny smile. "We'll see." She had to admit, having dinner with them did sound like fun. But once she found herself on the sidewalk in front of Lydia Ann's shop, the guilt she'd been suppressing gained the upper hand. Surely she wasn't so shameless that she would consider jumping the fence. And if not, was there a place in her life for rides in fast cars with handsome Englishmen? Emma was pretty sure she knew the answer to that.

Chapter Twenty-two
....

Kelly

The screen door closed with a bang and Kelly looked up from the flowerbed where she'd been weeding. Nick walked out, carrying a tray with a pitcher of lemonade and four glasses.

Aunt Irene was sitting at a table underneath a large umbrella. When she saw Nick walking toward her, she started to rise to her feet.

"No, ma'am." Nick gave the elderly woman a dazzling smile. "I can do it. You just rest for a bit."

"Thank you, dear." She accepted the glass of lemonade he handed her. "I'm supposed to be the hostess, though."

He grinned. "Oh, I don't mind at all. Tell you what? I'll let you serve me an extra helping of pie tonight."

Aunt Irene chuckled. "That I can do."

Kelly wiped her brow with the back of her hand. Part of the problem was that Nick could really turn on the charm. She watched as he sat down opposite her aunt, keeping up a steady stream of conversation. She knew a lot of guys would have grumbled and complained if they'd had to weed flowers and make nice with old ladies. But Nick hadn't so much as uttered a foul word all afternoon.

She glanced over at Andy. His University of Kentucky baseball cap was pulled so low she could barely see his eyes. He might have gone to OSU, but he'd always be a Kentucky boy at heart. He was hard at work, weeding a bed full of brightly colored zinnias. He'd been just as congenial today as Nick. It was times like this when she started to second-guess herself. They weren't *bad* guys. Just a little misguided sometimes.

Although…she thought back to the past few years and how many sleepless nights she'd spent because of Nick. Worrying what he was doing. Or if he was even still alive. Now that he was out of college, would he finally grow up? She wished she knew the answer.

"Once a cheater, always a cheater," Michelle said whenever the topic of Nick would come up. Maybe she was right. Would Kelly be foolish to give it one more try?

"Need some help?" Andy knelt down beside her. "I'm finished over in my area." He flashed her a smile. "And you looked like you weren't accomplishing much. Not many weeds get pulled when you're staring into space."

She laughed. "Yeah, I guess you're right. I'd love the help, though."

He got to work, careful not to disturb any of the new blooms. "Were you mad when Nick showed up this morning?"

"It's hard to stay mad at Nick. But I wasn't exactly the best welcome wagon when he banged on my door and woke me up." She sat back on her heels. "Look, Andy. You know him better than anyone. Is he for real when he says he's ready to settle down?"

He let out a low whistle. "As his best friend, I should say yes, hands down. As someone who has seen you go through a lot of pain with him, I will say that I'm not sure." He took his hat off and swiped his brow with his arm. "I think he wants to be that guy. Really, I do." He shrugged. "But we all know Nick's track record. So who can say? Who knows for sure?"

"That's what I was afraid you'd say."

"The wrecks have taken a toll on him, though."

She opened her mouth to protest but he cut her off.

"No, really. I know he didn't show it the way he should have. But he was torn up about you being in the hospital. And then, this last one. Whew."

"Was it bad?"

"You should've seen the Corvette. I don't know how he walked away. Barely a scratch." He shook his head. "I think those experiences together have gone a long way in showing him what's important."

She sighed. "Maybe."

"Just think about it. You know as well as I do that when Nick's good, he's very good."

"But when he's bad…well, that's when I get trampled on." She grinned. "It's a gamble."

"Indeed." He pulled the last weed. "Now why don't you go in and call your cute Amish friend? I need someone to talk to during dinner."

She raised a perfectly arched eyebrow at him. "Be nice to her."

He held his hands out and widened his eyes. "I'm always nice. Now go call."

Kelly rolled her eyes. "Fine. I'll go call."

* * *

Kelly pulled the SUV in front of the quilt shop and waited on Emma. She had to admit, she'd been a little surprised when her

Amish friend agreed to dinner at the inn. But Emma was new in town, and she didn't really seem to know many people.

Emma stepped out of the shop and climbed inside the X-Terra. "Thanks for picking me up."

"No problem." Kelly glanced over at Emma. "I don't know how you do it."

"Do what?"

"You always look so fresh. Your dress is always neat. Your hair is always tucked in your cap." She shrugged. "By the end of the day, I look like I've been running a marathon."

Emma chuckled. "Now I don't know about that." She grew somber. "But I look exactly the same every day. My hair in a bun, a kapp on my head. And my dresses are all the same, just in a variety of boring colors." She shook her head. "And of course, I don't wear any makeup, so it isn't like that needs touching up at the end of the day."

"You don't need to wear makeup. Your skin is perfect. And look at it this way, you don't spend a lot of money on clothes that you'll never wear." Kelly grinned. "I end up wearing the same things over and over, yet I have a closet full of expensive clothes."

"But at least you have variety."

Kelly glanced at Emma's furrowed brow. She had meant to compliment her friend, not cause her pain. A swift change of subject was in order. "So, I think Andy thought you were really something."

"He seems like a nice guy. I haven't really known many Englishers, though."

Kelly was puzzled for a moment, but then remembered Aunt Irene telling her the Amish referred to non-Amish as "Englishers," which was really confusing when you thought about it. It made Kelly feel like she was saying she was from England. "Oh?"

"I mean, we get lots of tourists in my hometown and all, but usually I just speak to them in passing. You, Nick, and Andy are the first ones I've spent any real time with."

"Well, don't judge all Englishers by the three of us. I'm not sure we're a great representation."

"I think you are. My thoughts on the two of them remain to be seen." Emma adjusted her seat belt. "So does this visit mean that you have forgiven Nick?"

"You mean forgiven Nick *again*, don't you?" Kelly shook her head. "I'm not sure. I don't want to get roped in again. But we do have a history together, and I guess that is the part that's hard to leave behind."

"Oh."

"I'm actually thinking of telling him we can start talking again. At least open the line of communication. If he behaves badly this summer, it will get back to me. So maybe not officially back together, but more like giving it some serious thought." She pulled the X-Terra into the space beside Nick's Jeep. "Here we are. I hope you're hungry."

"Starving." Emma climbed out of the SUV and followed Kelly onto the big porch.

Chapter Twenty-three

Emma

Emma stepped into the front room of the One Charming Inn and looked around. "This is beautiful," she exclaimed. The hardwood floors gleamed and the walls were dark green with white trim. Emma ran her hands along the back of the ornate gold and green couch.

Kelly stood in front of the fireplace. "Can't you just imagine it in winter? I think this is my favorite room. I'll give you the tour later."

"That would be wonderful. Is your room in the main house, or in one of the cabins outside?"

"See that staircase?" Kelly pointed. "If you go up those stairs and to the right, my room is there." She motioned for Emma to follow her through to the next room. "I hated to take up a whole room, knowing that would mean Aunt Irene would lose out on money, but she promised that if I weren't here, she'd have to hire someone to handle the things I'm doing."

"What all is that, exactly?" Emma asked.

"Roping unsuspecting visitors into weeding the garden," Nick said as he sauntered in. He grinned at them.

Kelly rolled her eyes. "I seem to recall you spending a lot more time on lemonade breaks than you did weeding."

"That's right." Andy stepped from behind Nick. "He was afraid he'd get a big, bad blister." He laughed and clapped Nick on the back. He

spotted Emma, and his mouth grew into a wide smile. "Hello again. I'm glad you could make it." His hair was still wet from the shower, and Emma detected the faint scent of aftershave when he passed by.

"Is everyone hungry?" Kelly asked. "Rather than eat in the main dining room, we'll just eat in the breakfast nook." She led them to the table. "It's smaller."

"Is Aunt Irene not joining us?" Nick asked.

Kelly shook her head. "She's turning in early. We're going to have a full house for the next several days, so she needs her rest. Besides, I told her we could handle serving and cleaning up."

"Does this mean we're going to get kitchen duty?" Nick grumbled. "We are paying guests, after all."

Kelly swatted at him. "Paying, but at a major discount. I think you can handle doing some dishes."

Emma hung back. She couldn't remember a time when she'd felt more out of place. She thought of Lydia Ann, eating at home with the twins, and wished she'd just stayed there. Her thoughts wandered over to Noah and the afternoon of fishing they had planned for Saturday. She smiled at the thought.

"Okay, guys, we're having lasagna. This is going to be a help-yourself kind of deal." Kelly took a rectangular dish from the oven. The cheese bubbled on top and the room was immediately filled with a delicious aroma. Kelly carefully placed the lasagna onto the stovetop. "Plates are there." She pointed to the counter. "Bread is on the table."

"No veggies?" Nick playfully whined.

"Listen here, you should just consider yourself lucky that Aunt Irene made the lasagna. If I'd been in charge we would've had cereal

and milk." She stuck a serving spoon into the lasagna. "Or we'd have been at the Homestead again."

The guys laughed. Andy leaned against the counter and met Emma's questioning gaze. "Let's just say that Kelly has tried to cook many a meal for us." He grinned. "Nick and I had an off-campus apartment last year. There is still grease on the ceiling from where she tried to make some kind of stovetop homemade rolls."

Nick joined in his laughter. "They exploded. All over everything." He reached out and pulled on Kelly's red ponytail. "Remember? You even had it all over you."

Kelly giggled. "See, Emma? I told you I couldn't cook very well. Unfortunately, I have these two to serve as witnesses to many of my cooking catastrophes."

"I think that even has me beat." Emma could see, for the first time, why Kelly was so torn about completely ending her relationship with Nick— what with the history portion of the issue and the fact that they seemed to have a solid friendship. But how could that be? A friend wouldn't treat another friend the way Nick had treated Kelly, right? It was all so complicated and confusing. Emma wondered what Kelly would think if she were in a room with Emma, Jacob, and Abby. Would she see the same camaraderie? Or would it be something else entirely? For the past several days, Emma had tried to push thoughts of Abby out of her head. She knew her sister wouldn't approve of the time she was spending with Englishers. And there was the chance she wouldn't approve of her talking to Noah, either.

Emma filled her plate and followed Kelly to the table. For a moment, she was unsure. Would they pray for the food? She decided that they likely would not, so she bowed her head and said a quick prayer of thanks. When she raised her head, she caught Kelly's eye.

Kelly flashed her a smile. "Would you like some bread?"

"Jah. Please." Emma took the bowl of bread from Kelly and plucked out a slice.

Andy sat down beside her, a steaming plate of lasagna on his plate. "This looks delicious." He accepted the bowl of bread Emma extended. "This is my kind of meal."

Nick sank into the remaining empty seat. "So, what's to do around here?" he asked Emma. "You know. Like for fun."

Emma froze. She was pretty sure her definition of fun wasn't the same as Nick's. In fact, they might not even be in the same dictionary. "I'm not actually from here. I've only been in town for a few weeks. But I do know there's a festival in October." Lydia Ann had just been telling her about the fall festival earlier today.

"A festival?" Kelly asked, interested.

"It's called Charm Days. They have all kinds of stuff to do. There are activities for the kids, music, food." Emma shrugged. "I guess normal festival-like things."

"Music?" Andy asked. "So like a real band?"

"I think it's more local music. Maybe fiddlers." She tried to remember what all Lydia Ann had told her. "All the proceeds from the auction go to the share-and-care fund."

"What's that?" Andy took a big bite of lasagna.

"It's a local charity fund that helps those in need of assistance."

"Wow," said Kelly. "That's pretty cool." She turned to Nick. "One thing I've noticed is that people around here are genuinely concerned about one another. Not like back home." She tore her bread in half and raked some of the sauce onto it. "There's a real sense of community, more than anywhere I've ever seen."

"Is it that way in your hometown, Emma?" Andy turned his gaze on her.

She looked into his deep blue eyes and felt her pulse quicken. "Jah. For the most part. We know our neighbors and look out for one another."

"I'll bet you miss it," Kelly said as she began clearing the table.

Emma sat back against the wooden chair. Did she miss it? She thought again of Abby and her family. "I do miss it." She smiled at her dinner companions. "But I'm glad to be here."

Chapter Twenty-four
....

Abby

Abby carried the stack of empty dinner plates into the kitchen. Her
little sister Sarah's birthday dinner was going very well. And since
serving as hostess was one of Abby's favorite roles, she was especially
enjoying herself. She put the dishes beside the sink and peered at the
German chocolate cake she had made earlier. It had turned out nicely,
and she couldn't wait for Sarah to see it. She'd practically had to tie
her up to keep her from peeking in the kitchen to see what was on the
menu. Abby carefully picked up the cake. Just as she turned to take it
into the dining room, Jacob entered the kitchen.

"Oh! You startled me, Jacob." Surprise made her loosen her grip
on the cake, which slid dangerously to the side.

"Sorry." Jacob reached out and steadied her hand on the cake
plate. "I just came in to see if you needed any help." He grinned at her.
"And to make sure you didn't drop the cake on the floor."

"If I had dropped it, it would have been your fault. Anyway, I've
got the cake, but since you're here you can bring in the smaller plates
and the forks." She nodded her head toward the dishes and utensils
on the butcher-block counter. "I appreciate your help."

"Well, I wasn't only being helpful. I also wanted to see what we
were having for dessert." He leaned toward the plate and sniffed.
"German chocolate. My favorite. Especially when you make it."

Abby ignored the blush creeping up her face. "It happens to be one of Sarah's favorite cakes." She reached for the door. "That's why I made it."

Abby entered the dining room, Jacob at her heels. "Here we go," she said as she set the cake onto the thick wooden table.

Sarah's eyes lit up. "Danki, Abby. It looks delicious."

Mamm helped Abby serve cake all around the table.

"This is the best cake I've ever eaten," Jacob said. "I may have to have seconds."

Abby beamed. "It's not nearly as good as Mamm's, but I'm learning." She looked over at Jacob's mamm. "It's not as good as yours either, Lottie."

"If I may weigh my opinion," Dat piped up, "I believe this must rank in the top three German chocolate cakes I've ever been privileged to eat." He looked at his own mother. "I mean, four. Top four German chocolate cakes."

Laughter rang out around the table.

"Sarah, you have one more card," Mamm said. She placed a pink envelope in front of her youngest daughter.

"I'll bet I know who that is from," Abby said to Jacob. "Just look at the color."

He looked at her blankly. "Who?"

"It's from Emma!" Sarah exclaimed. "She says to tell everyone hello and that she's having a good time and will see us at the end of the summer. She misses us, too."

The younger kids went out to play kickball, and the adults began to drift into the living room to let the meal digest and to enjoy conversation. "I'll do the dishes, Mamm," Abby said, hopping up from the table.

Her mother nodded. "Danki, Abby. It's a blessing to have such a helpful daughter."

Abby smiled and headed toward the kitchen.

"I'll help you, Abby," Jacob said as he followed her in to the kitchen. "So how'd you know that last card was from Emma?"

She looked at him incredulously. "Pink has been her favorite color since we were kids. I figured you knew that."

"Oh. I guess I forgot."

She stared at him for a moment. If he'd paid such little attention to Emma that he didn't even know what color she liked, what other details had he missed?

"I'll wash, you rinse." Abby filled the sink with hot soapy water and began washing the dishes, all too aware of the way Jacob's shoulder brushed against her whenever he grabbed a dish to rinse. She concentrated on each plate and tried to ignore her racing pulse. She reminded herself that Jacob and Emma were perfect for each other. Wasn't she the one who had first noticed that?

"You're awfully quiet tonight." Jacob carefully set the rinsed plate on to the drainer. "Is something bothering you?"

"Not really." If you didn't count wobbly legs and accelerated heartbeats. "I haven't heard from Emma lately, have you?"

"Emma?" It almost sounded as if he were trying to figure out who that was. "No. I haven't heard from her since she left. Just the same as I told you the other day when we got ice cream."

Peripheral vision told her he was staring at her, but she refused to acknowledge it. "Well, when she gets back, things will get back to normal around here, I'm sure." Abby pulled the stopper out of the sink and watched the water swirl down the drain. Just the way her life seemed to be going right now. Swirling out of control.

"I guess." He looked at her curiously. "Although things seem pretty normal right now. Maybe a little quieter." He grinned. "But normal." Jacob dried his hands and handed her the towel. "Want to go sit on the porch? Or... Wait a minute. I know how you love to play kickball. Want to do that instead?" he teased.

"Hah. No telling what would happen if I tried to play kickball." Abby hung the towel on the rack. "I'd probably end up in the hospital. Let's sit on the porch."

They sat in the porch swing. Was the swing getting smaller? Abby didn't remember having to sit this close when she and Emma sat out here. They sat for a few moments in companionable silence. Every now and then, a scream of laughter from the backyard kickball game made its way to her ears.

"So how was the quilt business today? I noticed lots of tourists when I came home for lunch."

"Hmmm?" Abby could practically feel Jacob's breath on her shoulder, and she couldn't concentrate on what he was saying.

"Abby? What is wrong with you? You're really acting weird." Abby didn't think it was possible for Jacob to lean closer but he did. He looked into her eyes. "Are you okay?"

"I'm fine," she said aloud. But her inner voice was reminding her that Jacob was Emma's future husband. "I think I'm going to Charm to visit Emma." That was a spur-of-the-moment decision. Although, really, when she thought about it, it made perfect sense. She needed to get away from here. It was weird for her and Jacob to spend so much time together without Emma there. It was making her feel different than she had ever felt before. "Yes." She nodded her head. "That's what I'm going to do. I have some vacation time coming, so I'm going to Charm."

Jacob looked at her as if she'd lost her mind. "Going to Charm?" he repeated. "Are you serious?"

"Why not? I would love to see Lydia Ann and the twins," Abby said truthfully. And even though that wasn't the main reason, it would do for now. "Why should Emma have all the fun?" Abby tried not to think of how much fun she had been having. With Jacob. Her sister's future husband. She knew she had to stop this before the fun turned into heartbreak for her.

"All the fun?" Jacob was beginning to sound like a parrot. "I thought you were having fun here hanging out with me and your family." He looked so disappointed.

"Well…"Abby hesitated, but honesty won out. "It has been fun." Too much fun. That was the problem. "I just need to get away, and I really do miss Emma. So if Mamm and Dat can do without me for a couple of weeks, I'm going."

"Just for a couple of weeks, though, right?" Jacob looked closely into her face again. "You aren't planning on 'jumping the fence' or anything, are you?" He quirked his lip in a half smile.

"Don't be silly." Abby allowed herself to touch his hand. "You know I'm not that kind of girl." She wasn't sure right now what kind of girl she was. Had she really developed feelings for the man intended for her own sister? Maybe she *would* have to stay in Charm for the rest of her life.

Chapter Twenty-five

Emma

"I've spent more time inside a vehicle over the past week than I have the whole past year," Emma told Kelly on the drive to Wal-Mart.

"Seriously?" Kelly asked.

Emma smiled. "Well, maybe not the whole year, but almost."

"Does it bother you? Riding in a car, I mean."

Emma shook her head. "I've always been fascinated by cars. Back home, we usually have a van that picks us up." She ran her hand along the inside of the SUV's door. "Riding with you or with Nick is different."

"Well, if you like cars, you should see Andy's sometime. He has the cutest little convertible. Some kind of British car that he and his dad restored last summer. It is really cool."

"Is it red?"

Kelly laughed. "Why, yes. It is. How'd you know?" She glanced over at Emma. "Did he already tell you about it? He's obsessed with keeping it shiny."

"Just a lucky guess." She didn't want to admit to Kelly that she often daydreamed about riding in a shiny red convertible. It would make her sound silly.

"So, speaking of Andy...he's pretty good-looking, huh?" Kelly flipped on her turn signal.

"Jah. He is quite handsome." Emma wondered if he had a steady girlfriend, but didn't want Kelly to think she was interested in him.

"I'm not really sure what the rules are." Kelly looked uncertainly at Emma. "So could you date a guy like Andy?"

Emma shifted uncomfortably in the seat. "It would be difficult. In order to marry an Englisher, either they would have to join the church and become Amish…" She trailed off. "Or I would have to leave my faith behind. And my family."

Kelly looked puzzled. "So, then you'd live like I do? With electricity and phones and all?"

"Right. I would have those things, but I would run the risk of losing my family."

A sad look came over Kelly's face. "Wow." She furrowed her brow. "So, I guess you've never been tempted then."

"I wouldn't say never." Emma clasped her hands tightly together. "Sometimes I do think about it."

"But not seriously, though, right?" Kelly asked as she pulled into a parking space.

Emma smiled weakly. "Right." Emma knew Kelly wouldn't understand the truth. After all, she was a girl who longed for family and community. And she would have no reference point for knowing what it was like to feel such limits placed on her life. She'd traveled to Europe and was getting a master's degree. Those were things that, for Emma, would only exist in a daydream.

"Come on," Kelly said over her shoulder. "I've got a long list, and I'm sure you do, too."

Emma caught up with Kelly's long-legged strides. "Lydia Ann needs a few things."

"And how does pizza sound for dinner?"

Emma grinned. "Delicious," she said, following Kelly into the store and letting her murky thoughts be chased away by the bright colors of the merchandise.

* * *

Lydia Ann was sitting in a wooden rocking chair, reading a well-worn Bible, when Emma returned from the store.

"Sorry it took us so long," Emma said as she carried the shopping bags to the dining room table.

Lydia Ann followed her and began removing things from the bags. "It isn't a problem." She pointed at the purchases. "Thank you for picking up this stuff for me. It saved me a trip, and I hate fighting the crowds."

Emma grinned. "It wasn't too bad." She smiled. "You sound like Abby. She's always happy to let me get whatever store-bought goods she needs just so she can avoid having to go. Unless it is a grocery store, and then she's in her element."

"Speaking of Abby..." Lydia Ann trailed off.

Emma jerked up her head. "What? Is there something wrong?" She felt a pang of fear in her stomach.

"Nothing is wrong. Don't be so worried." Lydia Ann smiled. "Actually, Abby is coming for a visit next week."

Emma's eyes widened. "Here? Abby is coming here?" This was shocking news. Abby hadn't mentioned that she was even considering a visit. And she'd been corresponding regularly. Most of Abby's letters had talked about Jacob and how he was a good man. Statements meant to make Emma miss him, she supposed, but she'd mostly just been entertained at her sister's continual attempt at matchmaking. You had to admire her persistence, however.

Lydia Ann nodded. "She called the shop just after you and Kelly left."

"She called?" Abby only used the phone in emergencies or times that she considered emergencies, like when she'd decided Emma needed to come to Charm. "Did she sound okay?"

Lydia Ann laughed. "Stop it. She sounded fine. I think she just misses you is all." She paused. "And if you ask me, it will do her some good to get away. Her letters have become way too serious as of late. She's worried about you." Lydia Ann looked pointedly at Emma. "Do you think she has a reason to be worried?"

Emma was silent. She knew what Lydia Ann was getting at. At least Abby didn't know about the time she'd spent around Andy and Nick. That would push her over the edge. "I think Abby is always going to be worried about me, unless I'm married to Jacob and living next door to her." She smiled. "She's just overreacting."

Lydia Ann didn't look so sure. "If you say so." She started down the hall then stopped and turned to look back at Emma. "But if you ever want to talk about anything, I'm here and would be glad to listen."

Emma watched her cousin walk down the hallway. Lydia Ann might be able to listen, but she likely wouldn't understand. There was only one person she'd been in contact with over the past weeks who seemed to have an inkling of what she was going through. Saturday afternoon couldn't come soon enough.

Chapter Twenty-six

Emma

Emma awoke earlier than usual on Saturday. She'd had trouble sleeping last night, despite the fact that Friday had been busier than normal at the store. She hated those nights when sleep wouldn't come, even though she could literally feel the exhaustion creeping through her body.

She tried not to make a sound as she began getting ready for the day. It was impressive that she was even up before Lydia Ann, who said the only way she could keep up with working in the store, keeping house, and raising twins was to be an early riser. Emma, on the other hand, had always been a notorious sleepyhead in her household, rivaled only by Thomas. Guessing which one of them would arrive at the breakfast table the latest was a running competition in their family.

She chose a light green dress that Abby had made for her last year. Abby's seams were so neat, she could've easily made a living as a seamstress. She couldn't help but wonder what had gotten into Abby to make her want to travel to Charm. She intended to try to catch her sister on the phone today to see if she knew what day she would be arriving. No matter the motives behind Abby's upcoming visit, Emma was thrilled at the prospect of seeing her and hearing all the news from home. Although she suspected much of Abby's news would contain tales of Jacob pining away. Emma was nearly certain that was wishful thinking on Abby's part. Since she'd arrived in Charm, she hadn't heard a peep from him. Of course, she hadn't tried to contact him either.

After brushing through her long auburn hair, she wound it into a bun and put on her kapp. Once her white tennis shoes were on her feet, she was ready to go. She stepped into the hallway and closed the bedroom door softly behind her. The soft rubber soles of her shoes barely made a sound as she walked to the kitchen.

Emma looked out the window that overlooked the kitchen sink. It looked like it was going to be a beautiful day. The sun was just beginning to rise, and there wasn't a cloud in the sky. She looked at the griddle and wondered if she should start breakfast. The tale of Kelly and the exploding dough came to mind and she thought better of it.

In the living room, Emma picked up the Bible that Lydia Ann had been reading from last night. She settled into a chair near a window, where light was already beginning to stream through. May as well put her extra time to good use this morning. She turned to Psalm 42 and began to read. It had always been one of her favorite passages. She wanted to live her life with a thirst for God, just as the deer thirsted for water. Was she living that way now? Technically, she hadn't done anything wrong. But was she on the narrow path she'd been raised to walk?

"Emma?" Lydia Ann stepped into the living room, startling her. "My, but you're up early."

"I couldn't sleep." Emma closed the Bible and placed it on an end table. "So, I thought it better to get a start to the day rather than lounge in bed until I heard you stir."

Lydia Ann smiled. "The girls were just waking when I walked past their room. If you'll get them ready for the day, I'll make breakfast."

"I'd be glad to." Emma started toward the twins' room.

"Oh, and Emma? The fishing poles are in the closet." She pointed to a door in the hallway. "Don't forget to take one with you when we leave for the shop."

"Thanks. You're sure you don't mind me leaving a little early today?"

"Not a bit. But if I remember correctly, Noah is a competitive fisherman. I hope you don't show him up today."

Emma giggled. "I'm sure I won't." She turned the knob on the little girls' room and was greeted with squeals and laughter. Her earlier worries vanished as she threw herself into the busy day.

* * *

"Well, are you ready for a little friendly competition?" Noah stepped to the counter where Emma was standing. "Everything is ready and waiting in the buggy."

She grinned. "I'm ready. I even brought a fishing pole from Lydia Ann's."

"A girl who is prepared. I like that."

"Well, I was afraid you'd give me a bad fishing pole to ensure you'd win," she teased. "I thought I'd better bring my own, just in case."

He winced. "I'd never do something like that. I'm the kind of competitor who only wants to beat someone fair and square."

"Good afternoon, Noah." Lydia Ann came around the corner carrying a stack of patterns. "How are your parents?"

"Dat's been having some back trouble lately." He grinned. "Mamm is making him go to her chiropractor today. He grumbled, but I think he realized just icing it down wasn't helping."

"I hope he feels better soon."

"I'll pass the word along. Mamm is getting the house ready for church next Sunday. I think Aunt Susanna is helping her out this week."

"If she needs me to help her with anything next week, tell her to let me know," said Lydia Ann.

He nodded. "I will." He glanced at Emma. "Are you ready?"

She grinned. "Let's go."

He held the door open for her and she walked through. "It's a beautiful day for fishing," he said as he helped her into the buggy. He climbed in and took the reins. "Don't you agree?"

"I think every day is a beautiful day for fishing. But I don't get to do it much anymore." She shrugged. "Grown-up duties call."

He chuckled. "I know what you mean." He turned the buggy onto the road and they headed out into the countryside.

Emma looked out at the lush green farmland, thankful the weather had held out. It was really a perfect day. It had clouded over around lunchtime, and she'd been worried their fishing trip was going to get rained out. But a couple of hours later, the sun had peeked through a smattering of puffy white clouds, and it had been that way ever since.

Noah slowed the horse and turned onto the road that led to the pond. In a moment, they'd come to a stop near several other buggies. He gave her a sideways glance. "It looks like fishing is a popular activity for this afternoon."

They climbed down from the buggy. Emma walked around to pat the horse while Noah unloaded their fishing poles and bait from the buggy.

"Do you like animals?" Noah asked, coming up beside her.

She nodded. "Abby and I always had a cat we'd play with when we were children." She laughed. "Once we got the bright idea to dress it up in a doll's clothes and try and put it in a bassinet like a baby. Somehow we got the dress on it, but when we laid it in the bassinet and tried to rock it…well, let's just say it didn't cooperate."

Noah laughed. "Sounds like you had a fun childhood."

"I did. Abby's only a year younger than me, so I always had someone to play with." She took the fishing pole from his outstretched hand. "I'm glad you brought chairs." She pointed at two folding chairs he'd set on the ground.

He shrugged. "I was afraid the fish might not be biting." He tucked the chairs underneath his arm and picked up his pole. "Can you grab the bait?" he asked, pointing at a small bait box.

"Jah." She picked the box up from the ground. "I'm ready."

"Follow me. I have a special fishing spot." He grinned at her over his shoulder.

She walked carefully along, trying not to step into any mud. It had rained a little overnight, and it looked like there were still a few puddles around.

"Here we are." He set up their chairs.

She fished a worm out of the box and baited her hook. She felt Noah's eyes on her and looked up. "What?"

"I was just making sure you were telling the truth about baiting your own hook." He grinned and picked up the box to find his own worm.

"Abby is a different story. She squeals a lot when she sees worms and crawly things." Emma cast her line and sat down.

"It sounds like the two of you don't have much in common." Noah's line hit the water with a *plop* and he settled into his chair.

"It probably does seem that way. But Abby and I are actually very close."

He looked over at her. "So does she share your uncertainty about our lifestyle?"

"No. I'm pretty sure she thinks I'm horrible for even having such thoughts."

He furrowed his brow. "And what do you think?"

"I think…" She trailed off. "Oh! I think I'm getting a bite." She jumped up from her chair.

Chapter Twenty-seven
....

Emma

Noah rushed to her side. "Are you sure you've got one?" he asked.

"Jah." She couldn't keep the excitement out of her voice. She brought the fish just to the surface, when it somehow wriggled off of her hook. "Oh, no."

"I can't believe it. That was a big one, too," he said. "Sorry."

"You sound genuinely sorry. Even though that means we're still even." She grinned and chose another worm for her hook. Once her line was in the water, she glanced over at him. "The last time we spoke, you said you'd tell me about Cleveland."

He nodded. "I did." He took a deep breath. "It was a few years ago, and I was starting to have some of the same feelings it sounds like you are now experiencing. I longed for travel and adventure. I felt boxed in." He shrugged. "So I left. I lived with a guy who I'd grown up with. He was working at a construction site in the city." He stretched his long legs out in front of him and looked over at her. "I picked up odd jobs here and there. I wasn't unhappy. But I wasn't happy either, at least not like I'd expected to be. Life was hard."

"How so?" she asked.

"I missed my family a lot. My parents took it hard when I left, even though I think they'd always expected that I'd at least give the English life a try at some point." He shook his head. "I was never like Levi. He never questioned things here. Never was even tempted by anything else. All he ever wanted to do was to marry Lydia Ann and live near his family."

Emma nodded. "They made each other very happy."

"Anyway, I had been courting a girl before I left. Her name was Miriam." He grimaced. "I don't know that we were right for each other, but she and I did have a few things in common. She had a brother who lived in the city, not too far from where I did. He and I knew one another, but not very well. And he was really into the party scene. I never was. Like I told you the other day, I may have explored a few places, but it never changed who I was. Not even temporarily."

"So what happened with Miriam? Did she end up with someone else because you were away?"

"Actually, she really wanted to visit me in the city. She arranged to stay with her brother one weekend, and I guess that was all it took. Pretty soon, she'd moved there. I expected that she was doing the same thing I was—just testing the waters, so to speak." Noah shook his head. "But I was wrong."

"Did you ever see her after she moved?"

"Jah. We saw each other a few times. And I thought things were going pretty well." He stared out at the water.

She waited for him to say more. When he didn't, she sat quietly and watched the rippling waves splash against the bank. A lot like life, one little ripple could cause a huge smashing wave.

Noah cleared his throat and glanced back toward her. "One day I got the call that Levi was sick. He was my older cousin, but we'd practically grown up together. I fell apart. All I wanted was to come home. And I wanted Miriam to come with me. She said she would."

"That was good of her," Emma said softly.

He nodded. "But when I went to pick her up, she answered the door holding on to an Englisher's hand. It turned out she'd been seeing him the entire time she'd been in the city. When it came down to it, she chose him and his lifestyle over me and mine."

"That's an awful lot of bad stuff for you to have dealt with in a short span of time." She looked at him, sorry for the hurt he'd experienced. "What ever happened to her?"

"She married him. That was the last I heard. But looking back, I should've known something was going on just by her appearance."

Emma furrowed her brow. "What do you mean?"

"At first, she looked pretty much the same even in English clothes. But the longer she stayed in the city, she started taking more interest in her appearance. You know, with skimpier clothes and a lot of makeup." He shrugged. "She'd started turning into someone I didn't recognize, but I was too blind to notice."

"So, then, you came home?"

He nodded. "And begged my family to forgive me. I joined the church later that year and have never looked back."

"And Levi? Did you get to spend time with him?"

"When I got back home, he'd just been diagnosed. They thought they caught it in time." His brown eyes clouded over. "The treatments seemed to take care of it, and soon he was able to work again." He met her gaze. "That's when we started working together at Keim. We had some good times..." He trailed off. "But then, the worst happened." He sighed.

"I remember. The cancer came back and it had spread."

Noah nodded. "There was nothing that could be done." He drew his eyebrows together. "I blamed myself for all of it for a long time."

"What do you mean?"

"First, if I'd never gone to the city, Miriam never would've wanted to come visit. And she wouldn't have left her family. And then…" He trailed off. "I guess I sort of felt like maybe if I'd have been here, I would've noticed how run down Levi was getting. He lost a lot of weight. If I'd have been here, maybe I would've encouraged him to go to the doctor even sooner." He looked at her with haunted eyes. "And then he'd still be here."

She let out a breath she hadn't realized she was holding. "Noah." She shook her head. "Neither of those things were your fault."

"I know that. Here." He pointed at his head. "But in my heart, it feels differently."

He stood and walked to the bank, gazing out at the water. "So I do know what it feels like to struggle." He turned toward her. "I don't want you to end up with the same kind of regrets I have."

She laid her pole down and went to join him at the edge of the water. "I guess I don't want to have regrets either way."

"So is that why you're spending time with Englishers?"

She had to force herself to meet his piercing gaze. "I think Kelly could turn out to be a good friend." She shook her head. "No matter if she is an Englisher. But I would be lying if I said I wasn't interested in learning more about her lifestyle."

He looked at her imploringly. "Just be careful, okay? I don't want you to get in over your head."

"I understand your concern, especially after what you've

been through. But I'm not going to do anything that makes me uncomfortable."

A clap of thunder made Emma jump. "Uh-oh."

"Sounds like we'd better hurry."

They scrambled around to gather their things and just made it to the buggy when the first raindrop fell.

"Think we have time to make it home before the bottom falls out?" Emma asked.

Noah glanced at the sky as he directed the horse out onto the road. "I think so." He looked over at her. "I guess we're equally bad fishermen."

"I did get one to the surface at least."

"If it doesn't make it into the cooler, it doesn't count."

She laughed. "It was a good day, even if we're returning empty-handed."

"It was a good day." He repeated and grinned at her. "A very good day."

She could no longer ignore the thrill she felt when he smiled at her.

Chapter Twenty-eight

Abby

It had taken all of Abby's courage to climb aboard the bus alone. She'd considered backing out more than once but had finally steeled herself against her fears. Abby couldn't fathom what was so appealing to Emma about traveling. It was crowded, the other travelers were often rude, and she always emerged from buses or cars feeling slightly gritty and in need of a bath. Besides, who in their right mind would want to get into a loud metal contraption when they could travel slowly in the open air pulled by God's own creatures?

At least she'd gotten an aisle seat. There'd been no way she was going to be near the window where she'd be able to see the world rushing by. Or worse, other cars that were separated from her by only a thin yellow strip of paint and what was hopefully good judgment on the part of their drivers.

Abby pulled a book out of her knapsack and opened it, hoping it could distract her from the things going on around her. But as much as she tried to concentrate on the world inside her book, she couldn't keep her thoughts from wandering. And unfortunately, Jacob's face was the one that kept swimming before her eyes. Had she totally lost her senses? She shifted uncomfortably in the seat.

Maybe she'd imagined the fluttery feeling in her stomach the other night. But looking back, she realized that most of her favorite memories from the past year or two included Jacob. How had she not realized her true feelings? This was definitely a problem, on many levels.

Emma would feel so betrayed if she ever found out. Abby knew her sister had spent a lot of time protesting their lifestyle lately. But Abby was certain that when all was said and done, Emma would choose to remain in Shipshewana and marry Jacob. And there was no doubt that he would choose Emma. He'd be foolish to pass up a woman like her.

Sure, her sister had faults. But she also had so many good qualities. Qualities that Jacob would want in a wife. Emma was loyal and brave and just a little bit daring. Life with her was never boring.

And Abby hated to think of what Jacob himself would say if he knew how she felt. She thought of how he teased her about sports or took her to get an ice cream cone when she'd had a bad day. He must perceive her as a little sister. And she'd gone and fallen for him. Like a silly schoolgirl.

She leaned her head back against the seat and suddenly jerked it upright. Had she forgotten where she was? She didn't know who else had leaned against that seat. Oh, how she hated to travel.

Finally, the bus rolled to a stop and the passengers filed out the door. Happy to have her feet firmly planted on the ground, Abby held tightly to her suitcase and scanned the crowd for a familiar face.

"Abby!"

Abby finally saw Emma waving from the sidewalk. "Do you need me to help with your bags?" Emma asked as she made her way over to where Abby stood.

"Can you get my backpack?" She pointed at the backpack at her feet. "I can get my suitcase."

Emma nodded. "Jah." She grabbed the backpack and slung it over her shoulder. "Then let's get out of here. We can talk better out of the crowds."

Abby picked her suitcase up and began to follow her sister out to the parking lot. She felt disoriented by all the people and voices. Once she'd taken a few breaths of fresh air, she began to feel better. When they got to a blue van, Emma turned and hugged her tightly. "I've missed you so much. I can't believe you decided to come visit. I didn't think you would leave home."

Abby hugged her back, wondering if Emma would be able to guess the reason for her visit. What if her feelings toward Jacob had been obvious to everyone but her? She felt a blush begin to creep up her face.

"Do you need some water?" Emma looked at her worriedly.

Abby sighed. Why must she be so fair-skinned? "No. I'm fine. It was a little warm on the bus is all."

Emma nodded. "I'm glad you're okay. For a minute there, you looked like you were going to be sick."

She was sick. Sick about her realization. What if Emma never spoke to her again? She'd just have to make sure Emma never found out. Time away from Jacob would probably kill any feelings she'd had anyway. And it wasn't as if they were reciprocated.

An Englisher hopped out of the van. He smiled at Abby, hoisted her bag from the ground, and placed it in the back of the van.

"Thanks, Derek," Emma called.

Abby looked at her quizzically.

"He's from Charm. He and his wife live just down the road from Lydia Ann." Emma took the backpack from her back and prepared to climb inside the van. "He also picked me up when I got here."

"Oh. I thought maybe you'd decided to start spending time with Englishers or something."

Emma was silent. She slid across the seat, allowing plenty of room for Abby to climb in. Derek started the van, and they began the drive.

"How long will it take us to get to Charm?" she asked Emma.

"About half an hour. It isn't a bad drive." Rather than meeting Abby's gaze, Emma was studying the van floor as if it held the secrets of the universe. Had she already guessed how Abby felt about Jacob? If she did, that would explain why she was acting so distant. But how could she know? Abby herself hadn't even known until Sarah's birthday party.

Eventually Emma looked up. "So how are Mamm and Dat? And Thomas and Sarah?" Abby was relieved that Emma hadn't asked about Jacob.

"Fine. Just fine." Abby glanced at her sister. "Sarah was so happy to get your store-bought birthday card. She loved it." For a moment, she thought about the pink card. "But we missed you at her party." Guilt nagged at her as she remembered washing dishes with Jacob and then sitting out on the porch swing with him. Abby reminded herself that she hadn't *done* anything wrong. It was more about the way she felt. "I made a German chocolate cake."

Emma looked interested. "That's always one of your best creations." She toyed with the tie on her kapp. "So who all was at the party?"

Abby's heart nearly stopped. She'd known Jacob's name was going to come up at some point. She may as well start practicing saying it without blushing. "Oh, the usual. Mamm, Dat, Sarah, Thomas, Mammi, Dawdi, a few school friends of Sarah and Thomas. Amos and Lottie Yoder were there, too." She paused for a split second. "And Jacob." She glanced quickly at her sister in an effort to read her expression.

Emma didn't even flinch. "That sounds fun."

Abby breathed an inward sigh of relief and stared out the window at the scenery. It was beginning to get dark. She yawned.

"Tired?" Emma asked.

Abby nodded. "You know I have a hard time sleeping on a bus."

"And if I know you, I'll bet you tossed and turned last night in anticipation of your journey." Emma glanced at her. "Am I right?"

Abby nodded. "You know me too well." Although, if that were true, she was in big trouble.

The van finally pulled into a driveway, and Derek got out.

"Here we are," Emma said.

Abby climbed down from the van and looked around. Lydia Ann was standing on the porch with a big smile on her face. She rushed down the steps and opened her arms to give Abby a hug. "I'm so happy to see you. I know how much Emma has missed you." She hugged Abby again. "I'm really glad you came."

Abby smiled. "Me, too." She would get over her feelings for Jacob while she was here. She was sure of it. Otherwise, she'd never be able to go home again.

Chapter Twenty-nine
....

Kelly

After a few weeks in Charm, Kelly had almost gotten used to holding her cell phone at various angles in the hope that she'd get a signal. She stood in the backyard of the inn and held the phone high in the air, thinking maybe it would pick up a strong enough signal for an outgoing call. Finally. Pay dirt. She hit a button and hoped for a connection.

"Hello." Michelle's voice was scratchy through the static.

"Hey." Kelly finally found a spot where she seemed to have a full signal. She froze. Maybe if she stayed in one place, she wouldn't drop the call. She just hoped no one looked out the inn's window and saw her posing like a statue.

"Well, well, well. I was beginning to get worried."

"I know. Sorry. I don't have good reception here." Kelly hadn't spoken to Michelle since the first day she'd worked at the bookmobile.

Michelle laughed. "Hmm. I seem to recall someone thinking you probably wouldn't. But you didn't listen. As usual."

"As usual? What's that supposed to mean?" Kelly asked.

"I talked to Andy the other night. He told me about their visit. I think he has a crush on an Amish girl." She laughed. "But he also told me you were back together with Nick."

Kelly sighed. "Okay. We're not exactly back together. Just talking again is all." She steeled herself for what she knew was coming.

Michelle had been the one to sit with her while she'd cried over Nick's careless treatment.

"Right. Just talking." Michelle's irritation came through the phone despite the poor reception. "Look, Kelly. The guy is no good for you." She let out a loud sigh. "I know you don't want to hear this. But you need to face the facts. There is no way he'll stay faithful."

"You don't know that for sure." Kelly's words sounded hollow. There was some truth to what her friend was saying, even if she didn't want to admit it. "People change."

"People change. Nick does not. It's that simple. Think of how disrespectful it is that he can cheat on you. Lie to you. Nearly kill you in a wreck and show no remorse. But yet you continue to let him."

"I know. But I think he really wants to commit this time."

"I don't want to go all Dr. Phil on you, but like he always says, the best predictor of future behavior is past behavior. And I agree. You might need tough love more than anyone I've ever known. Kel, you deserve so much more. You deserve a man who is going to respect you and cherish you and try his hardest not to hurt you by his actions. And, I know, there's no such thing as a perfect man. But believe me, there is one out there who is way better for you than Nick even has the possibility to be."

Kelly walked over to the nearest wrought iron chair and sat down. "But it's too hard to walk away."

"What? Kelly, you're breaking up. Can you hear me?" Michelle's voice was barely audible through the static. "If you can hear me, at least promise that you'll think about what I've said. Kelly?"

"I promise," Kelly said as she walked back over to the area where she'd had reception. But by the time she reached the spot, the call had dropped. She sighed. Was Michelle right? Was she totally foolish even to consider staying in a relationship that had caused her more pain than happiness?

* * *

Kelly looked at her watch. Nick and Andy should be here any minute. She wasn't sure what had prompted the spontaneous visit, but she hoped it was a sign that Nick had turned over a new leaf. Either that, or Andy really did have a crush on Emma. She wondered briefly about her new friend. It seemed like she'd had plans with Noah at some point over the weekend. Had that gone well?

The black Jeep pulled into the driveway right on time. She had to give it to him, he was trying. The vehicle was barely in park before both guys were out. Andy headed to the hammock and collapsed. Nick came close and pulled her into an embrace.

"I missed you," he said against her hair.

She pulled away and grinned. "That's nice to hear." And it was. Although, the conversation she'd had earlier with Michelle kept niggling at her mind. Was she totally stupid?

"What's on the agenda?" Andy asked from underneath his baseball cap. "Anything going on around here?"

She wrinkled her nose at him. "Can't you just relax? Read? Sleep?"

"Boring." He opened one eye and regarded her. "We are men of action."

"You are acting like a little kid who constantly needs to be entertained." She thought of the well-behaved children who came through the bookmobile when she was working in it. They were less trouble than Andy and Nick. Hands down.

"How about we just plan on going to dinner?" Nick asked.

Andy swung his feet to the ground and rose from the hammock. "Do I have to chaperone or can you two go alone?"

Kelly rolled her eyes. "If you don't go with us, what would you do?"

He grinned. "I was thinking about paying a visit to the local quilt store."

"I think you should leave her alone. She'll be working." The truth of the matter was that Kelly didn't want Andy bothering Emma if she couldn't be around to intervene. Emma might try and appear to be cool with his flirting, but Kelly had been around the Amish enough now to realize how uncomfortable he must make her.

"Don't spoil my fun." Andy looked at her imploringly.

"Tell you what. How about we all three run past the quilt store? But just so you can say hello. Nothing more." Her voice was stern.

"Okay, Mom." He made a face.

She glanced at Nick. He was staring into space and being oddly quiet. "What's gotten into you?"

No answer.

"Nick?" she asked.

Finally, he glanced up. "Did you ask me something?" He looked sheepish.

"Yeah, we asked you why you're such a loser." Andy laughed.

Kelly watched as they grabbed their backpacks from the Jeep. They'd only be in town for one night and, in typical guy fashion, had packed lightly. The three of them trooped into the front door, and she pointed them in the direction of their room. Was there something "off" with Nick, or was it her imagination? People always said you can trust your instincts, but hers had been wrong so many times, she wasn't so sure.

Chapter Thirty

Emma

Emma had to admit, it was very nice to be able to spend time with her sister. These past days had been lots of fun. She, Abby, and Lydia Ann had lingered over lunch today, talking and laughing. Even Mary and Katie had joined in the fun, pretending their dolls were named "Emma" and "Abby" and putting on an impromptu puppet-like show.

"Are you sure you don't want us to stay?" Emma asked Lydia Ann once they'd arrived back in the quilt shop. "I feel like I keep leaving you to fend for yourself."

Lydia Ann's eyes twinkled. "Go show Abby around. She's not had a proper tour yet. And you've been around Charm long enough by now that you'll be almost as good of a guide as a local would be." She gestured to the back of the store. "Mary and Katie are asleep and things are quiet. It will be a good time for me to do a little inventory. I need to place a fabric order soon."

"We won't be gone long," Abby assured her.

"Let's go then. The quicker we leave, the quicker we'll get back to work." Emma pushed the door open and let Abby out to the sidewalk.

They strolled at a slow pace. Emma found herself echoing Noah's story about the history of Charm as she pointed out the sights to Abby.

"I'm impressed. If I didn't know better, I'd guess you were born here." Abby grinned. "Did Lydia Ann teach you the town history that well?"

Emma shook her head. "Actually, Levi's cousin, Noah, was the one who gave me a tour right after I got here."

"Noah?" Abby inquired. "I don't know if I've ever met him."

Emma recalled Kelly's reaction to Noah's good looks. "I'm pretty sure you'd remember if you had." She started walking toward the Charm View School. "I think he'll be over at Lydia Ann's tonight, actually, so you'll get to meet him. He's doing some work for her."

Abby gave her a sideways glance. "I look forward to meeting him."

"This is the school," Emma said, pointing. "The bookmobile stops here sometimes." Emma couldn't remember the exact schedule but wanted to shift the topic from Noah. "You know how I love library books."

Abby laughed. "I'll bet you're a regular at the bookmobile. The librarian probably knows you by name."

Emma bit her lip. She hadn't planned to tell Abby about her English friend. But maybe just telling about Kelly would be okay. "Actually, I've become friends with the girl who works there." She explained the situation to Abby, careful to leave out Andy and Nick.

A flash of concern crossed Abby's face. "Oh? That's nice that you've made a new friend." The tone of her voice belied her words. "Is she going to be in Charm the entire summer?"

"Jah. Until she goes back to school in the fall. Let's head toward the Homestead Restaurant next." Emma motioned for Abby to follow her. "I ate there the other night. It was good food." She grinned at Abby. "Not as good as Mamm's cooking, though. Or yours."

Abby's mouth turned upward in a smile. "Danki."

"Next door to the Homestead is Charm General Store. They've got a little bit of everything," she said once they'd arrived at the front of the store. An Amish woman and little girl came out of the store. When they saw Emma and Abby standing in the parking lot, they waved.

"Everyone is very friendly here," Abby said, waving back at the pair. She glanced at Emma. "This is a quaint little town, isn't it?"

Emma nodded. "I'm really enjoying my time here."

"Our next stop is Keim Lumber." Emma led the way up the huge hill that led to the parking lot. "I know this hill is kind of steep, but it's the only way you can see the building." They were both a little out of breath by the time they reached the parking lot. It was full of a mixture of buggies and cars. "Inside of Keim is the Carpenters Café. If we have time while you're visiting, we'll eat lunch there." They made their way toward the entrance. "Keim is where Levi used to work." Emma started to leave it at that, but it somehow felt dishonest not to mention that she knew one of the current employees. "And where Noah still works."

"So, you've mentioned Noah's name several times. Is he a friend of yours, too? Or just a cousin of Levi's who helps Lydia Ann out?" Abby looked at her quizzically.

Emma cleared her throat. "Um. Both, I guess." She toyed with the tie on her kapp. "He's been a good friend to me since I got here."

Abby furrowed her brow but didn't say anything.

Emma had a pretty good idea of the thoughts that must be running through her sister's mind. Not only had she befriended an Englisher, but she'd also befriended a man other than Jacob. And Emma knew her sister well enough to know that those two things together had probably been earthshaking.

"Emma." A male voice drawled behind them. Only one person could draw out her name into that many syllables. She turned to see a grinning Andy standing before her. He was slightly out of breath.

"Are you out for a jog?" she asked. She looked behind him and saw that Kelly and Nick were halfway up the steep hill, making their way slowly toward the Keim parking lot. She waved in their direction.

"Nope. Just thought I'd try and surprise you. Your cousin told us you were out on a tour. We tried to catch up to you, but you were already almost up the hill." He noticed Abby for the first time and his eyes lit up. "And who do we have here?"

"This is my sister Abby."

Abby's startled expression made Emma wish she'd gone ahead and spilled the beans about her other English friends. But how was she supposed to know the two guys would come back to Charm so soon? "And this is Andy," she said with a flourish of her arm.

Andy grinned. "Abby, it is so nice to meet you." He looked again at Emma then back at Abby. "You must be the most beautiful sisters I've ever met." He comically raised his eyebrows. "And believe me, I've met a lot of sisters."

Emma rolled her eyes. Even though she had only been around him for a short time, she expected such things to come out of his mouth. But one glance over at Abby and she saw the blush beginning to creep up her fair skin. She needed to divert Andy and save her sister from embarrassment. He might comment on her flushed face, which would only serve to embarrass her more. "What brings you to Charm?" she asked sweetly. "I figured you'd had all of the small-town life that you could want for a while."

Andy let out a heaving sigh. "Love," he said dramatically. "Love brings me to Charm." He pointed at Nick and Kelly. "He's still trying to woo her back." He flashed Emma his movie-star grin. "And I came to see this girl I met in a quilt store." He hung his head. "She's Amish, I'm not. I guess we're doomed." He looked at her, his eyes sparkling with amusement. "Sounds like a movie, doesn't it? Or a book?"

"Sounds more like a tragedy to me." Emma raised one eyebrow at him.

Abby put her hand on Emma's arm. "We need to get back to the quilt store. Lydia Ann is expecting us." Her eyes were pleading.

Emma nodded. "She's right. Andy, it was good to see you again. But we need to get back."

"I can walk with you." He fell into stride beside Emma. "It would be no trouble."

"That isn't necessary. We made it fine by ourselves on the way here, and I'm pretty sure we'll make it fine on the way back." If she'd learned anything the other day, it was that Andy didn't need any encouragement.

They finally reached the spot where Kelly and Nick stood. Emma introduced them to Abby. The more new people she met, the more Abby seemed to withdraw. She barely spoke to Kelly, even though the English girl tried to draw her in to a conversation.

"We'd better be going. The store is still open and Lydia Ann needs us," Emma explained. "It was good to see you again, though."

They waved to the Englishers and started the short journey back to the quilt store. They walked in silence for a moment, and Emma could practically hear the wheels spinning in Abby's head.

"Why are you so familiar with them?" Abby finally asked.

Emma shrugged. "I told you I was friends with Kelly. Nick is her sort-of boyfriend. And Andy is Nick's roommate. They came by the store one day, and I ended up eating with them." She consciously left out the part about two meals in one day. No need to send Abby into a tailspin.

"Kelly seemed nice," Abby admitted. "But the men, especially Andy, seemed very forward." She cast a sideways glance at Emma. "Does he like you or something?"

"Oh, Abby. I only just met him. We barely know each other." She was glad the quilt store was busy when they arrived back. She wanted to avoid further questioning. One thing she wouldn't admit to Abby, of all people, was that she rather enjoyed Andy's attention.

Chapter Thirty-one

Abby

Abby watched the needle flash in and out of the brightly colored fabric. Even though she was now an accomplished quilter, she still enjoyed watching others work. When she was a small child, she'd sit for hours and watch Mammi, often interrupting to ask questions, an eager student. She'd always dreamed of the day that she'd get to teach her own daughters, and hopefully even granddaughters, the art of quilting. "You make such beautiful quilts, Lydia Ann."

Lydia Ann looked up from her work and smiled. "Danki. I love to quilt." She deftly broke off the blue thread. "I've always found it so relaxing." She leaned back in the rocking chair and dropped the fabric on her lap. "Levi always laughed at me and said 'just give Lydia Ann a needle and thread and she forgets all her problems.'" She grinned. "He loved to watch me work."

Abby grew somber. "I'm so sorry you lost him. I know you're still adjusting."

"I think it will take a lifetime of adjusting to get used to not having him around." Lydia Ann's hands stopped working, and she met Abby's gaze. "But I was blessed to have him be a part of my life for as long as I did." She motioned toward the hallway. "And just down the hall, tucked into their beds, are two pieces of him I get to hang on to." She smiled.

Emma rose from the rocker she'd been in near the window and came to join Abby on the couch. "I guess a love like the one you and Levi shared never fully goes away."

Lydia Ann nodded. "Levi was my best friend, but he was also much more. We liked to talk to each other. He was always interested in what I had to say or what I thought about things." She smiled at the memory. "And he was the first person I wanted to tell things to. Good, bad, or ugly. I mean, don't get me wrong. We had our moments." Lydia Ann re-threaded her needle with green thread. "We didn't always agree on everything, but when we didn't agree we still got along." She began working on another block.

Abby let out a loud sigh, and the other two women looked up at her. "Sorry. That was louder than I intended." She couldn't get the image of Emma flirting with an Englisher out of her head. Emma might deny it, but it had been easy to see she was flattered by Andy's words. And tonight, when Noah had stopped by to measure the windows, Abby was pretty sure she'd seen a spark between him and Emma. Had her sister completely lost her mind?

Lydia Ann smiled. "Abby, do you have anyone special back home?"

For a split second, Abby and Emma locked eyes. She could just tell the whole truth right now—that she thought Jacob could be all of the things Lydia Ann had just described. And maybe more. The news might shock Emma. But Emma had certainly participated in shocking behavior of her own today. It might make them even. Instead, she shook her head. "No. Not really."

"Well, I hope both of you find a love like the one Levi and I shared."

Emma played with the hem of her apron. "That is exactly what I intend to hold out for," she sighed. "I just hope I can find it."

Abby looked sharply at her sister. She couldn't help herself. "What about Jacob? Don't you think you could have a nice life with him?" Just saying his name was painful. She'd been telling herself for days that she needed to let him go. But she missed him something awful. And seeing how at ease Emma was with both Andy and Noah...well, maybe that meant she really didn't have any feelings for Jacob.

"Sure. I could have a nice life with Jacob." Emma leaned her head back against the couch and stared at the ceiling.

Abby sucked in air as if she'd been punched. She'd been hoping to hear Emma say those words for the past year. But now if her matchmaking proved to be a success, she would get no satisfaction from it.

"But 'nice' might not be enough for you, is that it, Emma?" Lydia Ann asked.

Abby watched the emotions dance across her sister's face as she tried to formulate her thoughts.

"That's exactly the problem." Emma shook her head. "Plus, I'm still trying to figure out how people make tough decisions. How do you know which path is the right one for you?"

"I think you pray about the issue, whatever it is. And you talk about it to people who not only know you but try to understand you. But in the end, you have to choose for yourself." Lydia Ann eyed her over the quilting. "Because the reality is that not making a choice is actually a choice." She grinned. "Did that make any sense? I'm afraid it's getting late and I'm beginning to ramble."

Emma and Abby chuckled.

"It made perfect sense to me," Emma said, stifling a yawn.

Abby rose from the couch. "Me, too. I think you're wise beyond your years."

Lydia Ann beamed. "I'm glad you think so." She put her sewing in a little woven basket sitting beside the rocker. "Now, let's go get some sleep."

Abby followed Emma down the hallway. She wanted to ask her sister to elaborate on how she really felt about Jacob, but it might be best to wait until they'd had a good night's sleep to have any more discussions. Didn't Mamm always say things always looked clearer in the morning? If she could get her nerve up, Abby might try to test that theory tomorrow.

Chapter Thirty-two

Emma

Emma carefully folded the quilt and encased it in plastic. She dropped the receipt in the bag and handed it to the customer. "Thank you for shopping with us, ma'am." She turned to the next customer and smiled as she looked at the small, framed prints in his hand. "You've made a good choice, sir."

"Yes, I think I have." He pulled some cash from his wallet and laid it in Emma's waiting hand. "My wife will love these."

After the last customer left, Emma put the CLOSED sign on the door. Lydia Ann and Abby had already left for the day, so it was up to her to close up shop.

She set out for Lydia Ann's house, waving to a couple of familiar people she passed along the way. Charm was a close-knit community, but everyone had accepted Emma with open arms. She was beginning to feel like she belonged here. Just as she passed the school, she heard the *clip-clop* of hooves behind her. Turning, she shielded her eyes from the late afternoon sun.

Noah stared down at her from his buggy. "Would you like a ride?"

Emma nodded and climbed in. "Thanks for being my knight in shining armor today and rescuing me from the heat." She fanned herself with her hands.

He pulled the buggy onto the road for the short drive to Lydia Ann's house. "Are you enjoying your sister's visit?" he asked.

"Jah. Although she's only here for two more days. The time has really flown by." She shook her head. "And I think she is enjoying herself, too, although…" She trailed off. "I think there's something on her mind. I've noticed that she's a little quieter than normal around me," she sighed. "She's fine with Lydia Ann, laughing and chatting. But for some reason, she's tense when she is around me."

"Tense?" He glanced over at her.

"Abby has always been a little, well, *uptight* is the word that comes to mind." She smiled. "But not in a bad way. She just likes to do things a certain way. And she rarely strays from her schedule."

"So what about you? Do you stick to a schedule?" Noah grinned.

"I probably shouldn't tell you this. But I like to sleep in sometimes. And sometimes I stay up late reading. And I've been known to eat dessert first."

"Would it help if I said I thought those were all admirable qualities?" he asked.

She laughed. "Maybe. Anyway, Abby is a little more traditional than I am. And I admire her for it. But these past days, I've noticed that there is definitely something different about her.
I even see it on her face. She's worrying about something."

Noah slowed the horse as they neared Lydia Ann's house. "Do you think she's worrying about you?"

Emma nodded. "I'm afraid so. And it makes me feel awful. I don't want to cause any strife for anyone. And she met my Englisher friends." She met his gaze. "That didn't go over very well."

"Well, you can hardly blame her." He stopped the buggy in front of the house.

Mary and Katie came running out toward them. "Noah, Noah," Katie called. "Will you take us fishin'?"

He grinned down at her. "Not today, but maybe soon."

The little girls scrambled off, chasing each other to the back of the house.

He looked at Emma. "Did you tell them about our fishing trip?"

"They wanted to know what I was doing with that big stick, so I told them about it. They were especially interested about how the fish eat the worms." She shook her head. "But they are girls after my own heart. Neither of them even wrinkled a nose."

"Maybe we can take them fishing soon, then. That would probably be an entertaining day."

She nodded. "That it would." She motioned toward the house. "I guess I should get inside. Thanks for the ride."

He grinned. "Anytime. I enjoyed being your knight today."

She climbed down from the buggy and watched him drive off. She never tired of talking to Noah. He was different from anyone she'd ever met. And she especially liked the way he always seemed to understand where she was coming from. She felt like she could share anything with him, and he would either identify or at least try to understand. For Emma, that alone made him knight-in-shining-armor material.

As soon as she walked through the door, she was greeted with a pleasant aroma. She followed her nose to the kitchen where Lydia Ann was stirring a savory stew.

"*Mmm*. That smells great. And I'm starving."

Lydia Ann looked up from the stove. "Did everything go okay at the store this afternoon?"

"Jah. I sold a quilt and a couple of those paintings."

"Uh-oh. No one bought the one hanging closest to the door, did they? I don't know what you'd stare at all day if someone took your favorite painting."

Emma grinned. "Would you be upset if you found out I'd been telling people that one isn't for sale?"

Lydia Ann laughed. "Not at all. Maybe it should just be considered part of the store's décor." She glanced at Emma. "Did I see Noah's buggy out front?"

"He gave me a ride home."

"That was nice. I thought about coming back to pick you up myself. It was pretty hot out there today."

"I know. It's at least beginning to cool down now." Emma washed her hands in the sink and dried them with a towel.

Lydia Ann began pulling bowls out of the cabinet. "We're almost ready to eat. Would you go out and call Abby and the twins inside?" Lydia Ann collected silverware from a drawer. "They're in the backyard playing chase."

"Abby is playing chase?" Emma widened her eyes. "She must just be watching them play. Abby doesn't play chase."

Lydia Ann laughed. "I'm telling you. I saw it with my own eyes. Abby was running around the backyard, pretending to be 'It' while the girls chased her. Maybe she's turned into an athlete while you've been away from home."

Emma grinned. "Somehow that's doubtful. Probably she just couldn't resist Mary and Katie."

"That's more likely. They can be pretty irresistible when they team up. I'd say Noah and the tea party is testament to that." She laughed.

"Now that is something I would've loved to have seen. Maybe next time he's over, we can suggest it?" Emma was still chuckling when she stepped out the back door. Abby came running around the corner, the two little girls right on her heels. All three of them were laughing.

Abby looked over her shoulder at Mary and Katie. "One more lap and we're through," she called, grinning. She ran to the far edge of the yard, and suddenly she crumpled to the ground.

For a moment, Emma stared in horror at her sister's lifeless form then took off running toward her. "Abby, are you okay?" she asked, once she'd reached her sister. She dropped to her knees next to where Abby lay trying to figure out what had happened.

Mary and Katie knelt down on the other side of Abby and peered at her. "Are you alive?" Mary asked softly, her face close to Abby's.

Katie looked at Emma. "Abby fell in a hole," she said somberly, pointing at the ground. "Abe Troyer brought us a puppy to play with." She brightened at the memory. "But we let him dig a hole." She looked sheepishly at Emma. "And we had to give the puppy back."

Abby groaned. "Don't worry, I'll be fine. I can't believe I did that. I even knew that hole was there." She sat up and shook her head.

But once she tried to put weight on her hurt ankle, it was obvious that she wasn't okay. Emma helped Abby into the kitchen, followed by the chattering twins.

"Oh, dear," Lydia Ann exclaimed. "What happened?"

Emma, assisted by Katie, told the story of Abby and the hole.

"Noah has been meaning to come fill that hole for the past several weeks. I think that puppy would've dug up the whole yard if we'd have let him." She took ice cubes from a tray and wrapped them up in a hand towel. "Here, let's try this."

Abby winced as the cold ice was applied to her swollen ankle.

"Do you want to go to the doctor?" Lydia Ann sounded worried. "I can take you if you need to."

"Are you kidding? Do you know how many times I've sprained my ankle?" Abby grimaced. "I am the world's biggest klutz."

"She does this sometimes when it's her turn to do dishes." Emma teased, but she was pretty sure the ankle was worse than her sister was letting on.

Abby propped her ankle up on a chair while they ate bowls of delicious stew.

The little girls babbled on about the day the puppy dug the hole and their hopes of going fishing soon with Noah. Emma was glad for their constant chatter, because the adults at the table were much less talkative. She looked around. Lydia Ann barely picked at her food. Worry was etched on her pretty face. She must realize Abby's rapidly swelling ankle wasn't just a simple sprain. And after her injury, Abby was subdued.

Emma was lost in her own thoughts. She'd meant what she said to Noah. Something was going on with Abby. She looked over at her sister. Something besides just a sore ankle.

Lydia Ann rose to begin clearing the table.

"Leave it. I'll take care of the dishes," Emma said. "You go ahead and get the girls ready for bed."

"Thanks." She went to attend to the twins.

Emma helped Abby into the living room, settling her onto the couch. "Here's a pillow to prop your foot on."

Abby raised her foot to allow Emma to slide the pillow underneath it.

"Keep the ice on it," Emma said. "Do you need anything before I go into the kitchen?"

Abby shook her head. "I'll be fine."

Emma perched on the arm of the couch and looked at Abby's swollen, purple ankle. "This looks pretty bad, Abby. How will you get home?" Emma looked at her sister. "You can't possibly ride the bus with your foot like that."

"Yes, I can," Abby said. "Besides, I'm not leaving until day after tomorrow. It will be fine then." She furrowed her brow. "I've worked with my ankle swollen like this plenty of times. Remember that time last winter when I tried to ice skate?" She adjusted the ice on her injury. "And that time I fell when we were running down the hill to the pond?"

"I know. But working in the quilt shop is not like the bus. The bus is crowded and smelly and there is no place to put your leg up."

"I'll be fine," Abby insisted. "And besides, I don't have a choice. I have to go back to work in a few days."

After another glance at Abby's ankle, Emma was pretty sure riding the bus wasn't an option. She kept her thoughts to herself as she went to do the dishes. She would go to the quilt store and use the phone. She looked at the clock. If she hurried, she might be able to catch Dat at the furniture store where he worked. The only way to convince Abby she wasn't able to ride the bus back home was to tell their parents about the injury. She hurried to get the dishes dry and then raced to tell Lydia Ann where she was going.

Chapter Thirty-three
....

Abby

The aching in her ankle told Abby she'd experienced more just
a typical sprain. She didn't think it was broken or anything, but she
was certain it was the worst sprain she'd ever experienced. Lydia
Ann had expertly wrapped it in an Ace bandage, which had helped
some, but Abby had a suspicion she was in for a long night.

She shifted on the bed and her ice pack fell off of her foot. She
groaned. Just when she'd finally gotten settled.

There was a tap at the door, and Emma stuck her head inside.

"How are you feeling?" Emma asked, putting the ice pack where
it belonged. "Does it hurt?"

Abby grimaced. "Not too bad. It aches, though. And you
should've seen me trying to get down the hallway and into bed."
She peered at her sister. "Where were you anyway? I could've used
some help."

Emma hesitated for a moment and then sat carefully on the
bed. "I went to the quilt store." She met Abby's gaze. "Now, don't be
upset. I called Dat."

Abby started to sit up, but Emma motioned for her to stay in a
reclined position. "What? You shouldn't have done that. I don't want
them to worry." She shot her sister a disgusted look. She would be
fine by the time she was supposed to catch the bus. Wouldn't she?

Emma sighed. "Your ankle is in no shape for you to travel on a crowded bus. You're still going to need to have your foot elevated, even the day after tomorrow."

"What did Dat say?" Abby was also curious if Emma had heard any news from home. Mainly, she was interested to know if there was any news of Jacob, but of course, she couldn't admit that to her sister.

"He's sending a van to pick you up."

"What?" Abby started to sit up again then collapsed back onto the pillows in frustration. "I don't want them to go to any trouble. You know I hate to have a fuss made over me."

Emma gave her a tiny smile. "No fuss. Just a van that will come to the house and pick you up. And you'll be able to lounge in an entire row of seats with your foot propped up." Emma leaned toward her sister with wide eyes. "And there'll be air conditioning," she said in a singsong voice. "And I'll bet you'll drive through for a milkshake."

Abby hit the bed with her hands. "Fine." She grinned. "But there'd better be a milkshake or you'll be in trouble."

"I promise. I'll pull the driver aside when he gets here and make the request." She grinned and then her face grew serious. "Actually, Abby. I wanted to talk to you." She picked up a pillow and hugged it to her. "I need to ask you something."

Uh-oh. This sounded important. She knew all the things that had been weighing on Emma's mind lately. And she wasn't sure she was ready to deal with the possibilities. "Well, maybe you should wait until I feel better. You know, until my ankle heals," Abby said. "Or until you get back home."

Emma shook her head. "I can see that you'd rather postpone this discussion. But I really think we need to get some stuff out in the open." She looked pointedly at Abby. "I've felt like something wasn't right between us ever since you arrived." Emma paused. "I've been thinking about it, and I'm pretty sure I know what it is."

Abby was startled. Had Emma figured it out? Did she know Abby had feelings for Jacob? She swallowed hard. "What's that?"

"You're upset with me, aren't you? Or maybe even angry because you've finally realized I'm never going to marry Jacob. Is that it?"

Abby froze. The desire to tell her sister the truth about her own feelings for Jacob pushed to the surface, but she still wasn't sure if she could share the news.

"I guess there's just something I don't understand," Emma said. "Why do you always insist that Jacob and I are perfect together? Maybe if I can understand your reasoning, I can better explain to you how I feel."

"Okay." Abby paused, sorting her thoughts. "Even when we were young, I could tell that you wanted more. That we might not be enough to keep you. That you might leave as soon as you were old enough." Abby shifted in bed, careful not to disturb the ice pack. "And I couldn't bear the thought of you being separated from us. Not just physically, you know, but cut off. And I was so afraid that would happen." Her eyes filled with tears. "So I looked around to find something that would keep you with us. And one day, while I was watching you and Jacob choose teams for volleyball, it hit me."

"What hit you? The ball?" Emma teased.

Abby smiled at her sister, grateful that she always knew when to lighten the mood. "Not that day, at least." She shook her head.

"What hit me was that Jacob was the answer I'd been looking for all along. What more could you want than a man like him? Even if we weren't enough, how could he not be?" She sighed. "He's always thought of me as a little sister, but he was so nice to me anyway. I just thought it would be wonderful to have him in the family and if you married him I would get both things—you would stay and be happy and he would be part of our family."

"If this were a fairy tale, that would be great," Emma said. "But it isn't. I mean, I do have love for Jacob, but it is definitely a brotherly kind of love. We never had the romantic love that a man and woman should have if they plan to get married." She shook her head. "And you heard how Lydia Ann talked about her marriage to Levi. That's what I want."

Abby was quiet. Maybe it was time to confess. "There was a time awhile back where I would've been upset to hear you say that." She took a deep breath. "But the truth is, now it makes me sort of relieved."

"Relieved?" Emma looked puzzled. "Why is that?"

Abby nervously rubbed the quilt edge between her thumb and forefinger. "I think I have romantic feelings for him," she whispered then closed her eyes. Even if Emma didn't have feelings for him, it didn't mean she would be supportive of Abby's.

"You do?" Emma squeaked. "Oh, Abby, that's wonderful." Her bouncing knocked the ice pack off of Abby's foot.

"No, it isn't. It's awful. What if he just sees me like some kid sister? I've always just been someone he has to watch out for."

"Looking back, he's always seemed pleased to look out for you, wouldn't you say?"

Abby shrugged. "Maybe."

Emma patted Abby's arm. "I'm glad you told me. Jacob would be crazy if he didn't return your feelings." She grinned. "Now, try to get some rest."

Somehow, having the truth off of her chest even made Abby's ankle feel better. And, although she knew Jacob's feelings for her remained to be seen, she couldn't shake the giddy feeling growing inside her. Sprain or no, she couldn't wait to get home to see Jacob.

Chapter Thirty-four

Kelly

"You're kidding," Kelly said into her phone. She tried to concentrate on the road between Millersburg and Charm rather than on the words Michelle was saying. "Are you sure?"

"I'm telling you. I've heard from several people and they all have pretty much the same story. Nick was out at a club Saturday night with some blonde girl. They were supposedly all over each other. And she was, like, nineteen or something." Michelle let out a snort. "Which is light years older than his emotional maturity level."

"But you don't have any real proof that he was cheating. Maybe they were just hanging out."

"Okay, I'm done." Michelle's angry voice flared through the phone. "I'm not holding your hand through this again. Stop making excuses for him."

Kelly was silent. She knew Michelle was right. But that didn't make things any easier.

Michelle continued, "I'm sorry. It just upsets me to see you let him get away with the same stuff over and over. But it's your life." She paused. "I'll call you tomorrow."

Kelly told her friend good-bye and ended the call. It was just as well Michelle didn't want to talk to her right now. She was about to enter the land of spotty cell service.

She sighed. It was probably a bad sign that Michelle's news hadn't come as a surprise. At all. She still felt inclined to give Nick the chance to explain himself. Although, she knew him well enough to know exactly what he would say. That the two of them hadn't "officially" been re-established as a couple. So he really was free to hang out with whomever he wanted and it didn't constitute cheating. Yes, that would be exactly the line of defense he would use.

Kelly thought about the things she'd experienced so far this summer. She'd wanted to come to Charm to rid herself of the turmoil she'd been going through. And she'd somewhat found a way to do that. She'd finally accepted that her parents weren't going to change. Even though it might not be the ideal situation, she'd made her peace. She knew that they both loved her the best way they knew how. And that had to be enough.

The time she'd spent at the bookmobile had allowed her the chance to have a trial run at her future career. And she was enjoying it so much. Especially when she could recommend a book to someone and they'd come back later and tell her how much they'd enjoyed it. Or when she got to introduce children to some of her favorite children's literature. She finally felt good about her upcoming graduate work. She was on the right path.

She pulled into the driveway at the inn and climbed out of the SUV. Aunt Irene's older model green Honda Accord wagon was parked in its normal spot, underneath a giant oak tree. Just as Kelly reached the porch, she heard her aunt calling from around back.

"Kelly? Is that you?"

"I'll be right there." She hurried around the side of the house to the backyard. Aunt Irene sat alone at one of the outdoor tables, a wide-brimmed sun hat on top of her head. The older lady grinned as Kelly approached.

"Did you have a good day, dear?" Aunt Irene asked, once Kelly had taken a seat at the table.

She nodded. "I did. Thanks again for helping me get the position with the bookmobile." She looked around. "Although I'm pretty sure I could've stayed busy here even without it."

Her aunt reached out and patted her hand. "You have helped me a lot. The bookkeeping aspect alone has been more than enough."

Kelly had been serving as the bookkeeper for the summer, paying bills and handling statements. She didn't mind doing it because she knew it was a chore for her aunt due to her shaky hands and failing eyesight.

Irene continued. "And the way that you've taken to greeting the guests and showing them around the grounds has been a tremendous help. It means I get to spend more of my time doing what I love the most." Her blue eyes sparkled. "Cooking and growing flowers."

Kelly smiled. "You do both of those things better than anyone I've ever been around."

"I won't tell your gram you said that," she said, winking. Her face grew serious. "There is something I want to talk to you about, though."

"What is it? Is something wrong?" Kelly ran through a list of things in her mind. Had she forgotten to do something?

"Nothing is wrong. I know your parents' divorce has shaken you up. And I know I'm only your great-aunt. But I hope you know you are always welcome here. If you ever need a place to call home, you've found it." Irene smiled and met Kelly's tearful gaze. "I've seen a change in you from the beginning of the summer."

"What do you mean?"

"You seem more content than you did when you got here. In fact, you're almost like a different girl."

Kelly shrugged. "I guess I've been around a few people who've made me realize my priorities might not have been in the right order." She reached out and grabbed her aunt's wrinkled hand. "And thank you for welcoming me into your life. You hardly knew me."

"When you get to be my age, dear, you learn that sometimes life is about taking a leap of faith." She looked thoughtful. "There is one other thing. Something I want you to consider."

"What's that?"

"It was the dream of your uncle Louie and me to have a place like this. He passed on ten years ago and I've been running the inn by myself ever since." She shook her head. "But I'm not going to be around forever. And I never had kids of my own. So I would like for it to be yours someday if you want it."

Kelly was speechless. Her aunt's kindness was overwhelming. "That's very generous of you."

"You don't have to answer right away. And, of course, if you wanted to stop running it as a bed-and-breakfast and just use it as a summer home or a vacation retreat, that would be fine." Her aunt smiled. "I'm glad you came here this summer. I've enjoyed having a young person around."

Kelly rose and gave her aunt a hug. She walked upstairs to her bedroom and thought about all her aunt had said. Was she a different person? She'd like to think so. And if she wanted to

continue to grow into the person she was becoming, she knew
a few other changes were going to have to occur. She knew what
she had to do. And even better, she had finally found a place where
she belonged.

Chapter Thirty-five

Abby

After a lot of protesting, Abby had finally agreed that riding home in a van was the best thing for her. Not that she'd had much of a choice. Between Emma and their parents, Abby's opinions on the matter would've been overruled anyway.

"Okay, you're all packed." Emma walked into the living room, carrying Abby's suitcase. "It must be fun to be waited on hand and foot."

Abby shrugged from where she was perched on the couch, her swollen ankle resting on a pillow. "Maybe a little." She offered a tiny smile. "I just hope my foot returns to normal." She looked down at her ankle. It was the size of a grapefruit and had turned a nasty shade of purple and blue. "I am thankful to be traveling in a van, though." She looked up at Emma. "The bus would've been miserable for me."

"The bus is miserable for you even when you're in perfect health." Emma grinned. "So maybe you're better off this way. If you'll stay off of your ankle for a few days, I think you'll be fine."

"The van is here," Katie called from the window. She and Mary had stood at the window for the past thirty minutes, hoping to see the van pull into the driveway. From the moment Abby had asked them to be her "van watchers," they'd thought it was a fun game.

Lydia Ann brought Abby's backpack into the room and set it beside the door. "I'll go out and talk to the driver," she said. "Girls, do you want to come, too?"

Katie and Mary ran outside after their mother.

Emma peeked out the living room window. "It looks like there is someone getting out of the van besides the driver."

Abby tried to see out the window from her position on the couch, but it was no use. "Who is it?"

"Oh." Emma turned quickly and looked at Abby, her brown eyes wide. "It's Jacob."

"Jacob?" Abby's voice came out shaky. "Why is he here?" She looked accusingly at Emma.

"I didn't have anything to do with it. I only told Dat about your accident. Jacob must've heard about it from him."

Abby's pulse quickened. She'd anticipated having a few hours in the van to give her the chance to figure out what she wanted to say to Jacob the next time she saw him. Instead, she would only have moments to choose her words.

Emma grabbed the suitcase. "I'll take this out to the van and see what Jacob is doing here," she said. Before Abby could say another word, she was out the door.

Abby ignored the shooting pains in her ankle as she hobbled to the window. She watched the interaction between Emma and Jacob. What was she saying to him? Their expressions were serious one minute and jovial the next. After a few minutes, Emma started up the path toward the house.

Abby quickly hobbled back to the couch.

"Are you ready to leave?" Emma asked as she stepped through the door.

"Why is he here?" Abby whispered.

"Remember how the other night you said he always had to take care of you? Well, I think that's exactly what he's doing here. He didn't want you to have to ride all the way home alone with an injured ankle." She offered Abby a hand and helped her rise to her feet. "It was mighty thoughtful of him, don't you think?" She grinned at her sister.

Abby tried to ignore the flutter of excitement. He'd come here for her. Even if that wasn't a declaration of his feelings, sometimes actions spoke louder than words.

* * *

"When your dat told me you'd gone and thrown yourself in a hole, I told him someone must've threatened to make you play volleyball." Jacob's dimpled grin was infectious.

Abby shook her head. "I didn't exactly throw myself in the hole. I just sort of fell in. But I was running when it happened, so that's my excuse." She grinned. "I believe that was my last game of chase."

"You're retiring?" he asked.

"Jah." She enjoyed their easy conversation. Having Jacob on the return trip with her had made it easier to say good-bye to Emma. Not too much longer and Emma would be home. Hopefully for good. Abby had promised Lydia Ann that she'd try to visit more. Maybe travel wasn't so bad if there was a loved one to greet you on the other end.

"I'm glad you came to get me," she said. "That was wonderfully kind of you." She thought for a moment. "Or did Dat ask you to come?"

He grinned. "I volunteered to come. I hated to think of you riding in the van without someone to keep you company, especially with a hurt foot." He shrugged "I know how you hate to travel."

She nodded.

"Plus, I've been pretty lonesome since you left." He grinned. "This way, I got to see you sooner."

Abby felt her face grow hot, but for once it didn't embarrass her that someone had caught her blushing. She grinned at Jacob, suddenly excited about what the future held.

Chapter Thirty-six

Emma

As was often the case, the summer that had once seemed like it would stretch on forever seemed to switch into fast motion. Emma was convinced it was an affliction that only hit schoolchildren and their teachers, but when she mentioned her theory to Lydia Ann, her cousin had only laughed.

"I think everyone experiences the feeling, although maybe schoolchildren and their teachers are the most affected by it," she said. "Summer seems to pass quickly for me because it is one of our busiest times of the year." Lydia Ann sighed. "But I know what you mean about time. It's just one of the many things we can't control."

Emma nodded. "I guess I'm just having a hard time realizing my time in Charm will be coming to an end before too long." It had been two weeks since Abby boarded the van back to Shipshewana, and Emma felt like she'd barely blinked.

"We've had a nice visit," Lydia Ann commented as she fluffed one quilt and twitched another into place. "Are you still glad you chose to stay in Charm for the summer?"

"Jah. This has been one of the best summers I've ever had. Maybe the best." She grinned at Lydia Ann. "Thank you for opening your home to me."

Lydia Ann's face lit up. "I'm glad you feel that way. And you've been a great comfort to me at home." Her smile faded. "In fact, it's going to be lonely once you leave."

"I promise to come and visit," Emma said, suddenly sad. She would miss Lydia Ann and the twins a lot. But there were others she'd grown close to this summer as well.

"I know your parents will be glad for you to get back home. And Abby." Lydia Ann began folding a stack of fabric scraps. "I'm glad you and Abby were able to clear the air about Jacob." Lydia Ann grinned. "I thought Abby was going to turn a cartwheel when she saw him, despite her injured ankle. But how sweet of her to be willing to sacrifice her happiness by offering you what she thought was the perfect gift—a man worth staying home for."

Emma nodded. "I think it was just that she and I have different tastes in the kind of man we each hope to find."

"I think you're right." Lydia Ann was quiet for a moment. "And I don't mean to pry…" She grinned. "But I've noticed you and Noah have spent a good bit of time together these past weeks." She peered at Emma. "I've known him for a very long time. And I can't remember seeing him look happier."

Emma was surprised. Was he happier spending time with her than he'd been with Miriam? A part of her wanted to ask Lydia Ann, but she wasn't sure she would like the answer. "I have a wonderful time with him, too. We never run out of things to talk about."

Lydia Ann sobered. "Abby told me she was afraid you might like one of the Englishers who comes to town to see Kelly. Her friend is handsome…." She trailed off and left an unspoken question in the air.

"I was afraid Abby had gotten that impression. It isn't that I like Andy in a way that means I'm going to run off to Columbus tomorrow or anything. But the attention is nice." She felt herself flush. "I guess the newness of everything can sometimes be exciting," she admitted. She hadn't seen Andy since the day she'd given Abby the tour, but Kelly assured her he might pop in at any time. And even though Emma knew there wasn't real substance between them, she still found herself thrilled to be the object of his interest, even if it was only for a few hours one summer.

Chapter Thirty-seven

Emma

Emma knew something was wrong when she woke up and heard the girls crying. She stumbled from her bed and ran into Lydia Ann in the hall. "Sorry if we woke you. I think the girls are coming down with something." She was clearly flustered. "Would you mind going in and opening the shop alone?"

Emma shook her head. "Not at all. Why don't you stay home all day? I can handle things at the store."

"I'm going to go and get Levi's mamm and see what she thinks. I don't want to take them all the way to the doctor unless it is necessary. She is a good judge of sickness."

"Do you want me to go get her so you can stay with the girls?"

"That would be wonderful, if you don't mind."

Emma got ready for the day with lightning fast speed. She set out on the short walk to Levi's parents' house.

She knocked on the door, and Levi's mamm, Susanna, answered. "Emma, what brings you here so early?" she asked, stepping out onto the porch.

"Katie and Mary are sick. Lydia Ann wants you to come over and see if you think they need to go to the doctor."

Susanna nodded. "Tell her I'll be right there. Just let me run and tell Ben where I'll be."

Emma made her way back to Lydia Ann's and relayed the news. "I'm going to go on to work now." She looked worriedly at Lydia Ann. "I hope they feel better soon. But don't give a second thought to the store."

"Danki." Lydia Ann turned and went back into the girls' room.

Emma set out for work, enjoying the morning. She passed the school and wondered where the bookmobile would be this week. She never could keep the schedule straight.

At the store, she went through the motions of opening and hoped the day wouldn't be too busy.

The bell jangled and she looked up to greet her first customers of the day. "Good morning," she said.

Two middle-aged women began to browse through the merchandise, laughing and talking. "Excuse me, miss?" The taller of the two women stopped at the counter and looked at Emma. Her wild, curly hair was black as coal.

"Jah?"

The woman pushed a strand of hair from her eyes. "Could you tell me if there is a way for you to ship a quilt to me? We've bought so much on this trip that I'm not sure Patsy and I will fit in the car ourselves, much less another purchase." She laughed and pointed to a woman across the store. "She has a shopping problem."

Patsy's head jerked up at the sound of her name. "I heard what you said, Barbara." She walked over to stand at the counter. "Most of the shopping bags in the car belong to her." She gestured toward her friend.

Emma smiled. "We can ship a quilt to your home. The price of shipping will have to be added to the quilt price, though." She motioned toward the quilts. "Just pick one out and if you'll bring it to me and provide your address, I can get it taken care of."

"Thank you for your help, honey. We need to look around a bit first."

Emma nodded.

"Barbara, come look at these. They're precious." Patsy cooed as she held up one of the landscape paintings that depicted Charm. "It's like you could walk right into them." Her raspy voice indicated a long-term devotion to cigarettes. The two women began an animated conversation about the fine quality of the artwork.

At long last, they brought their purchases up to the counter and, after much discussion, decided that they could fit two quilts and two paintings into the car. Emma was relieved. Shipping could be a difficult chore.

A few more customers drifted through the store, and before she knew it, it was lunchtime. She welcomed the break but struggled with a choice. Once she had placed the GONE TO LUNCH sign on the door, she was faced with a decision. Should she go back to Lydia Ann's house and check on the twins or go grab some food in town?

The temptation to possibly see Noah again was too strong to resist, and she set out for Keim. Maybe he would be in the Carpenters Café. She told herself that he definitely would not be there, in the hopes of being pleasantly surprised. She stepped in to the café and scanned the lunchtime crowd. Disappointment rushed through her. But she'd come all this way, so she was at least going to get a sandwich.

"Emma?" She heard the voice from across the café. She looked up and Noah was standing in the entryway. He walked over to where she stood in line to order.

"Hi," she said. "I was just about to order a sandwich to go and take it back to the store."

He held up a lunch pail, "I was just on my way to lunch, too. I could wait on you to get your sandwich, and then I'll drive you back to the store." He paused. "If you would like for me to."

She nodded. "I would like that. I'll meet you in the parking lot."

"I'll be waiting." He turned and walked out of the café.

Emma ordered a Café Burger and a bottle of water and headed out to the parking lot with her bag.

Noah was waiting right out front. "I'm glad I ran into you," he said as soon as she'd gotten settled in the buggy. He drove the buggy out of the parking lot and down the hill. After a car passed, he turned the buggy to the left and onto the main road.

"Me, too." She looked over at him. "Do you want to have lunch at the store?"

"How about the bench outside of the store? It's such a nice day, I don't want to be indoors any longer than I have to."

She nodded. "I know just what you mean."

"Did you tell Lydia Ann and the girls you were coming to the Carpenters Café? I'm surprised Mary and Katie let you go without them." He grinned.

"The twins are really sick. Lydia Ann had me go and get Susanna this morning to come see if she thought they needed to go to the doctor."

A worried look flashed across his handsome face. Emma knew instinctively that any trip to a doctor must bring back bad memories of Levi's lengthy illness and untimely death. She gave Noah a reassuring smile. "I'm sure there is nothing to worry about."

"God will watch over them," said Noah firmly.

Emma nodded. Her dat always said a strong man was one who believed in the strength of God.

Chapter Thirty-eight

Emma

"Tell you what," Noah said, once they were settled on the bench in front of the store. "Let's try to eat quickly and then go and check in on the girls."

Emma wasn't sure that was a good idea. She knew dealing with sick children was enough trouble without having to have other people afoot. "Maybe we should just go to Susanna's and see what she can tell us. I don't want to bother Lydia Ann, especially if the girls are in bed."

He grinned. "I never would've thought of that. Good idea." He took a bite of his sandwich. "How have you been doing?"

"The store is keeping me busy." She stared down at her burger. "But I'm starting to grow a little sad."

His brown eyes were full of concern. "What are you sad about?" he asked.

"My time in Charm is growing short. I have to go back to my teaching job and my family."

"Everyone is going to miss you around here." He took a sip of water. "I suppose I should really say that I'm going to miss you." He grinned. "I mean, you know about books and about fishing." He paused. "And you always make people feel at ease. I've watched you in the store and in line at the café." His eyes met hers. "You're like no girl I've ever met before."

She felt fluttery inside. "I'm going to miss you, too."

He finished his lunch and closed his lunch pail. "I hope you will keep in touch with me, even after you've returned to Shipshewana." He grinned. "You know, I have some relatives in Indiana. Maybe this will be the year I should go for a visit."

She smiled. "I think that would be a good idea."

"Are you ready to go check on the twins?" He rose from the bench.

"Jah. Let's go."

They climbed into the buggy and headed toward Susanna's house. "Do you spend much time with your aunt Susanna and uncle Ben?" she asked.

He nodded. "I try to visit them when I can. I think it helps them cope with losing Levi." He stopped in front of the house and they climbed down from the buggy.

His uncle opened the door and stepped outside. "You just missed lunch." He called to them from the porch.

"We've already eaten, but we wanted to stop by and check on Mary and Katie. Do you know how they're doing?"

"Susanna and Lydia Ann have taken them to the doctor. I think they're pretty sick."

"Well, if you see Lydia Ann, tell her we came to check in on them," Emma said.

"Will do," Ben said. "Good-bye."

Noah and Emma climbed back into the buggy.

"I hope they're okay," Noah said once they were on the way back to the store.

Emma nodded. "You know, it's probably just a summer cold or something." She tried to sound encouraging. "And you know, kids recuperate so quickly that they'll probably be right as rain by tonight."

"I hope you're right. What were their symptoms?" He pulled in front of the quilt store.

"I think fever. Maybe a sore throat." She shrugged. "Lydia Ann didn't give me many details because she was busy being a nurse."

"I'll check back by this afternoon." He grinned. "To see how they are and to see how you survived an entire day at the store alone."

"This could be the kind of day that requires a root beer float later."

He met her eyes. "Days that end with root beer floats are good ones in my book."

She laughed and climbed down from the buggy. She thought about Noah's declaration of how he would miss her. His words meant a lot. And she might not be ready to admit it to anyone else, but she would likely be leaving a little piece of her heart in Charm.

The jangling bell interrupted her whirling thoughts, and Lydia Ann hurried inside.

"How are the girls?" she asked.

Lydia Ann shook her head. "Can you believe it? They have chicken pox."

Emma's eyes widened. "Chicken pox? Oh, no."

"Have you had them? Please, please tell me you've had them."

Emma sank onto the wooden stool behind the counter. "I... I don't believe so."

Lydia Ann groaned. "The good news is that they caught it before they even have any spots. But the bad news is that they'll probably be contagious for ten days."

The door opened again, and Kelly walked up to the counter. She looked from Lydia Ann to Emma. "Have I come at a bad time?" she asked.

"We just learned Katie and Mary have chicken pox," Lydia Ann explained.

Kelly made a face. "Oh, no. Poor little things. I remember having them. It was miserable."

"Well, I've never had them," Emma said quietly. She looked at Lydia Ann. "I guess this means my trip is being cut short."

Lydia Ann sighed. "I'm not sure what to do. I could see if Susanna and Ben have enough room for you."

"Um, I have an idea." Kelly held her arms out in a dramatic way. "You could stay with me." She grinned at Emma. "You can even choose your own room at the inn."

"Oh, I couldn't do that. I know your aunt needs the revenue for those rooms," Emma said. Although, the thought was tempting. It would be kind of fun to stay in the fancy bed-and-breakfast.

"Don't think a thing about it. We always have at least one room empty. And if not, you and I could share one of the rooms that has twin beds." Kelly grinned.

"But I'd have to have a ride to work every day." Emma enjoyed the convenience of being able to walk to work from Lydia Ann's house. But the One Charming Inn was farther out. It really wouldn't be feasible to walk to work and back each day.

Kelly waved a hand in the air. "Don't be silly. I have to come through town on my way to the bookmobile. It won't be any trouble to bring you by here."

"I'll bet Noah would give you a ride, too, if you needed him to," Lydia Ann piped up.

"I'll go look around so you can discuss it." Kelly smiled at them and left the counter.

Emma locked eyes with Lydia Ann. "I'm sorry I can't stay at your house to help with the girls."

Lydia Ann shook her head. "We don't want you to come down with it, too." She flashed a tired grin. "Then I'd have three itchy patients. And I don't want that."

"I understand. Would you mind I stayed with Kelly?"

Lydia Ann shrugged. "Well...I'd feel better if you were staying with Ben and Susanna, but you are old enough to make your own decisions now."

Emma looked down. "I won't stay there if you don't think it's appropriate."

"Irene Abbott runs a respectable inn," Lydia Ann said, "and you have my blessing to stay there. But if you're ever uncomfortable, just know you'll have a place with Levi's mamm and dat."

Emma nodded and smiled her thanks. "I have always wanted to stay at a bed-and-breakfast. Thank you, Lydia Ann."

Kelly came back over to the counter where they stood. "Have you decided?"

Emma couldn't help but be excited. "I'm going to stay with you."

"Yay." Kelly grinned. "We'll have fun."

"I think I'd better go and pack your things for you, Emma. I don't even want you to step foot back in the house until we're sure they're no longer contagious," Lydia Ann said.

"How long will it take to pack her things?" Kelly asked.

"Maybe ten minutes."

"Do you want me to drive you home? Then I can just load her suitcase in my SUV."

"That would be wonderful," said Lydia Ann.

"Emma, I'll come by and pick you up after work. Okay?"

"I'll see you then." Emma looked at Lydia Ann. "Don't worry about the store. I can handle it on my own while you're home with the girls." She smiled. "Please tell them I hope they feel better soon."

"Okay. I'll at least get Susanna to stay with the girls for a few minutes each day so I can come by and see how you're doing."

"I'll be glad to see you each day, but if you can't make it, I'll understand," Emma said.

Lydia Ann nodded. "I'll try my best."

"Good-bye," Emma called to them as they left the counter.

Kelly and Lydia Ann waved to her as they walked out the door.

Emma watched them leave and couldn't help but wonder what was in store for her over the next couple of weeks. She remembered the nervous feeling she'd had when she'd first gotten to Charm. Those same pangs were back again as she was leaving the familiarity of Lydia Ann's house and stepping into the unknown. She was scared and excited all at the same time.

Chapter Thirty-nine

Kelly

Kelly poured lemonade into two glasses and carried them outside to the porch.

"Here you go," she said, handing Emma a glass.

"Danki." Emma took a sip and stared out into the countryside.

Kelly sank into the rocker next to Emma's and kicked off her flip-flops. "Are you enjoying your stay?" She glanced over at Emma. "Is it weird for you to be here surrounded by electricity and technology and all?"

"I'm enjoying my stay very much. And it was a little odd at first, but I'm starting to sort of ignore it."

Kelly grinned. "I'm trying to learn how to ignore it, too, at least the technology part."

"What do you mean?" Emma furrowed her brow.

"I'm trying to leave my cell phone in my car while I'm at work or in a store," Kelly explained. "And if I'm relaxing here on the grounds, I try and leave it inside my room." She laughed. "I know those may sound like small things to you, but that's a big step for me."

"So no more constant connection?"

Kelly shrugged. "I guess I'm trying to have more real connections. Like the two of us having a real, face-to-face conversation is way better than if we just texted." She grinned. "Of course, once you're back in Shipshewana, I guess texting would be convenient."

Emma's brown eyes grew sad. "I'll be back in Indiana very soon. I'm really excited about seeing my family, but I'm going to miss Charm."

"I know what you mean. I'll be in classes before you know it." She glanced at Emma. "So, what's been your favorite part of the summer? And I'll make it easier. You can't say meeting me." Kelly laughed.

"I probably should say spending time with my cousin and all." Emma flashed a mischievous grin. "But I'd have to say meeting Noah. Or Andy. But for very different reasons."

"I don't know that you could find two guys who are more opposite than they are." Kelly conjured a mental picture of both men. "But I've got to hand it to you. They're both hotties." She grinned. "Noah would turn bright red if he knew I called him a hottie, wouldn't he? And Andy would just think that was a given for him."

Emma giggled. "Maybe I'll tell Noah what you think. He's going to help out in the quilt store tomorrow."

"You sure can count on him to step in when you need him to." She shook her head. "He gives me hope that there are still good guys out there, you know?" Kelly said, taking a sip of lemonade. She glanced over at Emma. "Are you hungry? Aunt Irene said there are some leftover sandwiches in the fridge. Is that okay with you?"

Emma nodded. "That sounds good to me."

They went into the kitchen and Kelly pulled out a tray of sandwich halves. She placed it on the counter. "Would you like to eat outside? We can go down to the picnic table."

"Sure. It's a beautiful evening."

Kelly put two plates on the counter. "Help yourself. Do you want chips with the sandwich?

Emma nodded.

Kelly grabbed two small bags of chips from a basket. Aunt Irene always kept a snack basket out, in case guests got hungry between meals. They carried their plates and glasses of lemonade out to the picnic table in the backyard.

Once they were seated, Emma bowed her head. Once she was finished praying, she looked up. "This looks delicious."

Kelly nodded. "Can I ask you a question?"

Emma gave a tiny smile and nodded. "Sure."

"How do you know what to say to God? The last time I tried to pray, I just felt silly."

Emma's brown eyes were thoughtful. "I can understand why, if you only pray once in a while, it might feel that way." She pointed at her white head covering. "This kapp is to help remind me to constantly pray. When you begin to talk to God often throughout the day, not just before a meal, or when you need help with something, I think it gets easier."

"So it's okay to feel that way at first? I just never know what I'm supposed to say. What if I don't use the right words?"

Emma shook her head. "The words you use and the words I use might be different. But each of us has a different relationship with Him, so He understands." She smiled.

Kelly nodded. "I guess you're right. I've never thought about it like that before." Kelly took a bite of her sandwich. She was beginning to gain a new perspective about so many things. The drifting feeling she'd had when she first came to town was beginning to go away as she finally began to find an anchor for her life.

Chapter Forty

....

Emma

Emma watched as Kelly flipped through her stuffed closet, looking for items to get rid of. "You sure have a lot of clothes." She walked over to the closet door and looked at the shoe rack. "And shoes. Do you really wear all of these?"

Kelly grinned. "I guess you could say that I have a shoe problem. When I'm sad, buying shoes always makes me feel better."

"From the looks of this, you must've been sad a lot," Emma said.

"Well, I've had some of those for a long time. But I haven't bought a single pair of shoes this summer." Her green eyes sparkled. "That is a record for me."

Emma pulled a pair of pink heels off of the shoe rack. "Pink is my favorite color." Abby always said she shouldn't play favorites with colors, but she couldn't help it. Her favorite quilt in her bedroom at home had splashes of pink throughout.

"Do you want to try them on?" Kelly asked, grinning.

"Really?" Emma walked back over to the bed and sat down. She removed her white tennis shoes and slipped the pink sandals onto her feet. She stood up and wobbled across the room. The sandals pinched her feet with each step, and she finally collapsed back on the bed. "I don't know how you can wear these for more than a few minutes." She grinned. "Abby would've sprained her ankle just taking a walk around the room in these. Maybe just looking at them."

"Oh, but they look cute on you," Kelly said. "And you walk pretty well in them. A little shaky, but if you practiced you'd be fine." She smiled. "And I guess you kind of get used to the pain."

Emma removed the sandals and put them back on the shoe rack. "I've always wanted a pair of pink shoes. I saw a pair in a magazine once." She looked sheepish. "But maybe I'd do better with some flat ones. Or some flip-flops."

Kelly emerged from the closet with a stack of clothes and began stuffing the items into a box.

"I think I'm going to go to bed." Emma rose from the bed. "Tomorrow is going to be another long day."

"Okay. Hey, do you want to have lunch tomorrow? We could go back to the Homestead."

Emma bit her lip. "Actually, I'm meeting Noah for lunch. But you could eat with us if you want to."

Kelly laughed. "I wouldn't think of it. I know your time with him is nearly up. I just hope he'll be able to get by without you once you're back in Indiana."

Emma blushed. "I'm sure he'll be fine." She walked across the hall to the bedroom she was staying in. She was looking forward to her time with Noah tomorrow. As her departure date crept nearer, time with him was precious.

* * *

Emma blinked against the bright sunlight as she stepped out onto the sidewalk. "Thanks for getting me a sandwich." She grinned at Noah.

"You're welcome." His brown eyes twinkled. "How about we have a picnic today?" He held up a quilt. "I came prepared."

She laughed. "A picnic sounds fun. Where should we go?"

"Let's walk down to the schoolyard."

They set off on the short walk. "Have you heard from Lydia Ann lately?" he asked.

"The girls are starting to feel a little better. I think they're over the fever at least. But they're still spotty."

"So you're still staying at the bed-and-breakfast?"

She nodded. "Jah." She helped him spread the quilt onto a grassy spot underneath a large tree.

They sat down and began to unwrap their food.

"How do you like it at the inn?" he asked, a curious look on his face. "Do you feel comfortable there?"

"It was a little hard to get used to at first, but Kelly's aunt is a wonderful hostess. Both of them have done everything they could to make sure I'm happy." She pulled out the chicken sandwich Noah had gotten for her and took a bite.

"It's nice that they were able to take you in." He met her gaze. "I would've been very sad if your trip had been cut short. In fact, I might've tried to convince you to get the chicken pox just so you could stay."

She laughed. "I would've wanted to stay, but I don't know about purposefully catching a disease to do so." She grinned at him. "But it's nice to know I'm wanted here."

His eyes grew serious. "Emma, I hope you know what you've come to mean to me. And I know you still have some decisions to make. But no matter where you end up, I hope you know there's someone in Charm thinking about you."

Emma stared into his eyes. No one had ever said such sweet things to her. She searched for the right words. "Noah," she began. Before she could finish her thought, she was interrupted by a loud voice.

"Hello." An Englisher walked toward them. "I'm sorry to bother you while you're eating, but I was wondering if you could help me."

Noah jumped up. "What's the matter?"

The young man pointed in the direction where he'd come from. "We had a flat tire. I went to change it, but there isn't a spare." He wiped his brow with his arm. "It's a rental car and I didn't even think to look to make sure the spare was included." He sighed. "My wife and baby are in the car. I was wondering if you could tell me where I can get a tire."

"I can tell you, but you're going to need a ride," Noah said. "It isn't a far walk, but you'd have a hard time walking back, carrying a tire. I can give you a ride."

"Oh, that would be wonderful. Let me run and tell my wife. She and my little girl can sit here in the shade while you take me to get the tire. Thank you." He ran toward the vehicle.

Noah looked over at Emma. "I guess our lunch is over." He grinned.

She began to collect the trash from their meal and stuff it into the bag her sandwich came in. "That's okay. It's nice of you to help that man."

He folded the quilt. "It's the least I can do." He gave her a sideways glance. "You can go ahead to the store. I'll wait on him here."

"Okay. Thanks for lunch." She wished they'd gotten to finish their conversation about what would happen when she was back in Shipshewana. Her time in Charm was down to single-digit days.

"I'll see you soon," he said.

She turned to walk back to the store, her heart heavy. Leaving Charm might end up being the hardest thing she'd ever had to do.

Chapter Forty-one

....

Kelly

"Hi."

Kelly put down the book she'd been reading and looked up as
Emma stepped through the door of the bookmobile. "Is it lunchtime
already?"

Emma shook her head. "Susanna is with the twins so that Lydia
Ann could be at the store for a little while." She shrugged. "Business
was slow, so she told me I could take a break."

"That's nice. You have been working hard lately. How are the
girls doing?"

"Lydia Ann said they're much better. Their spots have almost
faded and they're nearly back to their old selves. She thinks I should
be able to move back in to her house in the next couple of days."

"I'll be sad for you to go, but I know you want to be back at
Lydia Ann's house for your last few days in Charm." Kelly gave a
tiny smile.

Emma held up a stack of books. "I need to return these."

Kelly took the stack of books from Emma and placed them on
the counter. She sank back onto the stool she'd been sitting on and
let out a big sigh.

"Is everything okay?" Emma asked. "You look like something's
on your mind."

Kelly furrowed her brow and nodded. "I have a lot on my mind. And actually, I needed to ask you something. I hate to ask, though," Kelly said. "Because believe me, I know it is some kind of favor."

Emma laughed good-naturedly. "You won't know the answer until you ask."

Kelly took a deep breath. "Okay. First I have to preface it, though." She sat down on a stepstool and stared up at Emma. "I've been doing a lot of thinking lately. You know, about the direction my life is going in." She sighed. "And, I've realized that over these past few years, I have spent the majority of my time worrying about Nick." She picked at a chipped spot in her nail polish. "He's reckless. Not just with cars. But with me." She met Emma's eyes. "And I've decided there can't be a place for him in my life anymore."

Emma pulled a stool over to where Kelly was and sat down beside her. "But haven't you tried that before? You've said yourself that you feel like you can't get away from him."

"That was before." She managed a tiny smile. "I believe I'm strong enough now to really end it. For good. I deserve to be with someone who treats me well. Someone who I don't have to always worry is feeding me a line or cheating on me with some girl he met at a Starbucks."

"You do deserve those things. But how are you going to do it?"

Kelly sighed. "I wish I knew. What I do know is this. I don't want to have to regret the past few years of my life. But I also don't want to keep going through this endless cycle. As long as he's known me, I've forgiven him for whatever he's done wrong and let him take his place in my life like nothing happened. The thing is, each one of those incidents has depleted a little bit of the love I had for him. And now, there isn't much left." She shrugged. "I figure at this point, it is a lot less love than it is addiction. I am drawn to him because I've convinced myself it is better to have him than no one. But you know what? I'd rather be alone than to spend any more sleepless nights wondering if he's wrecked another car or hooked up with some new girl."

"Okay. This all sounds promising. But where does the favor from me come in?" Emma smiled. "Do you want me to break up with him for you?"

Kelly laughed. "No, nothing like that." She played with the end of her ponytail. "Here's the deal. And believe me when I say that I know it is crazy."

"I'm a little nervous about what you have in mind."

"Nick and Andy are coming back to town this weekend. I think they're going to get here Friday."

Emma nodded. "And?"

"I don't want to just end things between us after they've driven all that way. So I was thinking…what if we had a double date of sorts on Friday night. Maybe go to dinner and a movie. Then Saturday, I can have some time alone with Nick to sort things out." She looked pleadingly at Emma. "I know you'd probably rather be spending time with Lydia Ann or Noah." She grinned. "Especially Noah. And I don't blame you. But I know you and Andy sort of hit it off, and it would only be for a few hours."

Emma was quiet for a long moment. "I don't know. I enjoyed hanging out with them last time they were here, but I felt uncomfortable."

"Was it Andy's constant flirting? I can totally ask him to stop."

Emma shook her head. "No. It's going to sound weird to you."
She stood up and began pacing the short length of the bookmobile.
"It was just that I don't fit in. I mean, I don't wear the kind of clothes
you do, and I don't have the same kind of life. I'd feel like a misfit,
especially if we're out in public. Here in Charm, there are more
Amish people than not. But if we drive to a town large enough to
have a movie theatre, people will wonder what I am doing with you."

"Do you feel that way around me?"

"No. But I don't feel like you're judging me, either, and I felt
that way about both Andy and Nick. They would never be able
to understand my lifestyle, and I'm not sure they'd even try." She
stopped pacing and sat down on the stool again. "Plus, I don't
know how it would be perceived by others. I don't want to make
people think badly of me, and I'm afraid if they see me out in a
fancy car, going to a movie, they'll think I'm disrespectful of my
upbringing."

Kelly nodded. "I understand." She patted Emma on the arm.
"Don't worry about it. I don't want you to do something you aren't
comfortable with."

"Unless…" Emma stopped. "No. I can't."

"Unless what?"

"I've always wanted to dress like you. Even just for a day. To see
how it feels." Emma bit her lip and looked at Kelly. "No one would
have to know, especially since I'm staying at the inn right now. I
could borrow an outfit from you, and we could go out of town to a
movie." Her eyes sparkled. "It would be like I was in disguise."

Kelly was astonished. "Emma. Are you sure? I wasn't asking you to
do anything like that." It hadn't even crossed Kelly's mind that Emma

might want to get so far out of her comfort zone. "But if you're sure, I'll let Nick know the next time I talk to him."

Emma nodded. "It will be fun. It's only for one night. What's the worst that could happen?"

The excitement in Emma's voice was the only thing that prevented Kelly from pointing out that those were often famous last words.

Chapter Forty-two

Emma

Emma was ready. She looked at the stranger in the mirror and wondered if she'd gone too far. Her hair fell in soft waves around her face, just as she'd always imagined it would. She leaned in close to the mirror and looked at the makeup Kelly had applied. She didn't feel like herself. Didn't look like herself. Would anyone who knew her even recognize her?

The odd thing was, she didn't feel happy, as she'd imagined she would be in this moment. This girl, this person looking back in the mirror wasn't who she wanted to be.

She backed away from the mirror, nearly tripping over a pile of shoes. She collapsed on Kelly's bed, suddenly sick. Her hands felt clammy and her stomach churned almost as bad as last year when she'd fallen ill with a virus. She stared down at the pink polish on her toes. It was the very color she'd admired on Kelly. But on her own feet, it seemed out of place. Each pink toenail seemed to scream *fake* and *fraud*.

This is what you wanted. What you chased after. She took a breath. Time to face the jury. It was only one night.

She slipped Kelly's high-heeled sandals on her feet. They felt different than they had a week ago when she'd just practiced walking in them. And now, with the fitted, dark jeans and a pink

251

top Kelly had helped her pick out, they even looked different. *Who am I?*

Emma couldn't stall any longer. She walked to the door and opened it quietly. She didn't want to make an entrance. Once on the landing, she heard voices coming from downstairs. She reached the balcony overlook and peeked over. Andy and Nick sat, talking and laughing.

She paused for a minute, listening. She hated to be an eavesdropper but couldn't resist. The image of Abby's frowny face flitted into her head, and she grinned. Eavesdropping had been one of the things Abby had always chided her about.

"Whatever, dude. Kelly is totally into you," Andy said. "Seriously. She'll take you back. She always does." He laughed. "As long as she doesn't find out that you cheated again."

"Maybe. It's not a sure thing this time, though. Must be the Amish influence." Nick snorted. "Think you can handle the Amish chick and give me some time alone to work my magic with Kelly?"

Emma peered over the balcony to see Andy's expression.

His smile was confident. "Emma is putty in my hands. She buys every line I feed her. And man, that sister of hers was way hot. But she was also a prude. But I'm not so sure Emma is, if you know what I mean."

Emma couldn't see his expression, but the way he punched Nick's shoulder and their knowing chuckles told her all she needed to know. She felt as if all the air had been sucked from the room. She wanted to turn and run. Or at least scream. But she stayed put. She grasped the balcony so hard, her knuckles turned white.

"No way." Nick's voice drifted up to her. "My money says Emma is as much of a prude. She's just a big talker. Besides, you really want to make a move on her?"

"I don't know about a move. But I've figured out what my research paper topic is going to be in that psych class I'm taking next semester."

"What's that?"

"I'm thinking something along the lines of *The Naïvety of Twenty-Something Amish Girls* or maybe *Amish Girls Gone Wild.*" Andy and Nick burst into laughter.

Emma blinked back the hot tears that threatened to spill down her face. So that was it. Andy didn't think she was interesting. Or refreshing. He saw her as a conquest. A story to tell to the guys back home. A research paper topic.

"Hey." Kelly's voice made her jump.

Emma turned toward her friend, still reeling.

"Whoa. What's wrong?" Kelly looked closely at Emma's face. "Are you okay? Are you sick?"

Emma shook her head and released the tight grip she had on the banister. "I'm not feeling well." She turned and rushed back into the bedroom, Kelly on her heels.

Emma sank down on the plush featherbed and put her head in her hands.

Kelly knelt down in front of her. "Seriously. What happened?"

"I don't want to talk about it." Emma's voice broke, and a tear trickled down her face.

Kelly rose and sat down beside Emma on the bed. "The guys are waiting downstairs." She glanced at her watch. "If we don't leave in like five minutes, we're going to miss the movie."

Emma glanced at the pink sandals on her feet. They looked out of place. Just like she felt. "I'm not going." She met Kelly's gaze and drew courage from the genuine concern she saw there. Her friend deserved to know the truth, and protecting those two guys would be stupid. She took a deep breath. "Andy and Nick were saying some pretty awful stuff about me." She closed her eyes. "I feel so stupid. I thought they liked me for me, you know? But it turns out I'm just some kind of school project."

Kelly's green eyes blazed. "What are you talking about?"

Emma filled her in on the conversation she'd overheard, careful not to leave out anything. Even though she felt awful, she hoped her friend would finally realize what kind of man her boyfriend was turning out to be.

Kelly paced the length of the bedroom. "I am so sorry. I never should've introduced you to them. I didn't think they would hurt you." She stopped in front of Emma, her eyes filled with pain. "Please understand that."

"You don't need to apologize." She stood. "This is partly my fault, too. Maybe all my fault." She gestured at her outfit. "I'm pretending to be someone I'm not. I don't belong in your world." Her eyes filled with tears again. "I should go."

"But what about the twins? You might catch the chicken pox."

Emma threw her things into a bag. "I'm sure it will be fine now. It's time for me to get back."

"Oh, no, you don't. You're not going anywhere. Those two losers downstairs are the ones who are leaving."

Emma shook her head. "No. I'm ready to get back to Lydia Ann's house."

Kelly must have recognized the resolve in her voice because she didn't argue.

Emma grabbed her bag and silently followed Kelly down the staircase.

Andy and Nick stood as they entered the room.

"Wow." Andy looked Emma up and down. "That is quite a change. You are one cute Amish girl." He slanted a knowing glance at Nick before turning back to her.

She was mortified at his leering glance. She should've taken the time to change into her own clothes. Why had she ever thought wearing English clothes was a good idea? She felt so ashamed. It was a good thing Mamm and Dat couldn't see her now. Despite her past tendency to push the limits, she'd never felt so rotten.

"Cut it out, Andy." Kelly spit the words out. "Look. We know what you guys were saying while you were waiting on us. I guess you never learned to use your inside voices."

The shock registered on their faces.

Kelly turned toward Andy. "You are a pig, do you know that? You don't deserve to even know a girl like Emma, much less get to spend any time with her."

Andy sputtered. "Now hold on just a minute."

"And you." Kelly turned her wrath in Nick's direction. "I have taken you back for the last time. I know that you've been cheating. And Nick, it is not going to happen again. You know why? Because we are through." Her voice was filled with rage, each word growing louder.

Emma couldn't take it any longer. She slipped out the side door of the inn and walked outside. It wasn't that far to Lydia Ann's house. And from the sounds of the raised voices, the breakup between Kelly and Nick could take awhile. All she wanted to do was get these clothes off, wash her face, and climb into bed.

She set out along the road, careful to watch for cars. The sandals that she'd once admired were now killing her feet. Five minutes later, when she felt a blister pop, she finally gave in to the truth. There was no way she would be able to make it all the way to Lydia Ann's house. She stepped over to the side of the road and fished through her bag, hoping against hope that she'd stuffed her tennis shoes in. Unfortunately, she hadn't.

"You look like you could use a ride."

She spun around to find Andy, sitting in his shiny red sports car beside her.

Chapter Forty-three
. . . .

Emma

Emma's mouth felt like cotton. He was the last person she wanted to see or talk to. Especially considering the way he was grinning at her—as if everything were fine.

"Come on. Get in the car." He leaned across the console to the passenger door and opened it. "Get in. It will be dark by the time you finally make it home if you go on foot."

"No, thank you," she gritted out the words. A clap of thunder made her jump.

"C'mon, you're going to get soaked if you don't get in. It's okay if you don't have anything to say to me."

She narrowed her eyes. She had plenty to say to him. About decency and manners. But he was right. She didn't intend to talk to him.

"We don't have to say a word." He grinned, showing his perfect white teeth. "I'll just turn up the radio."

She ignored him and took off walking as fast as she could, wincing with every step. From the corner of her eye, she could see the little red car keeping up with her. A drop of rain hit her arm and then one landed on her face.

"Emma, let me make it up to you for hurting your feelings. You don't need to walk in the rain."

She hesitated. Walking in the rain was much preferable to spending another minute with Andy. But the blister was hurting so bad that she felt like she might end up crawling rather than walking. Which would be ridiculous.

She glanced in the window at Andy. "You can just drop me at the quilt shop. I can walk from there with no problem."

She climbed into the low-sitting car and closed the door. It was amazing how hearing him say those words about her and about Abby made her see him in such a different light. She thought about Noah, talking about the Englisher whom Miriam had run off with. Was the man like Andy? Had he seemed nice at first but turned out to be dishonorable?

The car zoomed down the road, a little too fast for Emma's comfort. "You should slow down. There are children who live near here and they could be in the road." She didn't care what this man thought of her anymore. It was weird to think that only a couple of weeks ago, she'd have probably kept quiet in the hopes that he'd think she was like him. But now that she knew the truth, she figured he was only speeding to scare her.

Andy let up on the gas pedal. "Sorry," he said. "I didn't mean to make you uncomfortable." He turned the volume on the radio up and glanced over at her. "Is that too loud?"

Even though it hurt her ears, she was tired of arguing. She shook her head and looked out the window, wishing they would arrive at their destination so she wouldn't have to see him again. She leaned her head against the plush leather seat. His hand on her knee startled her. She looked over at him.

"Does that make you uncomfortable?" he asked. "You just look so great in those jeans." He waggled his eyebrows at her. Earlier she would've thought the facial expression boyishly charming. No more.

She pushed his hand away and scooted as close as she could to her door.

"Oh, come on, Emma. Lighten up."

She thought of how many times she'd said those very words to Abby. But now, they took on a whole new meaning. She looked into Andy's eyes. "I heard the things you said about me to Nick. I never meant to give you the impression that I was of loose morals." Her face flushed. "Because I'm not."

Lydia Ann's shop came into view and she breathed a sigh of relief.

He pulled the car over. "To tell you the truth, I don't exactly mind a girl with loose morals." He grinned, and she instinctively knew that smile had broken a lot of hearts. At least she'd never given him hers. "But the thing about it is that I don't think you are one. I think you're just experimenting. There's nothing wrong with that." He put his hand back on her knee and her leg practically burned against his touch. But it wasn't burning with desire, like she'd once read about in a book. Instead, his touch made her recoil.

She put her hand on the handle, but before she could open the door, he hit the automatic lock. Her heart pounded. "Let me out of here, Andy."

"Emma," he said softly. "I know you're mad. But you can't deny the attraction between us."

Attraction? Was he kidding? He reached again for her denim-encased leg. She pushed his hand away, but he grabbed on to her arm.

She gasped. She'd always been taught that there was no place in her life for violence, so the impulse to strike out at him took her by surprise. But instead of punching him, she tried to keep her voice calm. "No, Andy. I'm sorry. But nothing is ever going to happen between us." She pulled her arm from his grip and reached for the lock. In a swift movement, she'd extricated herself from the car. *Whew*. She could breathe easier now.

Andy jumped out of the car and hurried to where she stood. "Don't leave like this. I don't want you to be mad at me." He stood too close for her comfort.

She backed away, but he grabbed her forearms. She struggled against him. She heard a buggy coming down the street. Maybe whoever it was would stop.

"Andy. Don't." She tried to break free from his hold but he was too strong.

He bent down and pressed his lips to hers.

Horrified, she froze.

"Sweet Emma," he murmured against her lips. "That wasn't so bad, now was it?"

He stepped back and grinned, obviously pleased with himself.

Her eyes grew wide in horror as she saw the buggy that had stopped beside Andy's car. Noah.

Their eyes locked. She brushed away from Andy. "Noah, wait." She said as he prompted the horse into a trot. "Noah," she cried louder. "It isn't what you think." But it was too late. She watched as the buggy turned the corner, away from where she stood.

She turned and glared at Andy. "Why did you do that?" she demanded. "Do you force yourself on all the girls, or just the—what was it you said—'naïve Amish girls'?"

He sputtered. "I wasn't forcing myself on you. I was just giving you what you wanted… but were too scared to ask for."

Her mind was on the devastated look on Noah's face after seeing what he must've thought was a mutually desired kiss. She glanced down at her outfit again, then at the shiny sports car. After what he'd been through with Miriam, this scene must have made him feel like he was reliving it all over again.

She pulled her attention back to Andy. "That wasn't what I wanted, and you know it. I certainly didn't want to share anything like that with you." Her voice was icy.

"What, you'd rather be spending time with that buggy boy? What's his name? Nomad?" he jeered.

"He's twice the man you are. Maybe three times."

"Whatever." He glared at her.

A blue SUV careened around the corner and pulled beside Andy's car. Kelly jumped out and rushed to Emma's side. "Are you okay?"

Emma nodded.

Kelly put her arm around Emma. "You're shaking. Are you sure you're okay?" she asked worriedly.

Emma hadn't even realized she was trembling. "I am now."

What had been tiny sprinkles before turned into large raindrops. "Come on, let's get you out of the rain," Kelly said, guiding Emma to the SUV.

Without another word, Emma climbed inside and pulled the door closed without another glance at Andy.

"Go pick up Nick," Kelly called to Andy as she opened the driver's side door. "And you guys had better be gone by the time I get back."

Emma leaned her head against the seat, barely able to digest all that had transpired.

Chapter Forty-four
....

Kelly

As Kelly turned the X-Terra toward Lydia Ann's house, she glanced at Emma, worry evident on her face. Her friend was staring straight ahead, with the kind of expression you'd expect to see on a survivor of a horrible tragedy. What more had happened? It was bad enough that she'd overheard Andy and Nick saying ugly things.

Kelly cleared her throat. "Um. Emma? Do you want to talk about it?" Emma was one of the nicest, sweetest girls in the world. It turned Kelly's stomach to think that her friend was hurting because of people she'd brought into her life. Emma would never have met guys like Nick or Andy if it weren't for her.

Emma was silent.

"Did Andy say something else to upset you?" She felt compelled to keep trying. Even if Emma didn't want to talk about it, Kelly knew from experience that keeping hurt feelings inside wouldn't do much good.

"He kissed me," Emma said in a monotone voice.

Uh-oh. It was worse than Kelly had imagined.

"He put his hand on my leg. Then, later, after I got out of the car, he grabbed me and kissed me."

"I'm so sorry. I wish I'd never introduced you to him. I never dreamed he'd act like that."

"And Noah saw it happen."

Now they were getting somewhere. "What was Noah doing there?"

"I have no idea. Maybe he was on his way home from work." Emma's voice shook. "Sometimes over these last weeks, he'd come by the shop to see if we were still there. That was probably what he was doing."

"And you're sure he saw what happened?"

"Jah. He saw. And immediately took off. He couldn't get out of there quick enough." She turned to look at Kelly. "You know how I told you about the girl he used to see? Well, now he must think I'm just like her." Emma put her head in her hands and moaned. "And I'm really not."

"I'm sure you can explain it to him." But Kelly was unsure. Noah was so quiet, mysterious even. Kelly didn't know him well enough to know if he was the type of guy who would understand what had happened.

Emma shook her head. "See how I'm dressed? That, coupled with the sports car and the kiss..." She trailed off. "I imagine that will be enough to make him not want to consider seeing me anymore."

They arrived in front of Lydia Ann's house, and Kelly put the SUV into park. She glanced at Emma. "Oh, I'm sure you're wrong about that. I'll bet he'll come by and you'll have the chance to explain it to him." At least she hoped what she was saying was correct. Platitudes were all she had to offer.

Emma looked at her with a tearstained face. The eye makeup that had been painstakingly applied formed black rivulets down her cheeks. She shook her head. "I don't know. You didn't see his

face when he saw us." She sighed and slumped in the seat. "I knew I
shouldn't have gotten into the car with Andy after the way he talked
about me. I should've just walked home. But all I could think was
that I wanted to be at Lydia Ann's as fast as possible so I could get
into my own clothes and try and forget about my day."

Kelly reached out and patted Emma's arm. "Noah is an honorable
man. I feel certain he will listen." She gave her friend a sideways look.
"You really care about him, don't you?"

Emma nodded. "I never thought I could enjoy spending time
with someone as much as I do with Noah." She managed a tiny smile.
"It's like he understands me in a way no one ever has." She unbuckled
her seatbelt. "Or at least he did. But maybe you're right. Once he
hears that I didn't want to be hugged or kissed by Andy, surely he'll
understand.

Kelly watched Emma climb out of the car. She certainly hoped
they were right. But she had a nagging feeling that it might not
be so easy for Noah to get past what he'd seen, no matter how
unwanted the actions.

* * *

"You've been quiet all morning," Lydia Ann said the next day as they
were getting the shop ready for customers. "Sorry I didn't get the
chance to talk to you last night. It looked like you were already in bed
asleep by the time I got home with the girls. I hated to bother you."

Lydia Ann had taken the twins to have dinner with their
grandparents to celebrate their recovery from the chicken pox.
Emma had been thankful for the quiet house and had gone straight

to bed so she didn't have to tell Lydia Ann about her disastrous night. Plus, she was glad no one had been around to see her in English-style clothes. Although, she'd rather have been in a parade through the town in front of everyone if it could've meant Noah hadn't seen her.

"I was really tired."

Lydia Ann eyed her suspiciously. "I'm sorry things have been so hectic lately. And for your last few days here, too. I hate to see you leave tomorrow." She smiled. "It's been nice to have another adult in the house to talk to. I'm going to miss you a lot."

Emma's eyes filled with tears. "Let's try not to go so long without a visit again, okay? I hate to leave you and the girls. But school will be starting soon, and it's time for me to get back home."

"You must be missing your mamm and dat, too."

"Somethin' fierce." She grinned. "I even miss Thomas and Sarah. And I can't wait to see how my students have grown over the summer." She shook her head. "Ike Bellar has probably done some major damage over the summer. I'm sure I'll hear about it. In gory detail."

"Even though I'm not looking forward to you leaving, I'm looking forward to the get-together tonight. Susanna is going to make her famous bread pudding."

When Lydia Ann had mentioned having a get-together the night before Emma returned home, it had sounded like such a great idea. But after the events of yesterday, Emma wasn't so sure. Noah was on the guest list, and Emma's stomach fluttered as she thought about facing him. But at least she would get the chance to explain things to him before she left town.

"That sounds delicious." Emma's voice came out flat.

"Are you sure you're okay?"

"Jah. I can't wait." She forced a peppy tone. She didn't want to tell Lydia Ann about yesterday. So, she decided to let her in on the other part of her sadness. "It's just that after being away all summer, it feels weird to be going back home. I'd hoped to figure things out this summer, but I think I may be more confused than ever."

Lydia Ann looked up from the drawer where she'd been counting change. "How so?"

"In the beginning, I was trying to figure out where I belonged, and if I belonged, and all that." She shrugged. "I guess I blamed it on my roots. But after meeting Kelly, I learned that maybe having those feelings is just a part of growing up, you know? Because she's struggled with some of the same things I have, and she isn't even Amish." Emma sank onto a wooden stool. "And then spending time with Noah showed me that there are other people of our faith who are similar to me." She grinned. "Kelly says he 'gets' me. And as weird as that sounds, I think she's right."

Lydia Ann nodded. "Have you and Noah talked about what might happen after you leave Charm?"

"You mean have we talked about keeping in touch?" The truth of the matter was that Emma was sick at the thought of not seeing Noah on a regular basis. "Not in so many words. He has mentioned the future a few times, though."

Lydia Ann's eyes twinkled. "I'll just bet he has."

A flush crept across Emma's face. "I hope to talk to him tonight and exchange addresses so we can write to each other." She tried to ignore the nervous pang. What if Noah didn't want to keep in contact with her because of what he'd observed between her and Andy? She had been so foolish to have ever felt flattered by the Englisher's attention.

Lydia Ann winked. "Exchanging letters isn't exactly what I had in mind, but I supposed it is a start."

The bell above the door jingled, and they both turned to greet the customer.

Kelly rushed in, her face flushed from the August heat. "Good morning! I came into town to run some errands for Aunt Irene and thought I'd stop in to see how you were." She looked pointedly at Emma. "How's everyone feeling this morning?"

"The girls are fine," Lydia Ann gushed. "Just a few traces of their spots, but they are doing much better. The doctor doesn't think they will even have any scars."

Emma shrugged. She knew the question had been directed toward her. "I'm almost packed."

"I actually wanted to talk to you about that." Kelly's pale yellow T-shirt showed off a hint of her suntan. The denim skirt she wore came just below her knees, and on her feet were yellow flip-flops. Her red hair was pulled back into a loose ponytail, and there was barely a trace of makeup on her face. Emma made a mental note to mention how fetching her more subdued look was later. She'd noticed more and more lately that Kelly was less "made up" and more natural. Had living among the plain people been the difference?

"What about it?"

"I'd love to give you a ride home. Don't you dare think about hiring a driver or taking the bus."

"I don't want you to go to any trouble."

"Don't be silly. It isn't any trouble at all. We'll have fun. It'll be our last hurrah before we go back to our normal lives."

Emma smiled. "Okay, if you're sure. But I'll pay for the gas."

"You'll do no such thing. We'll talk about it more tonight and decide what time to leave." She turned to Lydia Ann. "Do I need to bring anything tonight?"

Lydia Ann shook her head. "No. I think we're covered. It will just be a small crowd anyway. The three of us, the twins, my in-laws, and Noah."

Kelly raised an eyebrow in Emma's direction. "It will be good to see Noah again." She turned toward the door. "See you tonight."

Emma watched her go. She was right. It would be good to see Noah again. She hoped to erase the hurt that had been on his face yesterday. Even if she had to beg his forgiveness.

Chapter Forty-five

. . . .

Abby

Singings just weren't the same without Emma around. Even
though Emma often said she didn't have much of a voice, Abby
missed hearing her sister's harmonizing. Tonight had been fun,
but sitting beside Naomi only made Abby miss Emma more.
Naomi hadn't laughed or commented to Abby between songs.
But tomorrow was the day Emma would be back home, and Abby
couldn't wait.

"Hi, Abby." Jacob caught up with her outside of the barn after
the singing was over. "I wondered if you might want a ride home
tonight?" Something was off with Jacob, but Abby couldn't quite put
her finger on it. His face looked a little flushed. Did he have a touch
of a summer cold?

"Jah. That would be wonderful." She flashed him a smile. Ever
since they'd gotten home from Charm, things were going better
than she'd ever hoped. All the tension she'd felt earlier in the
summer was gone. Once Emma had given her blessing, she'd been
able to allow her feelings for Jacob to blossom. It was almost as if
Abby had been allowed to enter a whole new world.

He grinned. "I'm glad you think so." He led her to his buggy and
helped her climb inside. "Do you need to go home right away, or
would you like to go for a ride?"

"Oh, I can stay out for a little while." Her stomach was jumping with excitement. She'd known Jacob for her entire life and still wasn't used to the fact that he made her feel so giddy. But lately, just one look from him had her feeling like she was going to burst with happiness.

He headed west, and soon they were in front of the one-room school they'd attended and where Emma now taught. Jacob brought the horse to a stop and turned toward Abby. "Would you like to take a walk?" he asked.

She nodded. He came around and helped her exit the buggy. She couldn't help but relish the touch of his hand, even though it only lasted for a moment. They walked toward a little wooden bench just outside the schoolhouse.

"Is this okay?" he asked.

"Yes. It is a beautiful night." The moon was full and bright, and the empty schoolyard seemed to glow.

"Remember when we were children and attended here?" He smiled at her. "I always knew you were special, even then."

She was happy to hear that he thought she was special. She grinned. "I knew you were special, too. The way you'd always look out for me." She chuckled. "Remember when I almost stepped on that snake?"

He let out a chuckle of his own. "What were you? Six? That poor garden snake was just as scared as you were."

"I squealed and squealed. You picked me up, and Emma picked up the snake." At the mention of Emma, she stopped giggling.

He reached over and took her hand. "Listen, Abby. There is something you should know."

She tried to read his expression. He looked serious. "What's that?"

Jacob reached out and traced lightly along her face. "I'm falling in love with you." He cleared his throat. "I've never told anyone that before. I know you wanted me and Emma to be together, but we never had the same connection that you and I do."

She nodded. "That's the same thing Emma told me." She smiled. "I just never thought you'd feel that way about me. But I knew I wanted to keep you around." She held tightly to his hand. "I'm falling in love with you, too. Maybe I've always been in love with you." She shook her head. "It's crazy that this has been right in front of our eyes all this time, and we just didn't know it."

"So you won't mind seeing me on a more regular basis? And maybe even thinking about a future together?"

Abby's smile was broad. "Nothing would make me happier."

He leaned closer and gently pressed his lips to her cheek. "I will always try my best to make you happy."

The rest of the evening passed in a blur, and when Abby's head hit the pillow, she said a prayer of thanks. Her life was full of blessings. And her sister would be home tomorrow. Abby's last thoughts were of herself and Emma, each finding the love they'd always hoped for. She just knew Emma would have news of her own when she finally returned home. She'd seen the spark between her sister and Levi's handsome cousin. Yes, things were turning out just as she'd always hoped. She and Emma were happy, loved, and were about to begin the next phase in their lives. With a contented sigh, she drifted to sleep.

Chapter Forty-six

. . . .

Emma

"What do you mean he couldn't make it?" Kelly asked shrilly.

"Shh. I don't want Lydia Ann to know how upset I am. She doesn't know what happened with me and Andy, and I don't want to tell her." Emma felt so stupid. She'd behaved in a way that went against her convictions. And now it seemed she was paying the price.

"Well, what did Noah say?" Kelly played with the white ribbon that was tied at the waist of her navy blue sundress. With a white cardigan sweater slung over her shoulders, and navy wedge sandals, she looked like she'd just stepped out of a magazine. Emma was secretly pleased at how demure her friend looked. Maybe her days of revealing clothes were over.

"Just that he was sorry he couldn't make it. I think his uncle said something about work." Levi's parents had relayed Noah's message when they arrived.

"Do you believe that?" Kelly asked.

Emma blinked back the tears. "Not exactly. I'm sure he really is working. But I'm also sure he could've made it if he'd wanted to. I ruined everything yesterday. And for what? So I could ride in a stupid convertible and wear lipstick."

Kelly shook her head. "It wasn't like that, and you know it. You've got to stop blaming yourself." She gave a one-sided grin. "You can blame me if you'd like."

Emma played with the tie on her kapp. "It wasn't your fault."

"But you make it sound like you purposefully set out to hurt Noah. And you and I both know that you had serious reservations about going out with Andy in the first place. And after the things he said and how he treated you…" Kelly trailed off. "Well, I believe Noah would understand," she added with less certainty.

"I can't exactly make him listen to me, though. And even if he understood, that doesn't change things. I chose to wear different clothes. I chose to get into the car with Andy. Those were bad decisions on my part. But they were mine." She met Kelly's gaze. "And even though Noah may understand, I'm not sure he would feel like he could ever trust me."

"Maybe you should give him the chance before you jump to that conclusion." Kelly pushed a wisp of red hair from her forehead. "Tell you what. On our way out of town tomorrow, we'll swing by Keim. You can tell him good-bye and maybe get a chance to clear the air."

Emma managed a tiny smile. That would be nice. She'd give anything to see him again and make sure the last image he had of her was not that of her being kissed by Andy. "Okay. That gives me the rest of the night to figure out what to say."

Kelly laughed. "I'm afraid you've learned from my scheming ways."

"Maybe you've just helped them along. Remember it was my sister's scheming that brought me to Charm in the first place."

Kelly was quiet for a moment. "And I'm so glad she did." She smoothed the skirt of her dress. "I don't know what I'd have done without you this summer." Her eyes began to fill with tears.

"Oh, you'd have been just fine."

"No. I've learned so much from you. Not just about friendship, but about faith. You have an amazing faith in God, and even though I don't plan to become Amish, I still plan to learn more about Him. And that is because of your example."

"You don't plan to become Amish?" Emma teased. "I'm sure I have a cousin you might think was cute."

"Don't joke. I'm being serious." Kelly grinned. "Really. There are so many things I've filled my life with that just aren't important. Distractions that keep me from becoming the kind of person I should be. You've helped me to see that." She motioned at her dress. "And I've learned that even though I love clothes. And shoes. And makeup... Well, those things are maybe not as important as I used to think they were. The next time I get into a relationship with someone, I want him to see me for me. Not for the label I'm wearing or the car I'm driving."

Emma nodded. "There is a wonderful man out there for you somewhere. But you've got to learn not to settle for someone who doesn't treat you well. You deserve to be respected, and I hope you'll carry that with you when you head back to Columbus."

"Are you ready to eat?" Lydia Ann poked her head around the corner. "Everyone is taking their seats."

Emma and Kelly scurried to the dining room. Emma tried to ignore the empty chair that should've been Noah's and concentrate on the delicious meal Lydia Ann had prepared. But it was hard to keep her gaze from drifting to the empty space. Would there always be an empty space in her life now?

* * *

The next day, Emma stood at the window, watching as Kelly pulled up in front of Lydia Ann's house. She left her SUV running and ran up the path.

Emma opened the door to greet her. "I'm almost ready."

Kelly stepped into the house. "Take your time. We aren't on a schedule." She grinned. "I've got nowhere to be for the next week. Then, it's back to the grind."

"Classes start that soon?" Emma asked.

"Yep. In just a week, I'll be sitting in class, writing papers, and studying again." She shrugged. "I'm actually excited about it."

"I'm so glad." Emma hoisted her bag over her shoulder. She bent down to grab her suitcase.

"I'll get that one." Kelly gripped the sturdy suitcase and carried it out to her X-Terra. She opened the backend and heaved the suitcase inside. "Goodness, Emma. What is in here? Rocks?"

Emma chuckled. "I'm taking some small gifts for my family. Sorry. I didn't realize it would be so heavy."

"It's a good thing I've been working out this summer." Kelly grinned and slammed the hatch shut.

They climbed inside the vehicle. "Well?" Kelly asked. "Is our next stop Keim?"

Emma was silent for a long moment. "Jah. I guess so." She buckled her seatbelt. "Do you really think I should stop by?"

"I think if you don't, you'll always wonder what would've happened if you had."

"You're probably right." She took a deep breath. Her heart was already beating faster at the thought of confronting Noah. "Okay. Next stop, Keim."

Kelly drove slowly through town, past the landmarks that had become so familiar to both of them over the course of the summer.

"I'm really going to miss this place," Emma said, staring out the window.

"I was just thinking the same thing. But maybe we can come back at the same time for a visit?" Kelly pulled into the parking lot and maneuvered the SUV into a space. She turned to look at Emma. "Well, do you want me to come in with you?"

Emma thought for a moment. On the one hand, she knew she needed to speak to Noah alone. But on the other, having Kelly nearby for support would make her feel better. "Why don't you come inside? You can maybe hang out in the café or something."

"I thought you might want some moral support."

They climbed out of the vehicle and walked down the sidewalk to the entrance. Emma's hands were clammy. In fact, she felt like she was coming down with the flu.

"Nervous?" Kelly asked as they came to the glass doors leading inside.

"You read me too well. I'm a wreck."

"You'll be fine." They parted ways, and Kelly walked toward the café.

Emma stopped by the nearest service desk. "Excuse me," she said to the older Amish man behind the counter. "I need to speak to Noah Weaver. He works here."

"I know Noah." The man scratched his graying beard. "But I believe he took the day off. Had some personal business to attend to. Let me check, though." He picked up the phone.

A minute later, he was back. "I'm sorry, miss. He isn't here. Would you like to leave a message for him for when he gets back?"

Emma's heart sank with the words. She wasn't going to get the chance to talk to Noah. There was no point in leaving a note for him. If he'd have wanted to see her, he would have. It wasn't as if her departure date were a secret. They'd talked about it.

"Miss?" The man at the counter looked at her worriedly. "Do you need to sit down? You've gone pale all of a sudden."

"What?" Emma said weakly. "Oh. No, thank you. I'm fine." She turned and walked slowly to the café. She needed to get out of there.

She paused at the café entrance and scanned the crowd. The last time she'd been in here, it had been with Noah. She saw a tall, dark-haired man at the counter, and for a moment she thought it was him. The man turned and caught her stare. He smiled tentatively and walked to a table.

"Any luck?" Kelly asked, coming over to where Emma stood. Emma shook her head. "He's not here today." She cast another glance at the dark-haired man who'd reminded her of Noah. "Let's go." She blindly followed Kelly to the vehicle. She'd really messed things up.

* * *

"We should be getting close," Kelly said. "Make sure I don't miss my turn."

Emma looked up, startled. She hadn't realized they'd covered so much ground so quickly. Once they left Keim, she'd tried to keep up with Kelly's chatter about the upcoming school year, but soon it became evident her heart wasn't in it. Kelly finally turned the radio onto a country station and stopped trying to draw Emma into conversation. "Oh. I haven't been paying attention to where we were." She glanced over at Kelly. "Sorry."

Kelly peered at her through oversized sunglasses. "Don't worry about it. I don't blame you for being upset. I wonder where he is today?"

Emma shook her head. "Do you think he expected that I'd stop by? And that's why he wasn't there?"

"Oh, I don't think so. Noah doesn't strike me as calculating. Maybe he genuinely had business to attend to." She slowed as they came upon a buggy crossing sign. "I feel certain you'll hear from him again."

Emma wasn't so sure. But for the time being, she wanted to pretend that her friend was right. Plus, she was starting to get excited about returning home. Home. The summer away had given her a new appreciation for it. Not that she hadn't had a good time, because she had. But it was good to be home. She turned to Kelly. "I'm going to miss you."

"I'm going to miss you, too. Promise you'll write?"

"Of course." Emma laughed. "Maybe I'll try to sneak someone's cell phone and text you every now and then."

Kelly joined in her laughter. "Yeah, right. A real letter will be fine. It will give me a reason to look forward to getting the mail every day."

"Right. But while I know I can handle actually writing a letter, can you?"

"Absolutely. I need to practice my penmanship anyway. All my texting makes me forget how to use proper English."

"Turn right here." Emma directed her down the road that led to her family's home. She was surprised at how nervous she felt.

"Well, this is it," Kelly said, once they had pulled up in front of the house. "Let me help you carry your stuff in."

"Wait. I have something for you."

Kelly's green eyes lit up. "You do? What is it?"

Emma reached into the back seat and pulled out her backpack. She pulled out a book and handed it to Kelly. "You may already have a Bible at home, but I underlined some of my favorite verses in this one for you. I hope you'll be able to find comfort in them, just as I do."

Kelly's eyes filled with tears. "Thank you so much. You have no idea how much this means to me." She took a breath. "I've got a whole new lease on life and it is largely because I met you." She met Emma's eyes. "You've been a huge influence on me. Thank you for this." She patted the Bible. "I actually have something for you, too. It's in the back." Kelly hopped out, still wiping tears from her eyes.

Emma followed, wondering what Kelly would pull from the back.

"Okay, I have two things. First, these." Kelly pulled the pink sandals Emma had borrowed. "I know you may not want to see them again. But I was thinking, maybe they could be sort of a reminder that you have exactly the life you want."

Emma grinned. "True. I guess they don't have the same allure they once did."

"And..." Kelly's eyes lit up. "I think you're gonna like this next one." She pulled out a large square object, wrapped in brown parchment paper, and placed it in Emma hands. "Open it."

Emma tore the paper away and gasped. It was one of the paintings from Lydia Ann's shop that she'd admired. "The town of Charm. Oh, this was one of my favorites."

"I know. I thought you might need something to remember the summer by. And I know you don't really hang paintings on your wall, but I thought you could at least keep it in a closet somewhere and pull it out every now and then."

"Thank you so much." She never would've bought one of the paintings for herself, but she was so glad Kelly had given one to her.

"Emma!" Abby called from the porch. "Welcome home." She flew out to the car, Sarah and Mamm on her heels.

Once the introductions were made, they carried Emma's things inside.

"Kelly, would you like to stay overnight? I know you must be tired after the drive," Mamm said, as they visited in the living room.

"Oh, no, ma'am. I'd better get on the road. I'm actually heading back to Columbus tomorrow, so this is my last night in Charm." She tightened her red ponytail. "I promised Aunt Irene I'd be back for supper."

Emma followed her out to the SUV. "Thanks again for driving me. And for the gifts."

"It was no problem. And thank you for the Bible. I promise to read it every day."

Emma laughed. "It isn't me you have to promise that to."

"I guess you're right." Kelly smiled. "Well, girl. I guess this is it. Promise you'll keep in touch?"

"Jah. And you do the same."

With one final wave out the window, Kelly was gone. Emma turned and looked at the house she'd grown up in. It seemed smaller, somehow. She headed up the pathway to visit with her mamm. The saying must be true. There was truly no place like home.

Chapter Forty-seven

Abby

"She isn't the same." Abby sat in the buggy beside Jacob. They were out for a drive. The days were beginning to get cooler, but it was still warm enough for short sleeves.

"How so?" Jacob asked.

"I can't quite put my finger on it. She doesn't have her head in the clouds as much for one thing. And she doesn't say things to shock me anymore." Abby furrowed her brow.

Jacob let out a chuckle. "But weren't those the exact things that drove you crazy before?"

She smiled sheepishly. "I guess. But I wish she'd talk to me. She's hiding something, I just know it."

He reached over and patted her clenched hand. "Do you think maybe you're just looking for something to be wrong?"

She jerked her hand away. "No. I'm not imagining it. I'm telling you, something's off with her. She's quiet and spending a lot of time alone." She looked over at him. "You know that isn't like her."

"Well, then I'd say you should confront her. Ask if she needs to talk or if there is something bothering her." He directed the horse to stop in front of Abby's house. "I have no doubt you'll find the words." He grinned at her. "And I'd say you should try and talk to her soon. I can see how much this is weighing on you."

Abby let out a huge sigh. "You're right. I'm sorry if I seem grouchy." She met his gaze. "I'll speak to her tonight. I'm worried about her is all. And…" She trailed off. "I want to tell her of our plans."

He smiled broadly. "She'll be happy, don't you think?"

Abby nodded. "I think she'll have nothing but good wishes for us." She told him good-bye and climbed down from the buggy. She watched as Jacob slowly drove away, giving her one last wave. She'd been dying to talk to Emma about things, but Emma had been so distracted in the few weeks since her return. Abby was determined that they'd get everything out into the open tonight.

* * *

"The meal was delicious." Emma carried a stack of dishes into the kitchen. "Lydia Ann was a good cook, but I'm happy to have Mamm's cooking again."

Abby began scraping the plates Emma had set on the counter. "Well, are you excited about school starting back?" She'd been thinking all afternoon about how to start the conversation with Emma, but hadn't come up with anything yet. She supposed she'd just have to start and hope things came out naturally.

"It might be hard to get back into the routine of things." Emma shrugged. "But I suppose it is that way every year."

Abby scrutinized her sister's expression. "Is it harder than normal for you this year?"

"Perhaps. I sort of enjoyed working in the shop and caring for the twins. It was a nice change of pace." Emma filled the sink with

warm water and added a few drops of liquid soap. "But I'm happy
to be back with my students. They've had some adventures over the
summer."

"They aren't the only ones." She glanced at Emma. "I'd say we've
both had adventures this summer, too, wouldn't you?"

Emma offered a tiny smile. "What was your adventure, besides
a bad sprain?"

Abby stopped rinsing the dishes and turned to face Emma. It
felt like there were jumping beans in her stomach. "Well, there's
something I wanted to tell you." She took a deep breath. "Things
have been going really well with me and Jacob."

"I was pretty sure you were going to say that. I noticed the
happy look on your face as soon as I got out of Kelly's car. I'd dare
say you've turned into the daydreamer." She finished the last of the
dishes and leaned against the counter. "Is he as happy as you are?"

Abby felt her cheeks flush. "I think so. Actually, I think... I
mean, I know...we're planning to be published in the fall." She
blurted the words out, hoping Emma would be happy for her.

Emma squealed. "Oh, Abby. That's truly wonderful news.
I believe you will be very happy together."

"Is everything okay?" Mamm stuck her head in the kitchen.
"I thought I heard a scream."

"Sorry. Everything is fine," Emma said.

The sisters exchanged glances. As soon as mamm left the room,
they burst out laughing.

"Why don't you come into my room? I want to hear the details,"
Emma said.

Abby followed her down the hallway to her bedroom.

Emma sat down on the bed, Abby in the rocker. "Well?" Emma asked.

"You were right. All that stuff you told me in Charm, about how he was so worried he traveled to see me and all. That was exactly what happened." She played with the tie on her kapp. "So we started spending time together. And I finally let myself believe that he could see me as something more than a kid sister." She grinned. "It turned out, he did. He had for a long time. But I'd tried so hard to get the two of you together, he assumed I didn't return his feelings."

Emma nodded. "How about that? If you hadn't been so determined to be a matchmaker, you'd probably be married by now."

Abby shook her head. "Oh, now. Don't say such a thing. I think it all just took some time for us to realize everything." She sighed. "But I am sorry I tried so hard to push you together. Deep down, I knew you didn't want me to, but I was so determined."

"Don't worry about that. I know it was only because you wanted me to be happy here." She met Abby's gaze. "And I have a feeling you want to know what my feelings are about that."

"I've wanted to ask ever since you got back. But I've been worried I might not like the decision." Abby tried to read Emma's expression. Was she going to leave their family for good?

"Actually, I have good news for you. I was able to do a lot of thinking this summer, and a lot of praying. I'm not proud of all of my actions over these past months. But the bottom line is that I've decided, with no question, that I want to remain here." She ran her hand along the quilt on her bed. "I'm going to join the church this fall."

"Oh, Emma. That is wonderful news. I'm so glad you're free from all the turmoil."

Emma's eyes flashed with uncertainty, and Abby wondered what could be lingering beneath the surface. Although she knew she may very well wish she didn't know, she decided to forge ahead. "What is it? You can tell me."

Emma sighed. "It isn't a pretty story."

Abby rose from the chair and went to sit beside her sister. "It's okay. Maybe it will help for you to get it out." She sat in silence as Emma explained to her how she'd dressed in Kelly's clothes. She felt the anger rise in her as Emma told of Andy's forced kiss.

"It sounds like a truly awful day," Abby said, once she heard about Noah's involvement. "Did you finally get to speak to him?" She'd only been around Noah a couple of times while she was in Charm, but she had seen the mutual admiration between him and Emma.

"No." Emma's voice was glum. "He skipped my going-away meal, and he wasn't at his work when I stopped by to see him on our way out of town." She shook her head. "It isn't any use. I believe he thinks the worst of me." Emma hung her head. "I was too ashamed to even tell Lydia Ann."

Abby placed a hand over her sister's. "I'll pray for you to find the peace you need."

"Danki. Prayers are exactly what I need." She stood. "In the meantime, I'd better get to bed. School comes early tomorrow."

"Good night, sister. I'm glad to have you home. For good." Abby turned and headed toward her own bedroom. But not before she glanced back one last time at the sad look on Emma's face. The first inkling of a plan began to form. Her sister deserved every happiness, and she would do all she could to see that she found it.

Chapter Forty-eight

....

Kelly

Kelly was overwhelmed. She'd only been back in Columbus for a few days and already the tranquility she'd felt over the summer was nearly gone. After hours in line for registration, she was finally ready for classes to begin. She'd gone and bought her textbooks this afternoon, and even secondhand, they had cost a pretty penny. It seemed that the money she'd saved over the past months might go quickly.

She flipped through the help-wanted ads, hoping something would jump out. It was time to find a part-time job to supplement her savings. She sighed. Things had certainly been simpler a week ago. Thankfully, Michelle was still on a late vacation with her family, so Kelly had the apartment to herself for a couple more days.

She went into her room and sat down on the bed. The quilt she'd bought at Lydia Ann's shop was draped over the foot of her sleigh bed. It perfectly complemented the blue and brown colors she'd chosen to decorate the room with. Her sky blue comforter was thick and plush, and the brown and blue striped accent pillows matched her curtains. She'd decorated the room in the hopes that it would offer a calm retreat. But right now, she wasn't sure it was serving its purpose.

Even the traffic was getting on her nerves. She could hear it right now, all those people trying to get home from work. She sighed. It was probably just anxiety over starting a new master's program. She closed her eyes and tried to remember those yoga breathing exercises she'd learned at the gym last year. Or maybe she just needed to find a mantra. She opened her eyes and her gaze landed on the well-worn Bible Emma had given her.

She picked the book up and stared at it in her hands. Memories of childhood VBS ran through her head. If you brought your Bible every day, you got a balloon at the end of the week.

Kelly flipped the Bible open. An underlined verse sprang out at her from the middle of the page. Matthew 6:34. *Take therefore no thought for the morrow: for the morrow shall take thought for the things of itself.* Hmm. Maybe she should try living that way. But wait. How would she possibly be able to stop worrying about the future?

She read a few passages ahead, paying special attention to any of the verses Emma had underlined. She flipped the page and paused on Matthew 7:7–8. *Ask, and it shall be given you; seek and ye shall find; knock, and it shall be opened unto you: For every one that asketh receiveth; and he that seeketh findeth; and to him that knocketh it shall be opened.* Could she pray? She'd watched Emma pray all summer. Emma had told her God would always listen, would always be there, no matter what.

Kelly bowed her head and was surprised at how easily the words came.

* * *

On Sunday morning she sat in her SUV in the church parking lot. She felt more nervous than when she was going on a first date or speaking in public. Why was this so difficult? She'd gone to church with her parents as a child, but once she hit her teens, her family had rarely found the time to attend. And even then, it almost seemed more social than anything else. Her mother enjoyed going to brunch after the service with some of the other families. And her dad had always found a way to make business contacts. Even so, their attendance had tapered off as they became busier.

She watched the families, walking inside together. The dads holding babies, moms leading toddlers by the hand. The teens seemed to gather outside and walk inside in small groups. Kelly took a deep breath. She could do this. Just because she didn't know anyone didn't mean she couldn't go in. She'd prayed that God would give her the courage to take the first step. And here she was.

She climbed out of the SUV, hoping she looked okay. Her black skirt came just below the knees, showing just a hint of a summer tan. She'd chosen an emerald green cap-sleeved sweater, because whenever she wore it, people always commented on how green her eyes were. She stood beside her vehicle for a long moment, watching the throng of people enter the building. Everyone was dressed up. Maybe not in designer fashion, but she could tell they were all trying to look their best.

"Miss Bennett?" A voice behind her caused her to jump. She turned.

The petite woman walking toward her looked vaguely familiar. "Good morning." The woman gave a bright smile. "I believe you're in my Foundations of Library Science class."

"Dr. Lewis. It's nice to see you." Kelly smiled. Though the class had only met once, she'd been impressed by the instructor's friendly manner in class. It looked like it carried outside of the classroom as well.

"I don't believe I've seen you here before. Are you visiting?"

Kelly nodded. "Yes, ma'am. This is my first time here."

"Well, we're glad to have you. There's a fairly large singles' group with lots of people your age. I'd be glad to show you where their class is."

"That would be great, thanks." Kelly walked beside her professor toward the brown brick building.

"It is nice to have you visit with us. I hope you'll consider making New Hope your church home." The older woman held the door open for Kelly and ushered her inside. "And don't hesitate to seek me out if you need anything."

"That's very nice of you." Kelly smiled back at the friendly faces that passed her by. Many of them called out greetings to Dr. Lewis.

"Here we are." Dr. Lewis paused outside of a set of double doors. "They are a fun group. You should make friends with no trouble." She smiled again at Kelly. "And don't worry, dear. It is the beginning of a new semester, and that means there will be a lot of new faces in there. You won't be the only one."

Kelly thanked her and entered the large room, with rows of seats. Several people were already seated, and others stood around the perimeter, laughing and talking. She spotted a girl sitting alone, a worried expression on her face. Looks like she'd found another newcomer. She made her way over to where the girl sat. The first step, just coming inside the building, was over. Now that she was here, she knew she could handle it.

Chapter Forty-nine

Emma

Getting back into the swing of things hadn't been easy for Emma. She only hoped her students hadn't figured out that her mind was miles away, still in Charm. But she finally felt like she'd settled into a routine, and for that, she was thankful. Rising early and reading the Psalms, breakfast with the family, and then heading to school. Her days were happy.

She was relieved that her old discontent about her life was gone. In its place was a deep appreciation for the life with which she'd been blessed. A family that had remained closely knit. Parents who still loved each other. Friends and church members who would be willing to pitch in and help if she were ever in trouble. Yes, it was the life for her. The Lord had blessed her more than she deserved.

And she was happy for Abby and Jacob and the new life they would soon begin. Even though there had been some murmuring within their community, it seemed that everyone accepted that Emma was perfectly fine with the turn of events.

The only thing that prevented Emma from being totally content was the lingering memory of Noah. Even though she wouldn't admit it to anyone, every time a letter came in the mail, she had a tiny glimmer of hope that his would be the name on the return address. But the letters that came her way were from Lydia Ann or

Kelly. Not that she would complain. She loved hearing about what was going on with the two of them. As happy as she was at home now, she still missed them. Every now and then, she would pull out the painting Kelly had given her. She loved the colors the artist had chosen. It was almost as if she could feel the emotion that had gone into the artwork.

She sat in the porch swing alone and looked out into the distance. She was surprised to notice the leaves beginning to change. It was time to face it. Summer was really a thing of the past. The calendar was already on October, after all. Where had the time gone?

"Lost in thought?" Abby joined her on the porch.

Emma sighed. "I was just realizing that it isn't summer any longer."

Abby chuckled. "You're just now noticing that? I've already had to get an extra quilt out for my bed." She motioned toward the large oak tree in the front yard. "Not to mention the colorful leaves everywhere."

"I guess I've just been distracted."

"Guess what? I have a surprise for you. I think it's going to make you very happy." Abby buzzed with excitement.

Emma looked warily at her sister. "What have you done?"

Abby sank onto the porch swing beside her sister, causing it to lurch backwards.

"Whoa, Abby. Don't knock us off the swing."

Abby giggled. "Sorry." Her face glowed. "Do you know what this weekend is?"

Emma thought for a moment. She couldn't come up with a single birthday or other special occasion that would be taking place. "No. But I'm almost afraid to find out."

"It's Charm Days." Abby's blue eyes twinkled. "Doesn't that sound like fun?"

"Lydia Ann and Noah both mentioned the festival while I was there. And it did sound like it would be nice." She shrugged. "But what does that have to do with us?"

"I've arranged for a driver to come pick us up in the morning." Abby practically shouted the words. "We're going to stay with Lydia Ann. And I contacted Kelly. She's going to be there, too."

"Oh, Abby. I have to work tomorrow. You know that."

Abby's smile was so wide it showed most of her teeth. "I've gotten someone to cover for you."

Emma was astonished. And not totally on board. "But you don't like to travel."

"Oh, Emma. Lighten up." Abby laughed. "I never thought I'd have to say that to you. But you've been a little sad these past weeks. I think another trip to Charm is just what you need."

Emma's stomach churned. A trip to Charm may mean a run-in with Noah. And she wasn't sure if she could handle his rejection. She looked over at Abby, who was quite pleased with her surprise. Emma couldn't help but grin at her sister. She certainly did try to keep everyone happy.

"Okay. I'm at least impressed with your spontaneity. And with your being able to keep all that a secret from me. When did you talk to Kelly?"

"I got her address from one of the letters she sent you. I mailed her the quilt shop's phone number and asked her to call me. She was excited about the surprise and said she can't wait to see you."

Emma shook her head. "You've really thought of everything."

"Pretty soon I'll be married and living in my own house. I thought a trip together sounded fun."

"It does. Thanks for the surprise."

Abby patted her on the leg. "Now, go get packed. My things are already in the suitcase. We leave first thing in the morning."

Emma watched as her sister rose from the swing and went inside. Abby never ceased to amaze her.

* * *

As soon as they were on the outskirts of Charm, Emma felt a lump in her throat. She couldn't help but be flooded with memories. Meeting Kelly in the bookmobile. Spending time with Lydia Ann and the girls. Realizing that Andy was not a good guy. And of course, somewhere along the way, falling for Noah only to see it all blow up. She let out a heavy sigh.

"Are you okay?" Abby asked.

"Jah. I'm fine. Just a little nervous, I guess."

"I have faith that everything will turn out fine. It will be nice to see your friends again, won't it?"

Emma nodded. It would be nice to see everyone again. But what if Noah didn't want to see her? Or even worse, what if he'd heard she was coming for a visit so he'd made it a point to be out of town? Only time would tell.

They pulled up in front of Lydia Ann's shop. The van driver got out and helped them with their bags. Abby thanked him for his service and reminded him of when and where they needed to be picked up.

The familiar sound of the jingling bell went off as they entered the store.

"Hi." Lydia Ann bustled toward them, relieving Abby of the bag she carried. "I'm so glad you decided to come for Charm Days." She gestured toward the people browsing the aisles. "Things are already very busy. In fact, I've got some extra helpers for the weekend."

Emma noticed two teenaged Amish girls behind the counter, one helping a customer and the other folding merchandise. "That's good. We can pitch in to help if you need us."

Lydia Ann shook her head. "Oh, no. I want you both to enjoy yourselves. In fact, I thought I'd run home and we could have lunch. Then you can go see some of the festivities while I tend to things at the shop."

Emma and Abby nodded. Soon they were settled in Lydia Ann's kitchen, eating a delicious meal. Abby chattered about Jacob and their plans for the future.

Emma was lost in thoughts of Noah. If she did see him, what would she say? What would he say? Suddenly, the silence of the room caught her attention. She looked up from her food. Both Lydia Ann and Abby were staring at her with strange expressions on their faces.

"What? Did you ask me something?"

Lydia Ann shook her head. "No. But you looked like you were going to be sick. Is everything okay?"

She didn't want to tell them her mind was on Noah. Honestly, she didn't even want to admit that to herself. "Jah. I think I just ate too fast." She managed a weak smile. "I'm so glad to be back, Lydia Ann."

"And I'm glad for you to be here. Katie and Mary were so wound up when I told them we were having company, they could hardly sleep last night." She laughed. "Of course, now they are all excited about the Woolly Worm Derby, so they may have forgotten about you two."

"Woolly Worm Derby?" Abby laughed.

Lydia Ann nodded. "One of the highlights of Charm Days. The younger children enter woolly worms to compete. The girls aren't quite old enough to enter, but they'll be there to watch. So will most people in town."

"When does that take place?" Emma asked.

"This afternoon. If you'll come by the shop, I'll go with you. We can meet up with Susanna and the girls there."

Abby jumped up as they began to clear the dishes. "Emma, why don't you change into a different dress? That one is well worn."

"Is that your way of saying 'old'?" Emma asked.

Abby grinned. "Maybe."

Emma came out of the bedroom a few moments later in a gray dress and matching apron. "Is this better?"

Abby looked her up and down. "Don't you have anything… brighter?"

"Who are you and what have you done with my sister? You've been trying to steer me away from bright colors my whole life."

Abby hung her head. "I didn't mean for you to wear a hot pink dress. Just that another color might be more becoming."

"For your information, I think this one is fine. And I didn't bring anything else."

"I thought you might say that."

"What?"

Abby sighed. "Emma, you've been wearing nothing but gray for the past few weeks. And truthfully, it worries me."

"Since when do you keep track of what I wear?" Emma asked, surprised. She hadn't noticed it at the time. But she guessed she had been in a rut lately.

"I have something for you." Abby hauled her own suitcase to the bedroom and opened it up. She pulled out a deep plum-colored dress and held it up.

Emma knew instinctively the color would go well with her skin tone. "What's that?"

"I made it for you. I saw the material over the summer and started working on it while I was waiting on my ankle to heal. Try it on."

Reaching out her hands, Emma took the dress from her sister. Her eyes filled with tears. "You didn't have to do that, Abby."

"I know I didn't have to. I wanted to." She shrugged. "As soon as I saw the color, I knew it would be perfect for you." She grinned. "And it isn't too flashy. So I figured it would make both of us happy."

"Danki. That was so sweet of you." Emma was touched by her sister's thoughtfulness. Abby had always been the better seamstress of the two, and Emma was elated at the thought of having a dress without the many imperfections her own creations always seemed to have.

With another smile, Abby left Emma to put on her new dress.

Chapter Fifty

Emma

Emma and Abby stepped into the quilt shop later that afternoon. The throng of customers had thinned some, but it was still busy.

"I want you to look at these paintings," Emma said. "I think they're so beautiful." She motioned for Abby to follow her over to the collection of paintings that hung on the wall. "I can never decide which one is my favorite. And it looks like there are some new ones to choose from."

"Those are wonderful. The artist is quite talented. Hey, look." Abby pointed to a painting that depicted two Amish women walking into the Charm General Store. "That girl looks like you."

Emma peered closer at the woman. Her face wasn't visible, but something about the way she stood in the doorway did seem familiar. "She's even carrying the same color backpack I do." Emma smiled. "I suppose all we Amish girls look the same from a distance."

A squeal came from the front of the store.

Emma turned to see Kelly barreling down on her.

"Emma!" Kelly said loudly. "It's so great to see you," she said, pulling Emma into a tight hug. "When did you get to town?"

"Just before lunch." She grinned. "You look great. Very happy."

"Thanks. I am." She linked arms with Emma. "And I have so much to tell you."

Emma motioned at Abby. "You remember my sister, Abby."

"Of course. She's the reason I'm here this weekend." Kelly smiled in Abby's direction. "It's nice to see you again."

"Likewise." Abby returned Kelly's smile. "I'm going to go see if Lydia Ann needs some help. You two catch up."

Emma followed Kelly outside the shop. "Do you want to walk through town or just sit here?" Emma asked, pointing at a bench outside of the shop.

"Let's sit."

"Okay. Now, tell me what's got you looking so giddy." Emma smiled at her friend.

"First of all, I love my classes. Library science was the right decision for me."

"That's great. I know you were worried about that decision."

"Yep. But not anymore. And…I have a date next weekend with a new guy. His name is Jason." Her green eyes sparkled.

"Oh? Is he in one of your classes?"

"No. I actually met him at church." She grinned widely.

Emma knew how much courage it had taken Kelly to go back to church. She'd describe it in one of her letters by saying she'd felt like she wasn't good enough to attend. But after a few weeks, Kelly wrote again, saying she'd been amazed at the outpouring of love and support from the congregation. "That's great."

"And I know…just because he goes to church with me doesn't mean he's perfect or anything. But we've slowly gotten to know one another, and I think he's pretty great."

"That's wonderful. I'm so happy for you."

"I just feel like I've been given such a wonderful second chance. Aunt Irene calls to check in on me often, and I've made a lot of friends within the church singles' group. It might sound silly, but it's like I finally have the stability I've looked for my whole life."

"That doesn't sound silly at all."

"It all started with me meeting you, you know. Seeing you live your spiritual convictions on a daily basis. It was a real eye-opener for me."

"I'm far from perfect. As you well know."

"Are you still dwelling on that?"

Emma glanced down at the sidewalk and felt her face grow hot. She pointed about three feet away. "Right there. It was right on that spot where things fell apart."

Kelly didn't look where she was pointing but kept her green eyes locked on Emma's face. "I take this to mean you haven't talked to Noah?"

Emma shook her head. "More like he hasn't talked to me. I kept thinking he would contact me, but he never did."

Kelly narrowed her eyes. "But maybe he was thinking the same thing. That you would contact him if you wanted to speak to him."

"He missed my going-away dinner. And I'm sure they told him at Keim that someone stopped by to see him. It wouldn't take a detective for him to figure out it was probably me."

Kelly was quiet. "Do you think you'll see him this weekend?"

"I don't even know if he's in town. And I hate to ask Lydia Ann. I don't want anyone to know how much it hurts."

"I certainly understand that." She patted Emma on the arm. "But maybe you could just casually ask. Lydia Ann knows how close you and Noah had gotten. She might have even talked to him."

"No. I'll just keep an eye out for him. I already have a little speech prepared."

Kelly grinned. "I'm sure you do."

Abby and Lydia Ann stepped out onto the sidewalk. "Are you two ready for the Woolly Worm Derby?" Lydia Ann asked.

Kelly and Emma stood.

"We're ready," Kelly said. "Too bad we're too old to enter our own woolly worms. I'm pretty sure we could take the trophy."

They set off toward the festival, following the sounds of laughter. Emma felt lighter than she had in weeks.

"Just be glad the weather is nice. It rained a couple of years ago, and it was miserable," Lydia Ann said as they approached the crowd.

"Of course it was miserable. Can you imagine a whole crowd of woolly worms having a bad hair day?" Kelly joked quietly to Emma.

Emma chuckled at her friend's offbeat humor. Odd that lately she was the one who needed the reminder to lighten up. "The weather today couldn't be any better." She tilted her face to the sky and relished the feeling of the warm sunshine on her skin. She had always enjoyed the crispness of fall, with warm days and cool nights. It really had the makings for a perfect weekend, surrounded by her friends and enjoying life. So why didn't she feel more peaceful?

"I see the girls." Lydia Ann pointed to where her in-laws stood, the two little girls in front of them. Mary and Katie were standing on their tiptoes trying to see what was going on.

"Oh." Kelly stopped.

Emma looked up, startled as she almost ran into her friend. "What's wrong?" she asked. And then she saw. It was Noah, standing next to Levi's parents. He'd picked one of the twins up so she could get a better view. His eyes met Emma's, and she felt her knees almost buckle. Kelly gripped her arm.

"Are you okay?" Kelly whispered.

"Jah." She took a deep breath. "I think so."

Noah set the little girl down and walked over to where they stood. He nodded to Kelly and Abby then turned to Emma.

"I didn't know if I'd see you again." His voice was as deep and pleasant as she remembered.

She froze. The speech she'd prepared collapsed somewhere inside her. All she could think was how she'd missed those eyes, that voice, and the dimple that hadn't shown itself yet.

"I came to see you at Keim."

He nodded. "I know." He glanced over his shoulder where the rest of her party stood, watching. "How about we go somewhere and talk? I see a bench behind the crowd that's unoccupied." He grinned. "Unless you'd rather see the Woolly Worm Derby."

She managed a shaky smile. "I was looking forward to seeing what the fuss is all about." She met his eyes. "But I'd rather talk. And we'll still hear the cheers of the crowd."

"So we won't really be missing any of the important woolly worm action, right?"

She nodded. "And if we do, we can get a play-by-play from the twins later. Their version will probably be as entertaining as actually seeing it for ourselves."

"Maybe more." He guided her away from the crowd.

She tried to collect her thoughts. How had she planned to start? She'd lain awake many nights, going over and over the first sentence she'd say to him. But no matter how she tried, she couldn't remember.

"I should've written," Noah said, once they were settled on a bench in front of a storefront. He shook his head. "I started to time and again but couldn't find the right words."

She took a deep breath. "I know you saw what happened on the sidewalk in front of Lydia Ann's store. And I know what you thought."

He cut her off before she could say another word. "About that. Do you know how I felt when I found out you didn't want that guy to kiss you? Knowing I just drove off and left you there with him? I should've had more faith in you."

She sputtered. "How did you know?"

"I only just found out. Lydia Ann told me a couple of days ago. I think your sister was worried about you, and she and Lydia Ann talked about the situation."

That figured, although it was hard to be upset with Abby. She might meddle sometimes, but her heart was always in the right place. "Oh. I wanted to tell you myself. But..." She trailed off.

"But I didn't show up at your going-away party. And I wasn't at work the next day. What must you think of me?"

She reached out and grabbed his hand. "I understand. After what happened with Miriam, what else could you think?"

He shook his head. "You and Miriam are nothing alike. I knew you better than to jump to the conclusion I did." He looked into her eyes. "I'm sorry. I think it was just my own pride that got in the way. The fact is, I found myself jealous of that guy. I thought you'd chosen him, when I'd always hoped you'd choose me."

Emma sat upright, stunned. "You did?"

He reached out and stroked her cheek. "Of course. My life hasn't been the same since you left."

"Mine, either. In fact, it's been pretty awful. So many times something would happen, good or bad, and I'd wish I could tell you. But I was afraid you didn't have any desire to see or hear from me again."

Noah shook his head. "I always want to see you and hear from you." He grinned at her. "There's something I never told you."

"What's that?"

"You know those paintings in Lydia Ann's shop?"

"Jah. I love those. I love the colors the artist uses." Emma smiled. "Kelly gave me one as a going-away gift. I pull it out and look at it when I'm having a bad day. For some reason, it can always make me feel better."

"I'm glad to hear it." He cleared his throat nervously. "I don't tell many people this, but I'm the artist."

She gasped. "You are?"

He nodded. "I don't like to make a big deal out of it. I enjoy painting them so much, and I know Lydia Ann can use all the extra funds she can get."

Emma smiled. "I can't believe you never told me. And neither did Lydia Ann. She's listened to me go on and on about them all summer."

"I begged her not to tell anyone. She just says a local artist did them. I have some in galleries in larger towns, too."

"Wow."

"But the thing is, ever since you left, it was like all the color went out of my life and my paintings. All the quilt paintings I did were so dull and lifeless I just threw them out." He took her hand again.

She thought about her recent penchant for wearing gray. "I know just how you felt."

"And then, one day, I was doing a painting of the town of Charm, and I decided to put some people in the scene. Before I knew it, there you were." His mouth turned upward in a grin. "So from that point on, all of my town scenes have you in them."

She chuckled. "Abby noticed it this morning. I thought maybe I just had a common look."

He shook his head. "There's nothing common about you, Emma."

She relished the tender look on his face as he said her name. She knew, just as she knew her own name, that she'd finally found the love she'd always hoped to find.

Epilogue

....

The following year

Kelly

Kelly opened the passenger door to her SUV and eagerly climbed out.

"Perfect weather, don't you think?" she asked.

Jason Thompson smiled at her. "We couldn't ask for a better forecast. I think Charm Days will be a rousing success."

She grabbed his hand. "I can't wait for you to meet my friends. And Aunt Irene. She's been asking me to bring you by for quite some time now."

He leaned down and kissed her on the forehead. "You know, any friends of yours are friends of mine." Jason held the door open to Lydia Ann's quilt shop and let her walk through first.

She walked up to the counter where Lydia Ann stood. "Are they here yet?"

"Any minute." Lydia Ann smiled. "It's nice to see you again."

"You, too. I'm going to show Jason around," she said, after she'd introduced them.

"Check these paintings out. Aren't they fantastic?"

Before he could answer, voices filled the small shop. Kelly turned to see Emma and Noah greeting Lydia Ann. She grabbed Jason's hand. "Come on. Here they are."

"Hello," Kelly called to them.

Emma grinned and embraced her friend. "I'm so glad you could make it."

"I wouldn't have missed it for the world. How does it feel to be newly married?"

Noah stepped over, his beard just beginning to fill in. "Pretty wonderful."

Emma laughed. "Exactly."

"And how is Abby? I thought she'd be here."

"Abby is with child. She and Jacob are thrilled. But she's a little queasy, so they thought it best to stay home this year." She laughed. "She hated to miss the Woolly Worm Derby this year, though, especially since Katie and Mary are entering."

"Well, give her my best when you get back home." Kelly turned to Jason and pulled him over to her. "And I have someone I'd like you to meet." She made the introductions.

"Jason, would you like to walk with me to the derby?" Noah asked. "I imagine these two have some catching up to do."

Jason nodded. "Yes." He leaned down and gave Kelly a quick peck on the cheek. "See you soon?" he asked.

She nodded. "We'll be right behind you."

Once the men were gone, she turned to Emma. "I'm so happy for you. It seems like things are going very well."

Emma nodded. "I've never been happier."

"You two go on. I'll catch up soon," Lydia Ann said from behind the counter.

They stepped out into the early October sunlight. "It seems that Charm was indeed a charm for me. I found the love of my life here."

Emma linked arms with Kelly. "I never expected to find a man like Noah. And yet, I did." She shook her head. "I was so nervous that he wouldn't want to leave his hometown." She grinned. "But he told me he'd follow me to the ends of the earth if he had to. And of course, we come visit here a lot."

Kelly grinned. "I'm glad it all worked out. I know it was important to you to stay near your family. Especially now that Abby is having a baby."

"How about you? Jason seems like a nice guy."

Kelly blushed. "I have news, too." She held out her left hand to show a sparkling diamond ring.

Emma squealed. "You're getting married?"

"Yes. Next summer." She paused. "And…we want to get married here. At the One Charming Inn."

"Oh, that's perfect. You will make a beautiful bride."

"Thanks." Kelly stopped. "One more thing. Is there any way you would be a bridesmaid? You know I don't have any sisters, and I know we come from different backgrounds, but you're about the closest thing to a sister I have."

Emma nodded. "Of course. Just as long as I don't have to wear those pink high-heeled sandals."

They giggled.

"You can wear whatever you like."

"There are the guys." Emma pointed to where Noah and Jason stood talking.

Kelly followed her friend, thankful she'd made the decision to come to this tiny town all those months ago. She guessed one never knew what God had in store, or how the tiniest of decisions could impact the outcome of things. She looked around at Emma and Noah, holding hands and laughing, and caught Jason's eye. Life might be hard sometimes, but it was also full of blessings. Some might even say it was charmed.

Want a peek into local American life—past and present?
The *Love Finds You*™ series published by Summerside Press
features real towns and combines travel, romance,
and faith in one irresistible package!

The novels in the series—uniquely titled after American towns with unusual but intriguing names—inspire romance and fun. Each fictional story draws on the compelling history or the unique character of a real place. Stories center on romances kindled in small towns, old loves lost and found again on the high plains, and new loves discovered at exciting vacation getaways. Summerside Press plans to publish at least one novel set in each of the 50 states. Be sure to catch them all!

Now Available in Stores

Love Finds You in Miracle, Kentucky by Andrea Boeshaar
ISBN: 978-1-934770-37-5

Love Finds You in Snowball, Arkansas by Sandra D. Bricker
ISBN: 978-1-934770-45-0

Love Finds You in Romeo, Colorado by Gwen Ford Faulkenberry
ISBN: 978-1-934770-46-7

Love Finds You in Valentine, Nebraska by Irene Brand
ISBN: 978-1-934770-38-2

Love Finds You in Humble, Texas by Anita Higman
ISBN: 978-1-934770-61-0

Love Finds You in Last Chance, California by Miralee Ferrell
ISBN: 978-1-934770-39-9

Love Finds You in Maiden, North Carolina by Tamela Hancock Murray
ISBN: 978-1-934770-65-8

Love Finds You in Paradise, Pennsylvania by Loree Lough
ISBN: 978-1-934770-66-5

Love Finds You in Treasure Island, Florida by Debby Mayne
ISBN: 978-1-934770-80-1

Love Finds You in Liberty, Indiana, by Melanie Dobson
ISBN: 978-1-934770-74-0

Love Finds You in Revenge, Ohio by Lisa Harris
ISBN: 978-1-934770-81-8

Love Finds You in Poetry, Texas by Janice Hanna
ISBN: 978-1-935416-16-6

Love Finds You in Sisters, Oregon by Melody Carlson
ISBN: 978-1-935416-18-0

COMING SOON

Love Finds You in Bethlehem, New Hampshire by Lauralee Bliss
ISBN: 978-1-935416-20-3

Love Finds You in North Pole, Alaska by Loree Lough
ISBN: 978-1-935416-19-7

summerside
PRESS